CW00376971

Dark Scotland

An Anthology

www.darkstroke.com

Copyright © 2021 by darkstroke
Artwork: Adobe Stock © Bernadett
Design: Services for Authors
All rights reserved.

No part of this book may be used or reproduced in any manner
whatsoever without written permission of the author or Crooked
Cat/darkstroke except for brief quotations used for promotion or in
reviews. This is a work of fiction. Names, characters,
and incidents are used fictitiously.

First Dark Edition, darkstroke, Crooked Cat Books 2021

Discover us online:
www.darkstroke.com

Join us on instagram:
www.instagram.com/darkstrokebooks/

Include **#darkstroke** in a photo of yourself
holding this book on Instagram and
something nice will happen.

To the Heart of Scotland

Thank you for purchasing Dark Scotland. We hope you enjoy it.

All royalties received will be split and donated to two Scottish charities: **ME Research UK**, and **The Halliday Foundation**.

The publisher is grateful to those who have contributed to the publication of the Anthology. Their work has been done without payment.

Dark
Scotland

Foreword

Wendy H. Jones

When I was asked to write the foreword for *Dark Scotland*, I was honoured, thrilled, and nervous, in equal measure. Honoured, because I know the deep importance of capturing and growing Scotland's literary heritage, thrilled because I knew I would be reading in my favourite genre, and nervous because I wanted with every fibre of my being, to do the anthology justice. The one thing I was not nervous about was that I would enjoy the book, as I knew the calibre of the authors involved. I trusted darkstroke to produce an anthology which would be not only of high quality, but absorbing, and worthy of its Scottish heritage.

Anthologies and short stories have been somewhat out of favour for many years, but they recently made a resurgence and a comeback with a vengeance. It would seem that readers cannot get enough of them and they continually top the bestseller charts. It would be difficult for me to speculate as to why they are so popular, but I suspect it may have a lot to do with the rise in digital reading, where short stories are the perfect length for reading on one's phone during the daily commute. Reading a whole novel on a phone can be somewhat daunting, but a short story is much more manageable. I also suspect it is because of the modern-day pressures on time where reading a novel can seem somewhat daunting. Whatever the reason, I am delighted they are back. I say this both as an author and as a reader.

As an author, I know the value of developing and honing my skills in an area where every word counts, where the substitution of one word for another can change the story entirely, and where plot, structure and pacing are crucial to the readers enjoyment. As an author, I know the importance of reading a wide variety of stories in order to develop my skills. As a reader, I soak myself in the story and await the shock or surprise which I know is sure to come. I read short stories because I know they will transport me to another world and leave me breathless and hungry for more. As an avid reader of crime fiction, I very much looked forward to reading this latest addition to the vast library of Scottish Crime Anthologies.

I was not disappointed in this book in any way; it ticked every box and met every expectation of my view of an anthology, giving me hours of reading pleasure. From the first word to the last, the stories drew me in, and kept me reading. The title of the book is *Dark Scotland,* and the stories are, indeed, dark. All of them had me waiting in breathless anticipation and many sent shivers down my spine. With tales based on fact and many others pure fiction, the authors hit every trope expected of a short story, and do it to the highest degree. They are to be congratulated on both the quality and originality of their work. I would like to pick up on the word originality – it can be difficult to be original in a country so deeply steeped in the crime genre. Scotland has a long history of crime-writing, and continues to dominate in the genre today. So anthologies can often have the feel of same old, same old. Therefore, I did approach the book with some degree of trepidation. I need not have feared, as the authors have risen above this, providing stories with a fresh, vibrant feel – something that can be difficult when writing crime. I would like to congratulate every single contributor to the anthology, in this regard. It can be difficult to impress someone who has been reading mysteries and crime for over fifty years, but every single author has managed to do so.

Dark Scotland is packed full of surprises, the first of which was the first story *Doomed Youth* by Sue Barnard. One would not expect a story based on the life of Wilfred Owen, the war poet, in an anthology of dark tales from Scotland; yet it worked. I wanted to know more and to find out where the story would take me. I could not put it down until I had finished. This was an inspired choice as the first story in the book, leaving me wondering how the other stories could equal or top this. The next story, *Keeper of Light* started off gently, and the tension built, little by little, until the final denouement; the approach sent shivers down my spine. It haunts me still, and I don't think I will ever forget it. Another ending which will stay with me forever is that of *Cats and Dogs*, by author Val Penny. It was truly visceral. Whilst I would love to give an individual shout out to every author in the book, I don't want to give the game away for readers, but allow them to choose for themselves. I will say all the stories are outstanding and it really is difficult to choose.

Page after gripping page, my stomach was tied in knots, and my chest tightened, as the stories kept me engrossed, each different, yet equally engaging and well-written. I could fully understand why these had been chosen for inclusion in the anthology. Each and every one is an example of what a short story should be. I was in awe of the talent shown within the pages and I was enthralled with the stories contained within the pages. This anthology is everything a good anthology should be.

I would like to congratulate all the authors in this book for the stories they have written. They demonstrate just how good Scottish writing can be, and celebrate all that is good about Scottish crime writing. I would also like to thank them for the time they have put into this charity project and hope that its success will benefit the charities greatly. Well done, darkstroke.

**Wendy H. Jones** is the President of the Scottish Association of Writers and runs two writing groups in Scotland, City Writers (Dundee) and History Writers (online). She is also a renowned international public speaker.

Wendy grew up in the beautiful Scottish city of Dundee. In a home full of books and with family who read extensively, she developed a passion for reading early in life. Having read all the books in the local library by the age of ten, she entered into a spirited discussion with a librarian as to why she should be provided with an adult library card. Showing steely will and determination, she won her battle and moved on to reading adult crime novels.

True to her adventurous side, she joined the Royal Navy to undertake nurse training after leaving school. After six years in the Navy she joined the Army where she served for a further seventeen years. This took her all over the world and fuelled her love for travel and visiting exotic lands. Postings to Hong Kong and Israel allowed her to travel extensively in the Far and Middle East.

Wendy is a committed Christian and a member of City Church Dundee, part of the New Frontiers Organisation of Churches. She enjoys spending time with her family, especially her nieces, both of whom are excited at their aunt being a published author. She still loves to travel and explore exotic locations, as well as spending time exploring the UK.

Doomed Youth

Sue Barnard

THE WESTERN FRONT
Spring 1917

"Come on, lads, and good luck!"

Wilfred fixed his bayonet, blew his whistle and scrambled up the ladder. He knew all too well what lay in store on the other side of the parapet. If he was lucky, as on previous occasions, he'd escape with his life. Otherwise, this could easily be the last time he'd ever see daylight…

Wilfred had no idea how long he'd been lying there. He eased his eyes open, rolled over on to his side and peered around him, seeing nothing but a blurred mixture of browns, greys and blacks. The sharp scent of cordite hung in the air, mingled with the smell of damp earth and another putrid odour which caught in his throat and made him retch on the spot. As his surroundings gradually came into focus, he froze in horror as he recognised the source of the stench: the rotting cadaver of one of his fellow-officers.

***

CRAIGLOCKHART WAR HOSPITAL, SLATEFORD, EDINBURGH
June 1917

"Who's the new patient?" Doctor Rivers asked.

"A junior officer, I think." Captain Brock closed the office door behind him and consulted the file in his hand. "Yes.

Second Lieutenant Wilfred Owen, Manchester Regiment. Neurasthenia." He sighed. "Another one? What on earth happens to them out there?"

"What indeed," Rivers muttered under his breath.

Craiglockhart Hydropathic had been requisitioned by the War Office the previous year as a military psychiatric hospital, and since then he and Brock had seen all too many broken young men pass through its doors. Until fairly recently, what was now known officially as neurasthenia (or, in everyday parlance, shell shock) had not even been recognised as a medical condition. In the early days of the war, any front-line troops who had become too traumatised to fight had simply been branded as cowards.

Rivers shuddered as he recalled the reports of terrified lads being court-martialled for desertion, tried (with nobody to speak in their defence) by pig-headed, narrow-minded officers, found guilty, then shot at dawn the following day by men from their own ranks.

And what, Rivers wondered, must have gone through the minds of those firing squads as they took aim and fired at someone who, only days before, might have been one of their best pals? Someone with whom they might have shared a joke and a smoke as they shivered in their filthy dugouts, united against an unknown and unseen adversary just a few yards away on the other side of No Man's Land? Such a memory would surely stay with them until their dying day, haunting their dreams just as fiercely as any traumas they might remember from the battlefields.

Today's youth was doomed. There was little hope even for those who managed to survive.

"Do you want to go and see him now?" Brock's voice interrupted his thoughts.

"What? Oh, yes, of course. Lead the way."

They found Second Lieutenant Wilfred Edward Salter Owen sitting up in his bed, staring into space. No, Rivers thought as he studied the young man's face, he's not staring into space. He's staring into hell. *Dear God. What has this poor chap been through?*

"Good morning, Second Lieutenant Owen," he began, and put out a hand. "I'm Doctor William Rivers, and this is Captain Arthur Brock. Welcome to Craiglockhart."

The patient slowly turned his head. His face was expressionless, and as he took the proffered hand his eyes seemed to look through Rivers and Brock without seeing them.

"Call me Wilfred..." He slowly focussed on his surroundings. "Where am I? What is this place...?"

Rivers detected a faint trembling beneath the chilled fingers as Wilfred returned the handshake. We'll need to tread very carefully with this one, he thought.

Aloud he said, "You're in Edinburgh, Wilfred. This is Craiglockhart. It's a special hospital for soldiers like you."

"Soldiers...like...me? You mean...?"

Rivers nodded. "Yes. We've had plenty more like you. You aren't the first, and you certainly won't be the last. There's nothing to be ashamed of."

"Ashamed..." Wilfred's voice was barely above a whisper. "Cowards..." He covered his face with his hands, and shuddered.

Rivers exchanged a quick look with Brock. The latter stepped forward.

"They were not cowards, Wilfred, whatever you might have been told to the contrary. They were just frightened young men, no different from you. We've helped them, and we're going to help you too."

Wilfred lowered his hands. His face showed a faint hint of hope, but he still looked and sounded bewildered. "So you're not going to...punish me?"

"Of course not," Rivers answered. "This is a hospital, not a prison. We're here to treat, not to torment."

Brock glanced at his watch. "It will be lunchtime soon, Wilfred. We'll leave you to rest for now, but is there anything you would like in the meantime?"

Wilfred was silent for a moment, then nodded.

"If it isn't...too much trouble, please may I have some paper...and a pen?"

After asking a nurse to deliver the pen and paper, the two

men returned to Rivers' office.

"*To treat, not to torment?*" Brock remarked as they sat down. "That was inspired!"

"Just the truth." Rivers grinned, then winced. "I could never understand the reasoning behind Colonel Graham's techniques. Those really do seem like punishments. And brutal ones at that."

Brock looked up, puzzled. "What sort of techniques? I've heard odd rumours about him, but I've never fully gathered the whole story."

Rivers grimaced. "He finds out what the patients' particular likes and dislikes are, then makes them avoid the likes and apply themselves to the dislikes. So those who hate noise – and, let's face it, very few don't after they've served on the front line – are deliberately given the noisiest rooms. And those who enjoy reading – schoolmasters, clergymen and the like – are forbidden to use the library and forced instead to do outdoor sports."

Brock's jaw dropped. "That's appalling. As if the poor buggers haven't suffered enough already."

"Indeed. Anyway, what do you suppose Owen wants with a pen and paper?"

Brock shook his head. "Goodness knows. Maybe he's an artist? Strange to use a pen for art, though."

"Hmm. Be that as it may, whatever he's doing, it could be useful."

"In what way?"

"Therapy. Keep an eye on it, will you, Arthur?"

"Will do. I'll go back and check on him this afternoon."

* * *

Noise. Constant, deafening noise. Gunfire. Explosions. Shrapnel falling…

Take cover… Close your eyes… Cover your ears…

Darkness…

Cold, grey light… Mud… Blood… Severed limbs… Staring, sightless eyes…

Corpses… Mangled, rotting corpses…

"No! No! NOOOO! Make it stop! Please, God, make it stop!"

"Hey, Wilfred, it's all right. It's just a nightmare. It's over. You're safe now."

Wilfred's eyes jerked open. He was shaking and sweating as Brock's calm voice eased him into consciousness.

"What…? Where…?"

"It's all right, Wilfred," Brock repeated gently. "You're at Craiglockhart. We're here to help you."

"The guns… The bodies…"

"Hush. Calm yourself. Take deep breaths. In, out, in, out…"

Wilfred's panting slowly subsided, and over the next few minutes he felt the pounding in his ears reduce. His violent trembling gradually ceased.

"I'm sorry… I shouldn't have—"

Brock held up his hand. "No need to apologise, Wilfred." He pulled up a chair next to the bed and sat down. "Would you like to tell me what you were dreaming about?"

Wilfred eased himself up to a sitting position as Brock helped to rearrange the pillows. Once he was comfortable, he took a deep breath and tried to keep his voice steady.

"It was the last thing I remember from the front line… We went over the top. I got so far, then there was a loud bang. The next thing I knew, I woke up in a shell hole…" His voice trailed off.

"Go on," Brock murmured encouragingly.

"When I realised where I was, I saw… I saw…" His nerves collapsed. "I'm sorry. I think I'm going to be sick."

Brock seized a bowl and held it as Wilfred emptied the contents of his stomach. When he had nothing left to bring up, he slumped back against the pillow, exhausted and embarrassed. Summoning up his courage, he spoke again.

"There were bodies everywhere! Some just looked as though they were asleep. Others were blown to smithereens. One of them was in bits all around me…"

"And that was your nightmare?"

Wilfred nodded. "Every time I close my eyes, I see him…"

The two sat in silence for a few moments, then Brock spoke again. "Wilfred, what did you do before the war?"

Wilfred relaxed slightly, grateful for the opportunity to talk about something different.

"I taught English at a school in Bordeaux, then I was a private tutor with a French family in the Pyrenees." He sighed. "That seems so long ago. It feels like a different world now."

"I think it's much the same for all of us," Brock said. "It's been a very long three years."

"How much longer do you think it will go on?"

Brock frowned and shook his head. "Who knows? I'm not sure if most of the chaps on the front line even know what they're fighting for any more."

"I can well believe that. It certainly felt like that amongst my men. Well, I say 'men', but a lot of them were little more than boys. Some of them had lied about their ages so they could join up…" Wilfred's voice trailed off. When he spoke again, his tone was sombre. "Poor buggers. They thought they were going on a grand adventure. '*It will all be over by Christmas*,' the big nobs said." He gave a wry smile. "They just didn't bother to tell us which Christmas."

"How did you get on with your men, Wilfred? Did you find that it helped having been a teacher?"

"In one sense, yes, but I'd also had some experience of pastoral care before I went to Bordeaux. When I first left school – before I went to France – I was a vicar's assistant in a town near Reading."

"For how long?"

"Just over a year. I had to do a lot of parish visiting, and I witnessed suffering I'd never seen before – poverty, illness, unemployment…" He winced. "To be brutally honest, the vicar wasn't much use. You'd expect a man of the church to care about his parishioners, wouldn't you? But this one was just full of lordly indifference. A bit like the brass hats we have to answer to now, come to think of it."

Brock smiled gently. "You really cared about your men, didn't you?"

"Oh yes. And I think they respected me, too. I hated it when

I had to lead them into danger. In many ways it felt like a betrayal…" His voice wavered.

"Don't blame yourself, Wilfred. You had no choice."

"That's what I keep trying to tell myself, but it doesn't make it any easier."

"Try not to think about it whilst you're here. I know that's easier said than done, but…"

There was another brief silence. Brock was the first to break it.

"Here, I've brought you something to read." He handed over the papers in his hand.

"*The Hydra*? What's this?"

"It's Craiglockhart's magazine. It will tell you a bit more about us and what we do."

Wilfred studied the cover thoughtfully for a moment, then asked, "The Hydra? Wasn't that a monster from Greek mythology?"

Brock nodded. "Yes. Well spotted. And it's also a reference to the old name of this place. Before the war it was a health hydro. Rich Victorians used to come here for water cures. It was called Craiglockhart Hydropathic. Rather clever, don't you think?"

"Yes, very. Thank you for these. I'll read them later." If nothing else, Wilfred thought, it might give me something else to think about for a while.

"Oh – one other question, Wilfred. Earlier, you asked for a pen and paper. May I ask why you wanted it? Are you an artist?"

"No." Wilfred hesitated, unsure how to continue. "I… I used to study poetry when I was younger. I even had a go at writing it. I thought I'd like to try my hand at it again."

"Writing poetry? That sounds very interesting. And very commendable."

Wilfred had been half-expecting Brock to dismiss this idea out of hand, so the latter's response took him by surprise.

"Writing can be very therapeutic, Wilfred," Brock went on. "Perhaps you could use your poetry to help lay those ghosts from the front line to rest?"

"How did you fare with Owen?" Rivers asked, as Brock returned.

"When I arrived, he was asleep, but tossing and turning. Then he screamed and woke up. He'd been having a nightmare about his last time at the front." Brock shuddered. "It turns out that he'd come round in a shell hole, with what was left of one of his comrades in bits all round him."

Rivers whistled under his breath. "No wonder he ended up here. His nerves must be shot to pieces."

"The strange thing is," Brock continued, "when he talked about the war, his speech was shaky and disjointed – yet when I asked him about his life before he joined up, he spoke perfectly clearly and fluently. If we can get him to focus on that, rather than on his bad memories, that ought to help."

"What did he do before the war?" Rivers asked.

"He'd worked with a vicar in Berkshire for a while, then he was a teacher. Went to France to teach English in a school in Bordeaux, then lived with a French family as a private tutor."

"Hmm. Quite an erudite chap, by the sound of it."

Brock nodded. "Oh, by the way, I left him a couple of copies of *The Hydra* to read. He spotted the mythology reference straight away."

"Did you find out what he wants with the pen and paper?"

"He said he used to write poetry, and he'd like to try his hand at it again. It will be interesting to see how that goes."

***

After Brock left, Wilfred turned his attention back to the magazines.

The first one was dated 9th June 1917. It began with a chatty (if somewhat brief) editorial, during which patients at the hospital were invited to subscribe to the magazine once they were discharged, then went on to give details of the hospital's various activities from the previous few weeks. There was an invitation to participate in a newly-revived

Camera Club, followed by reports on badminton, lawn tennis, cricket, and concerts. The remainder of the magazine appeared to be given over to contributions from readers, consisting of a varied selection of short stories, poems and memoirs, all published anonymously or under pseudonyms.

Intrigued, he turned to the second magazine. This was dated a fortnight later, and had a much longer opening editorial piece. It appeared to be a tongue-in-cheek narrative which began by lamenting the lack of availability of tea and sugar, then wandered off at a tangent detailing the apparent demise of the traditional spinster, and the total lack of cats on the streets of Edinburgh.

Next came a series of reports on badminton, lawn tennis, golf, swimming, gardening, poetry, and billiards, and a lengthy description of the hospital's most recent concert. Wilfred skimmed through these, then found himself reading a piece headed *MODERN ADVERTISING*. Its introduction claimed to "bring *The Hydra* up to the lowest ebb of modern journalism", and was followed by three pages of clever gallows humour. The final items in the magazine were, as before, a selection of contributions from readers.

Writing can be very therapeutic, Brock had said. The passages Wilfred had just read might not have been great works of literature, but if they had helped the writers come to terms with their own situations, maybe this was what Brock had had in mind.

Wilfred picked up his pen and paper.

***

July 1917

"Good morning, Wilfred. How are you feeling today?"

"Better, thank you. You were right about the writing. I've been jotting down a few ideas."

Brock smiled. "That's good to know. And it reminds me of something I need to ask you. *The Hydra* needs a new editor. How do you feel about taking it on?"

15

Wilfred blinked. "What? Me? What makes you think I'd be up to the job?"

"I know you would. I wouldn't have asked you otherwise."

"What would it involve?"

"Just sorting out the contributions from the readers and writing an editorial introduction to each issue. I thought it sounded like the sort of thing you could do."

"W-e-l-l... All right, I'll have a go."

"Good man!" Brock clapped him on the shoulder. "The latest issue has just come out, so you've got just under a fortnight to get the next one ready."

Wilfred swallowed nervously. "I suppose I'd better get on with it, then."

***

August 1917

"Wilfred, do you feel well enough for a visitor? There's someone here I think you should meet."

"Er – yes, I think so." Wilfred laid aside his pen and paper as Brock nodded, turned and left the room, returning a moment later accompanied by another man. Even before the stranger had spoken a single word, Wilfred could sense that his very demeanour oozed authority and confidence.

"Second Lieutenant Owen, meet Second Lieutenant Sassoon." After making the introduction, Brock quietly withdrew, closing the door behind him.

Wilfred gasped. "Second... Lieutenant... Sassoon? The poet?"

"Guilty as charged." The newcomer grinned, stepped forward and extended his hand. His handshake felt strong and warm. "And please, call me Siegfried."

"And I'm Wilfred. It's wonderful to meet you, Siegfried. This is a great honour. I love your poetry."

"Thank you. It's good to meet you, too. Why are you here?"

"Shell shock. And you?"

Siegfried sat down. "Officially, the same as you.

Unofficially, they sent me here because they said I was mad. And possibly dangerous."

Wilfred raised his eyebrows. "Mad? On what basis? Forgive me, but you look sane enough to me."

"Thank you. Yes, I am perfectly sane. But I had the audacity to question why the war is still ongoing."

Wilfred frowned. "I think that's true for most of us by now."

"Well, yes – but I did it publicly. I wrote to *The Times* and said I believe that those who have the power to end the war are deliberately prolonging it. Not surprisingly, the authorities didn't like that. By rights I should have been court-martialled and shot, but a friend of mine lodged an appeal suggesting that my mental faculties might have been affected by my time at the Front. So instead they declared me insane – sorry: '*suffering from neurasthenia*' – and packed me off here to Dottyville."

"Dottyville?" Wilfred chuckled. "That's a very good name for it."

"I don't know what they hope to achieve by sending me here," Siegfried went on, "other than perhaps rewire my brain so it stops being so mutinous. But if that's what they've got in mind, they'll have a long job." He scowled, then his face relaxed. "But that's more than enough about me. How about you? Captain Brock tells me you like to write poetry."

Wilfred sighed. "I try, but I know I'll never be as good as you."

"Let me be the judge of that. Can you show me something you've written?"

Wilfred hesitated, then shyly handed over a handwritten manuscript.

Siegfried read it, reciting every word under his breath, then looked up. "This is good, Wilfred. Really good."

"You think so?"

Siegfried nodded. "I know so."

"Would it be good enough to put in our house magazine? Anonymously, of course."

"I don't see why not. Who's the editor?"

Wilfred gave a sheepish smile. "I am. And I'm always looking for stuff to go in it."

Siegfried grinned. "Well, that settles it! Do you want one of mine to keep it company? I have something which might fit the bill." He winked. "A sonnet with a difference. It's called *Dreamers*. And it's very subversive."

Wilfred returned the grin. "Yes please. I'm starting to put Issue 10 together now. All contributions gratefully received."

***

Darkness… Fatigue… Trudging through mud… Flashes in the distance… Strange noises… The oddly familiar smell of mustard…

Struggling to fit the masks…

The man who didn't make it in time…

Following the wagon, watching him gasp… choke… retch… slowly and horribly die…

"NO! NO! NO!"

Wilfred's nightmare was ended by the sound of his own screams dragging him into consciousness. He had no idea of the time, but the early-morning Scottish sun was creeping round the edge of the curtains. Mercifully, he was alone. He lay back on his pillow gazing at the ceiling until his ragged breathing subsided, then eased himself to a sitting position and reached for the pen and paper on his bedside table.

***

September 1917

Siegfried closed Issue 10 of *The Hydra*, which contained two examples of Wilfred's verse and one of his own, and smiled.

"Well, Second Lieutenant Owen, how does it feel to see your words in print?"

"It hasn't really sunk in yet. But thank you for the vote of

18

confidence. I know I wouldn't have dared to do it without your encouragement. And neither of mine are in the same league as yours."

"Don't put yourself down. It's true that I've had a bit more practice at it, but that's all. You have the makings of a fine poet, Wilfred."

Wilfred's jaw dropped. "Really?"

"Really. And I can help you become a great one. Those lines you've used in the Editorial, for example, could be developed into something longer. In the meantime, do you have anything else you can show me?"

"Well, if you're sure…"

"Of course I'm sure. Otherwise, I wouldn't ask."

***

September / October 1917

ANTHEM FOR DEAD YOUTH

What passing-bells for these who die as cattle?
– Only the monstrous anger of the guns…

Siegfried read through the poem, then picked up a pencil.

"That's very powerful, Wilfred. Very powerful indeed. I think *silent minds* might be better as *patient minds*, but other than that, just a few very minor suggestions about sentence structure. You're getting very good at this."

Wilfred smiled modestly. "Thank you."

"Just the truth, my friend. Oh – one more thing: I think the title might be better as *Anthem for Doomed Youth*. 'Doomed' isn't necessarily the same as 'dead'."

Wilfred considered, then nodded. "I hadn't thought of it in those terms, but you're right."

***

October 1917

DULCE ET DECORUM EST

Bent double, like old beggars under sacks,
Knock-kneed, coughing like hags, we cursed through sludge,
Till on the haunting flares we turned our backs
And towards our distant rest began to trudge…

Wilfred watched nervously as Siegfried perused the draft.

"The first eight lines look fine," Siegfried said, when he had finished. "Perhaps lose the next four, and go straight in with '*Gas! GAS!*' That gives a much stronger contrast to the slow metre of the first verse. After that, it pulls no punches. Your description of following the wagon is so vivid that it almost turns my stomach."

"Thanks," Wilfred murmured. "It was based on memories of a gas attack." He shuddered. "It still gives me nightmares, even now."

"And those last two lines – they sum up exactly what I think. *Dulce et decorum est pro patria mori*? It's the biggest lie I've ever heard. There's nothing sweet or fitting in dying for one's country." He squared his shoulders. "The truth must be told, Wilfred. And between us, I reckon we can do it."

***

EPILOGUE

Wilfred Owen was discharged from Craiglockhart at the end of October 1917; Siegfried Sassoon remained there for another month. Thereafter, the two friends remained in regular contact.

Following a few months of home service (during which time he was promoted to Lieutenant), Wilfred Owen returned to the Western Front in August 1918. In October of that year, after leading an assault on the German front line, he wrote to his mother:

"My nerves are in perfect order. I came out again in order to help these boys – directly by leading them as well as an officer can; indirectly, by watching their sufferings that I may speak of them as well as a pleader can."

He was killed in action in France on 4th November 1918, exactly one week before the war ended. His family in England received the news of his death on 11th November as the church bells were ringing to celebrate the Armistice. He was just twenty-five years old.

Only five of Wilfred Owen's poems were published during his lifetime, including two (*Song of Songs* and *The Next War*) which were published anonymously in *The Hydra* in 1917, in Issues 10 and 12 respectively. An untitled and uncredited eight-line fragment which appeared in the Editorial section of Issue 10 was later adapted into part of *The Dead-Beat*. In total, he wrote forty-six complete poems, many of which were written or drafted during his time at Craiglockhart. These include the two for which he is probably best known: the haunting *Anthem for Doomed Youth* and the graphic *Dulce et Decorum Est*. Both of these poems appear in full below.

Siegfried Sassoon returned to active service after leaving Craiglockhart and was promoted to Lieutenant and subsequently to Acting Captain. Following a head injury in France in July 1918, he returned to Britain where he spent the remainder of the war. He lived until 1967, becoming a celebrated author, editor and outspoken anti-war poet. In 1920, with the assistance of Edith Sitwell, he edited and published a posthumous collection of Wilfred Owen's verse.

Wilfred Owen is now regarded as one of the greatest poets of the First World War. In a draft preface to his work, written in Spring 1918, he wrote:

"*I am not concerned with Poetry. My subject is War, and the pity of War. The Poetry is in the pity... All a poet can do today is warn. That is why the true Poets must be truthful.*"

As for Craiglockhart, it continued as a military psychiatric hospital until 1919, after which it was sold to the Society of the Sacred Heart and became a Roman Catholic convent and teacher training college. Since 1986, it has belonged to what is now Edinburgh Napier University.

The original building still stands. It is now home to the War Poets Collection. This permanent exhibition includes volumes of poems by Owen and Sassoon, together with three original editions of *The Hydra*, and forms a fitting tribute to this fascinating chapter in Craiglockhart's history.

***

ANTHEM FOR DOOMED YOUTH

What passing-bells for these who die as cattle?
– Only the monstrous anger of the guns.
Only the stuttering rifles' rapid rattle
Can patter out their hasty orisons.
No mockeries for them; no prayers nor bells;
Nor any voice of mourning save the choirs, –
The shrill, demented choirs of wailing shells;
And bugles calling for them from sad shires.

What candles may be held to speed them all?
Not in the hands of boys but in their eyes
Shall shine the holy glimmers of goodbyes.
The pallor of girls' brows shall be their pall;
Their flowers the tenderness of patient minds,
And each slow dusk a drawing-down of blinds.

DULCE ET DECORUM EST

Bent double, like old beggars under sacks,
Knock-kneed, coughing like hags, we cursed through sludge,
Till on the haunting flares we turned our backs
And towards our distant rest began to trudge.

Men marched asleep. Many had lost their boots
But limped on, blood-shod. All went lame, all blind;
Drunk with fatigue; deaf even to the hoots
Of tired, outstripped Five-Nines that dropped behind.

Gas! GAS! Quick, boys! – An ecstasy of fumbling,
Fitting the clumsy helmets just in time;
But someone still was yelling out and stumbling,
And flound'ring like a man in fire or lime…
Dim, through the misty panes and thick green light,
As under a green sea, I saw him drowning.

In all my dreams, before my helpless sight,
He plunges at me, guttering, choking, drowning.

If in some smothering dreams you too could pace
Behind the wagon that we flung him in,
And watch the white eyes writhing in his face,
His hanging face, like a devil's sick of sin;
If you could hear, at every jolt, the blood
Come gargling from the froth-corrupted lungs,
Obscene as cancer, bitter as the cud
Of vile, incurable sores on innocent tongues, –
My friend, you would not tell with such high zest
To children ardent for some desperate glory,
The old Lie: Dulce et decorum est
Pro patria mori.

***

The above poems and quotations are reproduced from *Wilfred Owen: the War Poems*, edited by Jon Stallworthy (Chatto & Windus, 1994), by arrangement with the Wilfred Owen Royalties Trust.

Many of Wilfred Owen's original handwritten manuscripts are now held at the British Library in London. Images can be viewed on the Library's website: **www.bl.uk/collection-items/the-poetry-manuscripts-of-wilfred-owen**

More details of the War Poets Collection can be found on the Edinburgh Napier University website: **www.napier.ac.uk/about-us/our-location/our-campuses/special-collections/war-poets-collection**

Special thanks are due to Catherine Walker MBE, Curator of the War Poets Collection, for her unfailing help, advice and encouragement during the production of this story.

———————————

Sue Barnard is a British novelist, editor and award-winning poet. She was born in North Wales but has spent most of her life in and around Manchester. After graduating from Durham University, Sue got married then had a variety of office jobs before becoming a full-time parent. If she had her way, the phrase "non-working mother" would be banned from the English language.

She has been with Crooked Cat/darkstroke since joining their editing team in 2013. Since then she has written six novels: *The Ghostly Father,Nice Girls Don't, The Unkindest Cut of All, Never on Saturday, Heathcliff: The Missing Years*, and *Finding Nina.*

Sue has a mind which is sufficiently warped as to be capable of compiling questions for BBC Radio 4's fiendishly difficult *Round Britain Quiz.* This once caused one of her sons to describe her as "professionally weird." The label has stuck. She speaks French like a Belgian, German like a schoolgirl, and Italian and Portuguese like an Englishwoman abroad.

She is also very interested in Family History. Her own background is far stranger than any work of fiction; she'd write a book about it if she thought anybody would believe her.

Sue lives in Cheshire, UK, with her extremely patient husband and a large collection of unfinished scribblings.

Follow Sue on Facebook @suebarnardauthor, Twitter @AuthorSusanB, Instagram @suebarnardauthor and Amazon - @Sue-Barnard/e/B00IF4ZJJU/, and visit her blog - broad-thoughts-from-a-home.blogspot.co.uk/ - for more about her and her books.

Keeper of the Light

J.K. Fulton

I don't know what made me call Uncle Michael. I hadn't spoken to him for years; not since my parents' funeral. He wasn't even my real uncle.

"You'll be after some money, then," he said.

"No, no, that's not what..."

"So you have savings?"

I had no answer to that.

"Come up to Edinburgh," said Uncle Michael.

"I can't," I said. The pips started, and I fed another ten pence into the slot. I jangled the few remaining coins in my palm. Add those to the crumpled pound notes in my trouser pocket and I might have managed to make it as far as Nottingham.

"Get yourself to King's Cross first thing tomorrow. There'll be a ticket waiting at the booking office." He paused. "I think I've got an opportunity for you. Something to tide you over for the summer at least."

I spent the train journey alternately staring out of the window and trying to read the cheap paperback I'd bought in the station with the last of my loose change. The further I got from London and that disastrous job, the worse I felt. I'd failed catastrophically at my first attempt to strike out on my own. And now here I was, running back up to Scotland with my tail between my legs.

Not that I had much choice. I was lucky my boss hadn't wanted to press charges, and I'd never get another job in banking once they called my previous employer for a reference.

Uncle Michael made me feel welcome, didn't press for too many details about what had gone wrong in London, but after dinner he shooed Aunt Morag out of the dining room and leaned in close.

"Have you a good suit?"

I nodded. More than one. I'd been expected to dress smartly for work. I had three jackets and five pairs of trousers, all matching, all tailor-made. Probably the only things I still owned of any value.

"Then here's where you're going. Tomorrow morning, ten o'clock."

He pushed a bit of paper across the table. "84 George Street," I read. "What's this?"

"A summer job, my boy," he said. "You need to clear your head. Get London out of your system."

I couldn't disagree.

"You heard I've been made a Commissioner of the Northern Lighthouse Board?" I hadn't. "No matter. A summer by the seaside is just what you need."

***

The interview was a formality. I was greeted with a limp handshake, as if the interviewer were expecting some arcane Masonic grip I couldn't provide, but most of the talk was of Uncle Michael, who seemed to exert an almost obsequious awe and fascination over my interviewer.

"One last thing," I was asked. "How's your cooking?"

"Cooking?" I frowned. "I can make beans on toast, or an omelette, at a push." Most of the time in London I'd eaten out with the guys from the office. If there's one thing London's not short of, it's restaurants. Socialising with the other juniors had been expected: work hard, play hard, drink even harder.

"Ah." The interviewer looked disappointed. There had been no questions about seamanship or knots or meteorology or whatever other nautical skills I imagined lighthouse keepers might need, but my lack of cooking skill had thrown him. "A relief keeper needs to take his turn making the meals, just like the other keepers. Your mammy'll not be there to make your eggy soldiers."

"Is it a problem?"

"Well, it's a bit of a disappointment, I'll not lie. We need someone for Muckle Flugga, Cape Wrath, and the Bell Rock, but they're all rock stations. They'd not thank me if I sent you out there and they had to live on beans on toast and omelettes for a month." He leaned back and scratched his head. "But we could do with a relief keeper to cover holidays for some of the shore stations, too. The keepers live there with their families, so you'd just be fending for yourself." He sighed. "It's a bit of a cushy posting for a first timer, and I'll need to shuffle things around a bit. But seeing as it's your Uncle Michael..." He stood up and extended a hand. "Welcome to the Northern Lighthouse Board."

***

My first posting was two weeks at a lighthouse just outside Montrose, covering the assistant keeper's summer holiday. I stayed in a spartan B&B in the port, ate in the local pub, and carried out the bare minimum of duties under the direction of the laconic principal keeper. He'd assessed me with a single look, found me lacking, and trusted me to wind the light every few hours, but nothing more.

I was so bored at the end of the two weeks that I was ready to jack it all in. But I had nowhere to go, and I wouldn't be paid until the end of the month, so when I got the letter sending me up to the Highlands for my next posting, I sighed, packed my duffle bag (Uncle Michael had said the keepers would laugh at me if I turned up carrying my fancy London-bought suitcase) and got on the train.

The scenery on the journey towards Inverness almost made it all worthwhile. I'd always been a city boy, growing up in Edinburgh, followed by university in Glasgow, then work in London. It was the first time I'd ever been that far north, deep into the wild Highlands. Even the light, unfiltered by city pollution, looked different, like a pale golden liquid washing over the craggy landscape.

I changed at Inverness onto the local service, then was met with another passive handshake at the station by the assistant keeper, a tall fair-haired man in his early thirties. He was wearing work clothes, heavy trousers and a green army-style jumper, both heavily spotted with paint, but on his head was a neat uniform cap, black-brimmed, white-crowned, with the golden NLB badge shining on the front.

He slammed the creaking rusty door of his Ford Escort and threw the cap onto the back seat.

"It's not far," he said.

I nodded, and fiddled with my seatbelt.

"You don't talk much, do you?"

I'd got out of the habit over the previous fortnight, and had almost forgotten how to make small talk. "You were wearing your cap," I said, trying to find a suitable subject. "Do you ever have to wear the full uniform?"

"Only when the commissioners come around," he laughed. "When the high priests honour you with their presence, you have to wear your Sunday best, ye ken? They like to see the little folk all turned out nicely for their lords and masters. I just wore the cap so you'd recognise me. I didn't fancy putting a rose in my buttonhole and carrying a copy of the Financial Times under my arm." He paused for a second. "No offence intended. Your uncle's the new commissioner, is he no?"

I nodded. "He's not really my uncle," I said, embarrassed. "He was a friend of my father."

He looked sideways at me. "No blood relation?"

I shook my head.

He seemed to relax a bit. "Ach well, a wee bit of nepotism never hurt anybody." The principal keeper at Montrose hadn't been of the same opinion.

We drove along winding roads, through a fishing village with nearly as many churches as houses, then along the narrow road out to the point. The lighthouse stood at the tip of a long, finger-like peninsula that jutted out into the North

Sea, and we could see the huge white tower with its red bands from miles off.

"Quite a location, is it no?" he said. "It's perfect for a lighthouse. Over there to the left you can see clear across the Dornoch Firth, then there's the far side of the Moray Firth to the right, and the North Sea is dead ahead. Clear views of the sea all around. There's aye been a beacon here. The fisherfolk from the port used to light a fire on a mound near the point to guide their boats home, and there's a local legend that the lighthouse was built on the site of a Roman signal fire."

"I didn't think the Romans got this far north," I said.

"Maybe not the army, no, but after the battle of Mons Graupius, the Roman governor Agricola sent his fleet all the way up to Orkney. They'd have sailed right past the point." His voice tailed off dreamily, as if he were imagining triremes surging up the coast.

The honey-scent of yellow gorse flowers wafted through the open windows, and then I caught a glimpse of the iron-grey Moray Firth.

He saw where I was looking. "We get dolphins around here, ye ken."

"Really?" I had no idea. I'd always associated dolphins with sunny places. Didn't Flipper off the telly live by the Florida coast? The North Sea didn't seem quite exotic enough.

"Aye," he said. "Magical beasts. The Greeks and Romans thought they were sacred to the god Apollo. If you're lucky, you might see a pod or two while you're here. I saw one just this morning. Always a good omen."

He brought the car to a halt and popped the boot. "Here's your bag." Beside the tower was a building containing the keepers' accommodation, single-storey and flat-roofed, painted in the same bright white as the tower, with mustard trim around the doors and windows. He led me past the cottages, out of the lighthouse courtyard, to a driveway containing an old caravan that looked even more dilapidated than his ancient Ford. "Welcome to your new home."

The caravan creaked as we stepped inside, and there was a

faint smell of cabbage and socks. "Not quite what you're used to, eh?" A tiny black-and-white television with a wire coat-hanger for an aerial sat on a chipped Formica shelf, and the dust-smeared windows looked out onto the blank outside walls of the courtyard.

"I've stayed in worse," I lied, trying not to think about my flat in London with its panoramic views over the city and colour telly. "I didn't think I'd start my career as a lighthouse keeper in a caravan, though."

He frowned.

"Don't let the principal hear you say that."

"Say what? Caravan?"

"No, 'lighthouse keeper'. There's no such thing. We're *light*keepers. We don't keep the *house*, we keep the *light*."

"Sorry," I muttered.

"Aye, well," he said, pushing his face close to mine, suddenly grim and intense, his brows stitching a frown across his face. I tried to back up, but there was nowhere to go, and I sat down hard on the bench that doubled as a bed. He loomed over me. "The light is the most important thing. Let the tower fall, let the buildings crumble, let the world fall to hell and damnation, but *do not let the light fail*."

"No, no, of course not," I said, holding my hands up.

He took a step back, and seemed to calm himself with an effort. "Sorry, lad, but this is serious. You have to learn how important this is. It's a sacking offence to let the light go out. It's like..." He paused as if unsure, then continued. "You've heard of the Temple of Vesta?"

"In Rome? With the, what were they called, Vestal Virgins?"

"They were priestesses of the holy fire, dedicated for life to their goddess. It was their sacred duty to make sure the flame didn't go out. When Theodosius, who was one of the first Christian Emperors, ordered the fire to be put out in 394 AD, that was what started the decline and fall of Rome."

"Right," I said, uncertainly.

He nodded. "Earlier, when the Roman general Sulla sacked Delphi, he extinguished the eternal flame in the temple of Apollo – the flame that the Greeks had kept alive for centuries. Greece was never the same again; the Romans had broken their spirit."

"OK," I said in answer to his earnest gaze. He seemed keen for me to take this all in.

"And even further back, in Babylon, they kept a sacred flame burning in their temple, and only extinguished it at the death of the Great King. Alexander the Great ordered the sacred fire put out for the funeral of his friend Hephaestion – and that was a bad omen that foretold his own death less than a year later." His eyes glinted. "The fire, the light – *that's* what's important. That's what's *always* been important."

"You're saying lightkeepers are Vestal Virgins?" I said, then immediately regretted it and wished I could keep my smart mouth shut. Just for once. For a second he looked as if he wanted to hit me.

"Ach!" he spat. "You're just a daft laddie." He turned to leave. With one hand on the caravan door, he turned back. "Get settled. You'll be on two until six tonight. Get some sleep."

"What about dinner?" I asked. I'd had nothing but a curled-up British Rail sandwich since lunchtime.

"The office called ahead. There're some supplies in the wee fridge." The caravan shook as he closed the door behind himself.

I let out a breath. I'd got off to a bad start with the principal in Montrose, and it looked like I'd messed things up here, too. When Uncle Michael had suggested the job, I'd imagined something more like a monastic existence. Isolation and silence – that was what I'd wanted after the noise and chaos of London. That was what my soul was crying out for. Instead, I just couldn't help rubbing everyone up the wrong way and making more trouble for myself.

I opened the fridge and, despite my gloom, laughed. Inside were beans, bread, and eggs. All the fixings for beans on toast and an omelette.

***

I had my meagre meal, then lay on the hard bed and tried to relax. The sun was still high, and would be for some hours. I checked the date window on my wristwatch; it was the 20th, the eve of the solstice. Come midnight, it would be the longest day, the shortest night, and that far north it would be like the sun would never set. Not that the long daylight did me much good; the caravan was trapped in a shadowy angle of walls, and I couldn't even read my paperback without switching a light on.

I pondered my strange colleague with his surprising enthusiasm for ancient history. I hadn't expected much in the way of erudite conversation from keepers, not after my experience with the laconic principal in Montrose, but I supposed it made sense. Particularly on rock stations where the keepers spent an entire month away from civilisation, there probably wasn't much to do *except* read. The assistant keeper had no doubt been reading some book on ancient history recently, and had wanted to impress the fancy London boy with his knowledge.

But his mercurial attitude, congenial one minute, almost threatening the next, would make for a stressful posting. I hoped the principal keeper was more reasonable.

I finished my paperback, wished I'd brought more than one, and realised the sun had actually set at last. It was gone half-past ten.

It was strange, though. I hadn't heard anyone open the big heavy door to the tower. Maybe the principal had overslept? That would annoy the god of the sacred fire! I craned my head out the window and looked up at the tower. Against the inky-blue sky swept four bright white beams, smooth as a Swiss chronograph's second hand. I timed them with my watch. Four beams, repeating every thirty seconds exactly.

I shrugged then went back to lie down.

I hadn't expected to fall asleep, but I was suddenly awakened from a dream of flames and clockwork and Roman maidens in flowing white robes by the assistant keeper banging on the flimsy caravan door.

"Get your lazy arse up those stairs."

33

I stared blearily at my watch. "It's not quite two yet." My travel alarm clock hadn't even gone off.

"There are two hundred steps up that tower," said the keeper. "You've to be up there to relieve the principal at two, not a moment after."

"I'll be there in a minute," I mumbled, pulling my boots on. I pondered making some coffee, but the keeper's stern face at the window made me think again. Surely there had to be a kettle at the top of the tower, anyway? With shorter towers, keepers tended to go up to the lightroom to wind the mechanism, then come back down. With a monstrous tower like this one, it made more sense to stay at the top for the entire four-hour shift. I hoped there was at least a comfy chair. And maybe a book or two. I pondered asking the assistant keeper for a loan of his history book but decided against it.

**

The spiral stairs seemed to go on forever, their red-painted edges like blood in the dim light. At regular intervals there were windows, deep-set in the thick walls, affording me an occasional glimpse of darkened seas, their wave crests etched in pale moonlight.

At last, slightly out of breath, I made it to the lightroom. The central mechanism whirred away in its cast-iron cabinet, brass governors spinning like children's toys, as the vast clockwork converted the slow earthwards fall of a weight down the central shaft of the lighthouse into the rotation of the lens assembly. The sharp tang of Brasso was in the air. Above me the light sat at the centre of its nest of Fresnel lenses, the whole thing smoothly rotating on a reservoir of mercury.

"Hello?" No answer. That was strange. The principal was supposed to be up here already. It wasn't like there was anywhere to go. There was the lightroom, the gantry above that allowed access to the light itself, and...

The door to the balcony. The heavy hatch was shut, but its

three-quarter-inch diameter bolt was drawn. The principal had to be taking the night air. I heaved the door open and called out again. "Hello?"

The air had been still at ground level, but up there, hundreds of feet above, the wind whistled through the balcony railings like a distant haunting and a shiver ran through me. I'd never had a problem with heights, but this was something different. I could swear I felt the tower sway.

I stepped outside and gripped the handrail, firmly anchoring myself to the tower. "Hello?" I called again. This was getting silly. Were they playing some sort of prank on the new boy? It was all a bit juvenile. It was the sort of thing I'd have expected from the lads in the London office, not the grizzled sea dog I expected a principal keeper to be.

That made up my mind. I'd had enough. Keeping a light was not the job for me. I'd call my uncle in the morning and tell him. Or better yet, just walk away. Get a job in a bar or something. Leave *everything* behind.

And then I saw him, standing on the balcony, staring out towards the thin sliver of land to the south-west. It was the only direction where the beams of focused light didn't sweep overhead; the landward panes of the lightroom were painted to block the light. His skinny frame leaned out over the rail, as if his whole body were yearning for the land.

In the dim light, he looked gaunt. His hair was long and lank, shot with grey, and when he turned to me his eyes were sunken and black, more like eye sockets in a skull.

His mouth opened, his lips moved, but nothing but a hiss came out. He closed his mouth, swallowed, and tried again. "Wh-Who are you?" he whispered, his voice hoarse and cracked as if through long silence.

"I'm the relief keeper," I said.

He slumped, and a susurrus escaped his lips. "At last."

I looked at my watch. It was just turning two o'clock. "I'm right on time," I said, but the old man pushed past me, his bony frame shouldering me aside with surprising strength, and ducked through the hatch into the lightroom.

"Hey!" I followed him back inside, and slammed the

heavy door shut. The bolt screeched as I jiggled it home.

The principal keeper was hunched over the desk, scratching in the log book. "It's been so long. Such a long, long watch."

"I can imagine," I said. I didn't much like the ten until two shift myself. The long hours straddling midnight always seemed to drag.

"But the next watch will be even longer." He looked on me with what seemed like pity, then headed down the stairs. His footsteps echoed into the distance. I stood there until the sound of his departure faded to silence, finally punctuated by the sharp report of the tower door at the bottom slamming closed.

The silence was broken by the noise of the mechanism needing to be wound, so I grabbed the winding handle and began to turn, raising the weight from the depths of the tower back up to the top so it could begin its descent and power the light's rotation once more.

I straightened up and rubbed my back. It was a long wind – but the advantage of a tall tower was that you had to wind it less often, so I had some time to myself to get my bearings. Disappointingly, there was no sign of a kettle. I looked at my watch. Just after two. I'd have plenty of time to go back down to my caravan for a coffee, then head back up before the mechanism next needed winding. I had a feeling I'd need the caffeine.

I found myself counting the steps under my breath on the way back down. How many steps had the assistant keeper said? Two hundred?

One hundred steps. Then a hundred more. And the bottom was still out of sight. Each step was the same as the last, with only the occasional window to break up the constant monotonous placing of one foot in front of the other, round and round the spiral.

The assistant must have been mistaken. There were more than two hundred steps.

I reached two hundred and fifty before I started to wonder. Had I lost count? Missed out the eighties or something? The oddly hypnotic motion, step after step, round and round, made it difficult to keep the numbers from dancing in my head.

Three hundred steps, and still no end in sight. The night-obscured view from the windows didn't reveal much, but certainly gave no indication of getting any closer to the ground.

Four hundred. Five hundred. That was impossible. I ran a rough calculation in my head. If each step was six inches (and they looked higher than that) the stairs had taken me two hundred and fifty feet down from the top.

The tower wasn't even two hundred foot tall, from the tip of its weather-vane to the door at the bottom.

I kept going for another hundred steps, then a hundred more. Then stopped.

I don't know how long I stood there, staring down at the impossible spiral, but eventually I looked at my watch and realised the next winding was due.

I turned around and headed back up the tower.

***

There were two hundred and three steps back up to the top of the tower. I wound the mechanism, then sat with a defeated thump at the desk.

After a minute or two I idly opened the log book. The principal keeper's scrawl was incomprehensible. And so was the previous entry. And the one before. Page after page I flicked backwards, and only slowly did the writing look more legible.

The details were banal. Sunrises and sunsets, along with watch times, going back years.

I flicked back a few more pages. Twenty years. Fifty. A hundred. A hundred and fifty – right back to the founding of the lighthouse in 1830.

All in the same hand. There was a steady progression from a clear, elegant script through to the later incomprehensible chicken-scratch.

I flipped back to the end and picked up the pen.

I've been sitting here now, pen in hand, for what seems like hours. I know what I have to do, but the courage – or perhaps resignation – is slow to come.

But there is no escaping my duty. I must keep the light until the end of my watch.

J.K. Fulton lives in Leicester, but as his father was a lightkeeper, he grew up at lighthouses all around the Scottish coast. His short stories have appeared in Uncharted Constellations (Space Cat Press, 2020), Best of British Science Fiction 2018 (NewCon Press, 2019), Leicester Writes Short Story Prize Anthology (Dahlia Books, 2018) and Shoreline of Infinity (The New Curiosity Shop, 2016).

Under the somewhat transparent pseudonym John K. Fulton, he has also written Scottish children's historical fiction: The Wreck of the Argyll (Cargo 2015, republished Cranachan 2018), and The Beast on the Broch (Cranachan, 2016).

For more information see www.johnkfulton.com or find him on Twitter: @johnkfulton

In Hiding

Ross Alexander

CHAPTER ONE
EVEN FLOW

I have always had a fascination with the surgeon's scalpel. I remember as a child watching too much television and learning the word 'scalpel' before fully understanding what it meant. It seemed that any television show that depicted a life-saving operation began with the surgeon asking for the scalpel, something that, then, in the playground, I would copy, much to the bewilderment of my friends. It was inevitable that I would follow the calling and seek out a career in medicine.

I can't recall exactly when my scalpel collection began, but it must have been some time before I went off to St Andrews University. I would have been around sixteen years old when the first one was purchased, spotted it in a charity shop window, it was an antique blade with a bone handle, and was in its original box. My parents were not told at the time and the legislation to buy knives was more relaxed in those days than it is now. It was surprisingly inexpensive and, based on current value, it must be my best ever investment.

Once university started, I began to buy an assortment of scalpels, both modern and older. When my graduation came, my parents bought me a ridiculously expensive model and had my name, 'ALEX', engraved into the handle. They knew that despite my desire to become a surgeon, I would not be able to use it, but they were happy for me to add the knife to my ever-growing collection. If they worried about my weird obsession, they never showed it. They were just proud that their only child graduated with a First in Medicine and would be starting their career in Edinburgh.

After graduation, I withdrew somewhat from society. Fortunately, life as a junior doctor gives you a believable excuse for missing so many social events. Relationships were also areas I had no interest in, and again, the ridiculously long hours working hours convinced my parents that I had no time to think about meeting someone.

Things started to take a dark turn in my second year at the hospital. I managed to convince my parents that moving out of the family home and getting a place of my own would give me more independence. I earned enough, now, to be self-sufficient, and a mixture of long working hours and a lack of desire to spend money on material things meant most of my money remained in the bank. I still bought the odd scalpel, however. My collection had grown to fifty at this point. God knows how much I must have spent on some of the more vintage models.

I had experience of using the hospital-issued scalpels as well as the ones from university. I was fascinated to know how those in my collection would compare. Would the cheaper, modern, disposable scalpels perform better than ones that were over one-hundred years old? An unlikely friendship, that had been built up over a number of years would allow me to discover this.

Alan worked in the butcher's shop in Stockbridge, right next to my flat. I was particularly fond of their traditional steak pies and would visit often to treat myself. Alan knew my profession. We learned similar skills in our respective training, albeit for very different purposes. After getting to know him a bit better I approached Alan with a proposition. A suitable carcass was required, one that I could hone my surgical skills on. Alan agreed that he could do a good deal on part of a pig and would also be happy to dispose of it afterwards for me. He gave me tips on how to keep the meat fresh and how long it could be used before it had to be disposed of. I also agreed to remove all the stitching before returning it to him. I wasn't sure how legal or ethical this practice was, but we had become good friends over the period and considered we could trust each other to keep it between ourselves.

The first carcass I received from Alan was a loin section of the animal. For my purposes, I didn't need anything overly-expensive, and it was just big enough for my requirements. I would not be using all my scalpels, but it would give me an opportunity to test out a number of my collection for their intended purpose.

Choosing ten scalpels to begin with. I had purchased a special moleskin notebook to record my findings. One by one, I made two incisions with each blade. First I would use the palmar or dinner knife grip. Secondly I would use the same scalpel to make an incision using the more delicate pencil grip. A sense of pure joy was felt with the even flow of each cut. In my hand it felt like the artist's paintbrush or the sculptor's chisel. I noted the performance of each scalpel methodically; weight, comfort, ease of incision and end result. This was recorded twice for each scalpel, once for each grip.

I had to sew up each incision and then remove the stitching so that Alan would not suspect my real motive. He was happy to continue to provide and dispose of more pig-flesh. The exercise was repeated a further four times over a number of weeks. I was both surprised and delighted that the final scalpel that I used was the most effective, achieving the highest mark in my perverse scoring system. The scalpel that I had been deliberately kept until last. The 'ALEX' scalpel given to me by parents. The one that I would shortly use on human flesh.

Only it would not happen in the hospital, under anaesthetic or with the patients' consent.

CHAPTER TWO
IN HIDING

David Jones sat by the converted outbuilding that was now his home. The property was miles away from the nearest village in rural East Lothian, with beautiful views of the coastline towards the North Sea. The rustic property sat on the edge of farmland. He had purchased it from an old farmer for a steal, given the derelict state of the building. The farmer's own house was a number of hectares away and David was left alone to get on with his solitary life. That was just they way he liked it.

David Jones is not his real name, it was part of his new identity as well as a new life. He was keen to leave his past behind. Initially he had scoffed at the name, thinking that he was neither a member of The Monkees nor Welsh. He never had a choice in the matter, however, and soon embraced the name, his new persona and his new beginning.

His upbringing was pretty normal and was certainly not an early indication of what would happen to him in his early adult years. He grew up in a small village in East Lothian within a comfortable three bedroomed semi-detached house. His father was an area manager for an insurance company and his mother worked part-time in the local school. He had no siblings, and the majority of his extended family lived in Aberdeen, where his parents grew up. David also had a good circle of friends and did the sort of things that most children do at that age: he had a number of good relationships with girls from high school and then in college where he went to study computing.

It was through his college years that the first traumatic event of his life occurred. Coming home from an evening out together, David's parents were involved in a car crash. A young, newly-qualified driver was speeding his way through the back roads of East Lothian in a far-too-powerful car. He overtook at a blind spot and careered straight into David's parents' car. The evil twist of fate was that David's parents were killed outright and the young driver escaped with only a broken leg and whiplash.

David had been exceptionally close to his parents and never really recovered from what happened. He threw himself into his college work, passing his courses before gaining a place at university. Financially secured from his inheritance, David could have easily gone off the rails. He knew how important his education was to his parents, so wanted to do them proud should they be watching down from a higher place. It was upon leaving university that things started to turn sour.

He graduated at a time when a degree no longer guaranteed employment. Although he did not have the financial worries of his fellow alumni, his lack of employment started to affect his mental health. He had worked incredibly hard over the previous four years securing his degree, working towards his chosen profession. The lack of opportunity made him question his decisions, whether he had wasted time studying for a degree that may be useless to him.Within the first few month of leaving university, the global financial crisis hit, making finding employment almost impossible. His particular branch of computing was geared towards the financial sector and he was unable to find work in his chosen field, or any other computer related roles. After a year of rejected applications and unsuccessful interviews, a chance encounter took his life down the darkest of roads, and into drug addiction.

It started with speed, a little something to pick him up when he was feeling down. A little before a Friday night out and a little more before a Saturday night out. Soon he was having more than a little on a Friday and Saturday until he was consuming every day of the week. In what seemed like no time at all, the drug was no longer having the desired effect and the small step towards cocaine use was completed. Within two years of graduating, he had spent almost his entire inheritance and found himself serving a five year sentence in jail.

Life in Edinburgh's prison was tough. He was targeted for attack, had unthinkable things added to his food and drink, and was verbally abused continually. Even the guards appeared to turn a blind eye to these events. It was hell on earth with one major exception. It got him off of drugs for good.

David was released early due to good behaviour and

arranged to sell the family home. It was in a popular location, ideal for the Edinburgh commute, and he got a good price for it. He had also learned property maintenance skills in his time inside and wanted to put that to use. With house sale proceeds, along with what was left of the inheritance, he bought the outbuilding and the materials he needed to covert it into a habitable place to live. A mixture of skills learned in prison, studies from books he obtained and online instructional videos allowed him to complete his project in six months.

David wrapped his hands around a steaming cup of peppermint tea and sat on the bench outside the rear door. The view from there was stunning. He watched the waves crash against the rocks off the shore. The area was a goldmine for geologists and he would often see students out with their field notebooks and equipment. He missed the student life enormously, but knew that he was destined to remain in this place. In hiding from his family, in hiding from his friends and in hiding from himself.

Most importantly, in hiding for those who wanted him killed.

CHAPTER THREE
LIFE WASTED

I have thought long and hard about killing a person. Not any person, of course. That would make me some kind of psychopath. Maybe by wanting to kill just one person I am putting myself into that category nonetheless. Being a doctor does, however, place me at odds with this practice, especially given that my professional purpose is to save people's lives. If we can't save a person's life, then I have to find a way to make them as comfortable as possible.

Being a doctor is the greatest feeling and perhaps one day I will go on and train to be a surgeon. Life as a junior doctor was pretty tough, especially working the ridiculously long hours during my initial training years. I had previously imagined a life working in General Practice, perhaps in some remote town or village. This would suit my introverted lifestyle, still, as I am, without many friends and continuing to avoid relationships. How could I have a serious relationship with someone if I am planning on murder?

I spent years planning this attack and have studied countless criminal cases. During this time I have taken up writing crime novels, but this is all a smokescreen for what is planned. The material studied has fitted well into my novels, rather than being an obvious link to my future plan. My particular interest has been in forensic science and the killers who nearly got away with their crimes.

Under the cover of a researching crime writer, I met a fascinating scientist based in Dundee. We met numerous times over a twelve month period and my determination to get the forensic science correct in my book masked my real motives. With what was learned, I created a killer that would have got away with their murdering, had it not been for a large slice of luck in my detective's case. After she read my novel, my forensic scientist was so impressed with the accuracy of the killer's preventative measures that she agreed he was indeed unlucky to get caught. This gave me the belief that I could carry out the killing without being detected.

My interests also led to my researching a number of true-life killers who very nearly got away with their crimes and how they acted to avoid detection for so long. Many of them moved around various cities and countries, and although this wouldn't be an option for me, being quite content living and working in Edinburgh. It may be a risk, but it is one that I am willing to take. Others nearly got away with it as the deaths were made to look like natural causes: a syringe filled with air injected into a vein to cause cardiac arrest, for example, or a difficult-to-trace poison injected somewhere that was not immediately obvious to the pathologist, such as between toes or in the armpits. Neither of these options would fit my planned modus operandi. My best hope of escape, on top of protecting myself from detection by the forensic scientists, would be to not have a connection with the victim. I just hope that my killing is far enough away from detection in this regard.

I've heard it be said that sometimes there is one case which stays with a police officer for their whole career, perhaps a particularly gruesome car accident for a traffic officer, or a brutal murder for a detective. The same might be said for medical professionals and, for me, it happened on a night shift in the accident and emergency ward. The events of that night, and what happened a few months later, have stuck with me since and have led me to where I am today. Thoughts of a tranquil life in rural Scotland, working as the local GP, were extinguished that night. Working in the A&E department would be calling from that day on.

The boy was barely sixteen and his wounds were horrendous. I stayed with him from the moment he arrived with the police, and I gave him as much mental support as possible, knowing that we could not be able to treat his physical wounds until evidence had been gathered. The hours that passed until it was possible were unbearable for the boy, and pretty unbearable for myself. The boy recovered and was discharged a couple of days later. Police had captured the culprit, but the story was far from over.

Less than three months later, on another long night shift at Accident and Emergency, the same boy returned. He had been saying my name to the paramedics in the ambulance and as soon as they got him to the hospital, a call was put out for me. The boy had been found in the bath by his father, both wrists deeply slashed and he was going in and out of consciousness. When I arrived at his side, he opened his eyes and met mine. He only spoke one word before he passed away. 'Sorry'. His life had been wasted by the actions of one sick, evil and disgusting individual.

I later learned that his attacker had pled guilty of a lesser charge and in return had achieved a light prison sentence. This is when my determination for justice began for real. There was no way anyone could accept that this boy's life was taken by the evilness of this person. If the boy had died as a result of his original injuries, the attacker would have received a life sentence. Now, for the same crime, he would be out in a matter of years.

I have kept a close eye on him ever since, needing to know when he was released from prison and what he was doing. The chances of him remaining in Edinburgh were slim, so I had to use all my resources to find where he would end up. The family home was sold shortly after his release and I managed to find out when his moving date was by casually talking to one of his neighbours in passing. On the day in question, I followed the removal van from a distance and found out where he would be living now.

It's a shame that such a beautiful spot would soon be tarnished by his gruesome murder.

CHAPTER FOUR
PENDULUM

David had good days and bad days.

On the good days, he focused on the home that he had built himself and the amazing transformation that would not look out of place amongst the many property shows on television. He had managed to get a job as an IT support worker, that he did entirely from home. He had managed to get a decent internet connection despite the remote location. The role gave him something he had been missing since he first moved here: a connection with other adults.

On the bad days, he felt lonely and afraid, unable to shake the pain of being banished into self-isolation. He wondered if he would have actually been better off in prison. At least you had people around you then, albeit people that wanted to make you as uncomfortable as possible. No, he thought, even in the worst of days here at least he was free of the bullying, the beatings and the death threats. Also in these dark days he was reminded of his previous addiction and would often feel the itch of needing another fix. Today was one of those dark days, but he was now experiencing something new.

Paranoia had started to build up steadily over the last few months. It began with little thoughts, a plug turned on when he was sure he had switched it off, forgetting to lock the door at night and getting up in the middle of the night to find it was locked, even though he had no recollection of doing so. A few times he had thought he had seen a figure lurking in the nearby fields, especially at night.

There were times when David hated himself. He hated what he was, what he became and for the mistakes he had made when he was younger. Perhaps if he lived in the modern era it would have been different. Growing up in the 1990s, things were starting to change, people were starting to change, but there was still a long way to go. Today, people are more understanding and tolerant of individuals who are different. Diversity is widely accepted in today's society and David had no doubt that if he had not made his previous mistake, he could be open and be his true self. Instead, he had not only let himself down all those years ago, but had let down the genuine and kind people like him. His actions intensified the unfair stigma between what he was and the evil of others who would never be able to show love or affection.

He always woke early, four o'clock most days, and would take a herbal tea out to the bench and look down at the sea. In the milder weather, he would sit at this spot and watch the sun rise and the day begin. In colder weather he would wrap up warm in his outdoor jacket and sit with a fleece blanket around his legs. One of his favourite sights in East Scotland, is the haar (or what some call sea fog) rolling up from the North Sea, covering the fields like a blanket of cloud. It is a truly beautiful sight to behold.

David was unaware of the figure approaching from the west, dressed completely in black, and completely camouflaged amongst the crops of the neighbouring farmer's field. The figure crouched low to the ground, carefully picking its way through until it reached the front of the property, out of sight of David and his beloved bench. The next part would be the most tricky for the attacker, but it was imperative that it came off as planned or the rest of the mission would be ruined.

The figure was slight in stature, but powerfully build.

Years of endurance and muscle-building exercise had been done specifically for this moment. Very carefully, it took the rucksack from its back and reached inside for the tools required to undertake the important first stage of the process. Already gloved, it reached inside for a bottle and folded square of cotton material. Carefully unscrewing the top, it poured the required amount of chloroform that would have the desired anaesthetic effect. David had to be knocked out for only enough time as to undertake the second stage of the mission. Too much chloroform and the action could be fatal. Too little, he would awake too soon. It was a risk, but one that had to be taken to succeed.

Armed and ready, the figure crept around the side of the house, pausing momentarily. From the inside pocket of its jacket, it extracted a dental mirror which it used to view around the corner, checking that David was still sitting on his bench. So far, everything had gone to plan. David was slightly taller than his would-be killer, so the element of surprise would move the pendulum back in the killer's favour.

The figure rushed at David, placing the chloroform-soaked rag over his nose and mouth. Fingernails scraped at the gloved hands, but were unable to get any purchase in the smooth leather. Soon the scraping eased and David slumped back into the figure's arms, where he was pulled through the back door into his house.

Death would not be far away now.

CHAPTER FIVE
NOTHINGMAN

Stage one had gone so smoothly that it had made all the planning and preparation worthwhile. How many hours had I spent researching, studying and observing to get to this part in the proceedings? There was still work to do, and I would have to ensure my tracks were covered. There had been no-one around at this time of day, and the back roads had been empty in my drive over. My car was hidden in a remote spot, well away from this location, and parked so as not to leave telling tyre marks behind. The tyres would be replaced and destroyed shortly anyway.

I dragged the heavily-sedated body through to the only bedroom in the property and threw him onto the bed. The next part was to remove his clothing, required for the final stage of my plan, but this would also humiliate my victim. I took out metal chains from my backpack and secured him to the bed, his unresponsive body lying in a cross-shape on top of the duvet. I had a mouth-gag, but that would not be needed just yet. I had some questions that he was required to answer first.

I took the opportunity to check the surrounding area to ensure that we would not be disturbed, the remote and isolated location was perfect for my requirements. It was a beautiful part of the country and once more I wondered how we got here. Was this the right thing? Would this give me the closure sought? Would I get away with it? Was the risk of ruining a highly successful career and a comfortable lifestyle worthwhile for my personal vendetta?

I knew this feeling of uncertainty would come, and I was prepared for it. The feeling could almost be compared to a nervous actor, readying himself to go on stage, only to find the butterflies in his stomach. Many of the most famous and accomplished actors still got the same feeling, despite being in the business for decades. I heard many embraced this feeling of uncertainty, saying that if they ever lost it they would find it had to go on being an actor. I have also heard them say that they channel this nervous energy into their performance. That is exactly what happened.

A single weathered chair sat next to the kitchen table, undoubtedly this man ate alone and was unvisited here. I dragged the chair through to the bedroom and sat beside the prone body, making sure we were face to face for when he awoke. This was always going to be the hardest part, waiting for him to regain consciousness and ensure that he was recovered enough to know what was happening. I waited patiently, going through the final stages of my plan in my head to ensure everything was ready and prepared.

A flutter of an eye lid caught my attention and a return to consciousness was imminent. My eyes were fixed on his as they begin to open fully with a stone-faced expression. I could see the confusion in his eyes as they met mine, before he looked around to take in the full horror of his situation. He tugged at his restraints, the metal chains clucking against the metal frame of the bed. No one would hear the noise, no one would be coming to his undeserved rescue. His dry mouth started to speak.

"Wh...what's happening?" I remained silent to begin with. He was still coming round from the anaesthetic. I felt joy in the sight of his suffering, a suffering that others had endured, a suffering felt within myself. His reactions were quickening, his pulling of the restraints getting more frantic. He was now fully aware of his senses, fear now the overriding emotion.

"Your time has now come, David." I deliberately used his assumed name, partly so that he knew that I had found out his secret identify, partly because of the sick feeling that came to be stomach when he was referred to by his given name. David started to scream, so I rose from my chair and hit him hard on the face with the back of my gloved hand. It felt good, albeit it was only a warning shot to gain his attention.

"No one will hear you David," I told him. "There is little point wasting your remaining energy in such a feeble act."

The fear in him intensified, and his bladder gave way involuntary. I looked down at the wet floor and gave him an evil smile. Walking through to the bathroom, I retrieved a towel and rubbed his body, absorbing the traces of the urine from him. I resisted the urge to rub the towel on his face and threw it to the floor. It was time for the questions. His answers would not impact his ultimate fate, but they might reduce his suffering.

"Do you like young boys, David?" The question came out more calmly that I had expected it to. He looked confused, before the horror of realisation kicked in.

"No...no...no. It was a mistake. I...never knew, I would

never have…" He could not find the words to justify what had happened. In sheer desperation, he changed tact and begged for mercy.

"Please don't do this. I'm a nothing. I keep away from others now. I just want to live my life away from everything and everyone. You…you don't have to do this."

"You are both correct and wrong, David. You are indeed a nothingman, a scab on society, the lowest of the low. But I'm afraid you are very wrong in your other point. I *do* have to do this…"

I reached for the mouth gag and tied it tightly around his head. He trashed his head from side to side, trying to dislodge it without success. I reached into my bag and withdrew my scalpel of choice, ready for the final stage of my mission.

Then, using the delicate pencil grip, I cut open his scrotum.

CHAPTER SIX
GETAWAY

Alex turned on the television to catch up with the local news. As expected, it had made the headline report.

"Police investigating the brutal murder of Simon Taylor are appealing for witnesses to come forward, exactly three years after the discovery of his mutilated body. Taylor, who was also known as David Jones, had previously spent time in prison, having been found guilty of sex offences. Police confirmed that they had not made any links between his murder and his previous conviction."

The report confirmed that the police were baffled by the murder, and previous lines of enquiry had failed to lead to any suspects. Nothing in the report gave Alex a cause for concern, and confirmed that this one-time killer would continue to get away with it.

Alex continued to buy scalpels, and the collection had finally reached three figures. The ALEX scalpel had been cleaned throughly and Alex took special care of this most-prized possession. The curators of the so called 'Black Museums' would pay a small fortune for the scalpel, especially since the murderer had got away with the crime.

Alex flicked through the channels absentmindedly, stopping at an episode of Agatha Christie's Poirot. It was one of Alex's favourite episodes, 'Cards on the Table', with David Suchet in the lead role. It had just began, and Alex awaited the scene at the dinner table. There was a line in particular that came up, the police officer said it.

"Woman are highly successful criminals."

Alex smiled to herself, thinking they certainly were.

Ross Alexander *is a Scottish author who writes crime and thriller novels and short stories. He started writing in his thirties and completed his debut novel 'Alive' in 2012, sharing it with family, friends and colleagues before being encouraged to self publish in 2016. His second novel 'Christie's Early Cases' is a collection of short crime stories based around Edinburgh Detective Inspector Joanne Christie. During the lockdown of 2020, Ross wrote 'Five Against One', a full crime novel starring DI Christie.*

Ross has also written a number of short stories, some of which are available to read at his website. One of these stories 'Speak To Me' was included in an anthology in aid of Mental Health UK.

He lives in East Lothian and is married with two grown-up daughters.

Visit his website - www.rossalexwriter.com

The Rowan Tree

Penny Hampson

"It's got to go."

Sarah sighed, watching as Dave thumped his fist against the gnarled bark of the trunk.

She quite liked the rowan tree.

It was one of the things that had caught her eye when she'd first driven past all those months ago. The spreading branches had nearly obscured the *For Sale* sign, and it was only when she'd parked up and retraced her steps along the road, checking house numbers, that she knew she was in the right place. The house was perfect, just on the outskirts of Milngavie, and not too far from their now overlarge home in Bearsden.

Dave was still muttering to himself. "Bloody tree."

"What's wrong?" she asked. "I think it's lovely. We could even make our own jelly when it fruits." Rowan trees were also said to deter witches, or so she'd heard. Not that she believed such nonsense.

"Well, I don't," Dave snarled back. "Nearly hit the damned thing with the car last night in the dark. Could've sworn I had plenty of room, and then the next thing I knew the sensors went off." He gave the tree trunk another thump, wincing as his knuckles made contact. "If I hadn't slammed on the brakes that would have been the offside sill buggered."

Sarah bit her tongue. There was nothing to be gained from pointing out that he'd had a drink or two on the way home. He hated her bringing up the subject of his drinking. Said it felt like she was keeping tabs on him, and it shouldn't matter if he had the odd dram with the lads. She went out with her girls too, after all.

Yes, but I don't come home in a foul mood, she thought.

She forced a smile and started to lug the shopping bags out of the car boot. "I'll get this stuff put away, then start dinner. Sausages ok?"

Dave grunted and ambled behind her up the path to the front door, but not before giving his pride and joy a loving rub on the bonnet with the sleeve of his jacket. "I'm going to get changed and work on the old girl for a bit. Call me in when dinner's ready."

Sarah rolled her eyes as she dumped the heavy shopping bags on the kitchen table. When she decided to work from home, moving house had seemed like a good idea. The kids had left, and they were on their own now, so the plan had been to downsize and use some of their cash to do some travelling. But three months and a compact new house later, things were still the same. No trips planned, not many cosy evenings together, just the same excuses of "too much on at work" and "give it a few more weeks, and I'll book something". Same old. Same old.

For the first time that week, they sat together on the patio after dinner. Gone nine, but it was still light, and if you didn't mind the midges there was nothing better than enjoying the quiet of the garden at the end of the day. Even Dave's mood had mellowed. It wasn't often that he came out to join her, usually too busy on his computer. She looked over to where he sat, gazing at the screen of his iPad. His frown of concentration told her he was probably looking at something car-related. If only she could share his enthusiasm, but she'd never really got it. Cars and engines left her cold. Now if he could feel the same way about books as she did... She smiled. That would never happen.

"What's going through your mind to bring a smile to your face?" he asked, watching her and breaking the silence.

"Nothing much." She shrugged. "Just thinking. We don't have much in common, do we? You and your cars, me and my books."

He grinned back at her. "Well, they say opposites attract." It had been a while since she'd seen him looking at her like that. "I've been thinking," he said. "I've been going through our finances. I think we can afford a short break. We haven't had a holiday this year what with moving, but if we're careful, we could manage a few days away. What do you think?"

"I'd love to," she answered, wondering whether she ought to cook sausages more often. If this was the result, they'd be going on the menu every week.

The next day, Sarah spent time on the computer checking out places that accepted bookings for short stays. They'd both decided Mull might be nice. And it wasn't too far to travel from Milngavie. The last time they'd been there was when the kids were small. They'd stayed in a small cottage with a metal roof that made the rain sound like thunder when it landed. It had rained every day. Still, the kids had loved running round the field trying to make friends with the sheep and skimming stones across the water at the beach to see how many splashes they made. Despite the dreadful weather, they'd enjoyed themselves, laughing themselves silly when Dave realised he'd chopped up the wooden prop for the washing line as firewood. Even though it was summer, they'd needed the warmth of a fire every night.

This time they were going to stay somewhere less rustic, Sarah decided. Somewhere that didn't mean she'd have to cook. She was fed up with cooking every night, but Dave refused to do what he called "women's work", even when they both had demanding jobs, and she was as exhausted as he at the end of a long day. How she had wished that he might change.

It didn't take her long to find the right place. By lunchtime everything was booked – ferries, hotel, and even a restaurant for the first evening. How often did that happen? Sarah felt great as she pressed send on the text to Dave, letting him know everything was sorted. As a reward to herself she decided to go for a walk; maybe pop into that new deli for a coffee and get a couple of cakes as a treat for after tea?

The sun was shining as she stepped out of the front door. A

whiff of wild garlic, made intense by the recent rain, assailed her nostrils. In the window of the house across the way the curtain twitched. Sarah looked over but couldn't see anyone. Even though they'd moved in three months ago, she still hadn't met all the neighbours in the little cul-de-sac she and Dave now called home. But at least she wasn't too far from her old friends back in Bearsden; when they'd decided to move that was one thing she and Dave had agreed on, to stay near the place where they'd put down roots.

As she came level with the house where she'd seen the curtains move, the front door opened. Sarah turned, a smile on her lips and ready to issue a greeting. Her eyes widened momentarily. It wasn't an elderly lady, as she'd assumed, but a tall, slim woman about her own age and quite glamorously dressed for an afternoon excursion. The woman's jet-black hair was worn up, and her eyebrows – equally as dark – arched elegantly over hooded eyes. Sarah was reminded of Morticia Addams.

"Hello there," the woman called, her bright red lips enunciating the words. "I've been meaning to introduce myself." Her high heels made clicking sounds as she came down the path to the front gate where Sarah stood. "I'm Melissa. I was just about to walk to the library. Do you mind if I join you? I assume you're going that way?"

Sarah nodded. The library was just along from the shops, and it would be nice to have some company. Most of the other residents of the cul-de-sac seemed to be out during the day, making it some time since she'd had a face-to-face chat. "That would be lovely. I'm Sarah, by the way. Have you lived here long?"

"Oh, Gwen and I have lived here forever, or rather it seems like it." Melissa laughed, revealing yellowing teeth. Sarah adjusted her assessment of Melissa's age upwards. "Gwen's my sister. She's decided to stay at home today. Now, tell me all about yourself. I'm terribly nosey, you know."

Sarah jumped as Melissa linked an arm round hers, but quickly covered her unease with a nervous giggle. She wasn't quite comfortable with this sudden level of intimacy, and the pungent smell of Melissa's perfume was cloyingly unpleasant. What was it?

"There's not much to tell, really. Just Dave and I. The kids are both away now, and we moved here for a bit of peace and quiet."

"Don't tell me," Melissa gave her a conspiratorial look. "I bet you're finding it a bit too quiet, am I right?"

"Well…" Sarah wasn't going to admit to loneliness – that would be revealing too much and would tell this woman far more about her relationship with Dave than she was ready to share.

"Go on, admit it." Melissa's voice had a cajoling tone. "I can think of just the thing for you. I run a little social group. We meet once a month for a few drinks and nibbles. We've got one coming up this Friday, if you're interested."

"I'm not sure at the moment. Dave and I…"

Melissa cut her off. "It's ladies only, I'm afraid. All girls together and all that." She gave Sarah another wide smile. "I'm sure your husband won't miss you for a couple of hours."

"I'll think about it," Sarah said decisively. She didn't want to be bullied into something. She might be lonely, but she wasn't desperate. Glancing sideways, she saw Melissa's mouth was now a thin line.

Sarah got the impression that she'd upset her neighbour, so attempted another topic.

"I do like your garden. You've got some unusual plants, ones I don't recognise."

To be honest, Sarah knew nothing about plants, but thought gardening was something safer to discuss.

"Oh, it's Gwen who's the gardener. You'd have to ask her," Melissa replied. "Why don't you come round for coffee tomorrow morning and we can get to know you? We've been dying to meet you."

Sarah refrained from pointing out that Melissa and her sister could have popped over any time to introduce themselves if they'd really been eager to make her acquaintance. Instead, she said, "Sorry, I'm waiting for a delivery tomorrow. Why don't you come over to me?" A flicker of something crossed Melissa's face. It passed so quickly that Sarah thought she'd imagined it.

"No, I insist that, as the newcomer, you should come to us. Why don't we make it for the following week? Wednesday, say ten o'clock?"

"That would be lovely," said Sarah. Somehow the fact that she was finally getting to know one of her neighbours didn't fill her with enthusiasm.

They'd nearly reached the High Street. Sarah could see a couple of young mums pushing buggies towards the play park. Was it her imagination, or did they really cross the road as soon as they saw Sarah and her neighbour coming towards them? Sarah told herself she was being daft. Unhooking her arm from Melissa's, she pointed to the delicatessen. "Well, I'm just going in here for a few bits. Enjoy your library trip. I joined the other week. It's quite well stocked for a small place, isn't it?"

Melissa's silvery-grey eyes locked onto Sarah's face. A feeling that someone had walked over her grave slithered down Sarah's back.

"Yes, Gwen and I positively haunt the place. They're very good at getting specific books for you if they haven't got them." Melissa gripped Sarah's hand. It was a surprisingly strong grip. "Now don't forget: ten o'clock, Wednesday."

Rubbing her hand – she could still feel the imprints of Melissa's fingers – Sarah watched for a moment as her new acquaintance sashayed down the road towards the library. Still shaking her head at the strange encounter, Sarah opened the door of the deli. She couldn't quite put her finger on it, but there was something about Melissa...

"Hello, thought I recognised you. You've just moved into that house that backs onto mine."

Sarah looked over and saw a woman about her own age.

"Do you live on Weston Avenue?" Sarah asked.

"That's right." The woman grinned at her. "You bought Mrs Gibson's house. I'm right, aren't I?"

Sarah nodded. "Yes. She had to move into a home, her son

59

said. Poor soul went a bit doolally, apparently."

The woman tutted. "She seemed alright to me. We got on fine."

"Well... I only know what her son told me." Goodness! Sarah wondered what other minefields she would be crossing today.

"Oh, I'm sure that's what he thought." The woman frowned, then as suddenly the frown was replaced with a smile. "Do forgive me; it's just that Helen Gibson was a friend of mine. We often used to chat across the fence. I'm Katie, by the way. There's a gate, a bit overgrown now, that joins our two gardens. It was already there when we bought our house thirty years ago. That's how Helen and I met."

Sarah held out her hand. "I'm Sarah. Nice to meet you, Katie."

They shook hands then Katie indicated the empty table in the section of the deli reserved for customers eating in. "Do you fancy a coffee? The cakes are pretty good too."

Fifteen minutes later they were chatting like old friends. Sarah learned that Katie did voluntary work at the library, had three grandchildren, and a husband, Sam, who apparently was as into his cars as Dave. Sarah hadn't met them previously because Katie and Sam had been away for three months in Australia, visiting Sam's brother and family.

"I couldn't believe it when I saw Helen's house up for sale," Katie said, wiping carrot cake crumbs from her lips. "It was too bad it happened just before Sam and I were due to fly out, otherwise I'd have gone round to see her." She frowned. "I feel bad about that, I can tell you. When I got back, I got in touch with the estate agents to see if they could let me know where she'd gone, but all they said was that clients' information was confidential and promised to pass on my inquiry." She shrugged. "But I've heard nothing."

Sarah felt sorry for the woman, who seemed genuinely upset.

"I only met the son once. He showed me and Dave round. A nice chap, I thought, though he did say he was worried about his mother. Seemed she'd been having delusions, and that's why he thought she'd be safer in sheltered accommodation."

Katie gave Sarah a searching look. "Can I tell you something, Sarah? Promise me you won't tell a soul."

Sarah hesitated. "Erm…"

Katie turned anxious eyes towards the door. "It doesn't matter. Forget I mentioned it."

A hand landed on Sarah's shoulder. "Enjoying your coffee, ladies?" It was Melissa.

Katie stood up. "Well, I'll be going." Her eyes flickered to Melissa. Sarah wasn't sure, but she got the impression that some hidden message was being passed between her two new acquaintances. "Hello, Melissa," continued Katie as she swiftly gathered her things from the table. "So you and Sarah have met?"

Melissa took hold of the back of Katie's newly-vacated chair. "Yes, we have, but only today. Don't rush off on my account, Katie."

Sarah watched bemused as the two women edged round each other. There was something going on that she didn't understand. At last she found her voice. "I have to go too. Dave will be home from work soon."

Melissa grinned at her from across the table. "You don't strike me as the little woman type, Sarah. Surely he doesn't expect his dinner on the table as soon as he gets home?"

Sarah felt herself flushing. No, she wasn't downtrodden at all, not really, but she needed some sort of excuse to leave. She wasn't sure she could take any more of Melissa's prying questions for one day.

Katie came to her rescue. "Didn't you say you were expecting a package or something?"

Sarah smiled gratefully and made a show of checking the time on her phone." Yes, I had a text this morning to say it would be delivered after four. My goodness, it's quarter to already. I'd better get my skates on."

She removed her jacket from the back of her chair and shoved her arms into the sleeves, all the while conscious of Melissa's eyes steadily watching her. Sarah could tell Melissa didn't believe her excuse, the same one she'd used for refusing the invitation to coffee, but frankly she was past caring.

Once outside, Katie spoke under her breath, "Thought I'd help you there. Melissa can be a bit overpowering, don't you think?"

"Thanks. I didn't know what to say. I didn't want to upset her but...well, I do need to get back."

Katie winked at her. "Sure."

They parted at the turn off to the cul-de-sac. No further mention had been made of whatever it was that Katie had been about to disclose, so Sarah didn't ask.

Sarah didn't see any of the cul-de-sac residents over the next couple of days, but she had met up with Jane, one of her mates from her office days, who'd expressed surprise at the fact that Sarah didn't yet know her new neighbours despite now working from home. By Friday she was feeling guilty at not making more of an effort, so when in the evening she saw a group of ladies trooping into Melissa's house she decided to make amends.

"I'm just popping out for an hour," she shouted as she passed the open door of the garage. Dave's legs were sticking out from under the car. A muffled grunt was all the reply she got. Rolling her eyes, she continued down the front path.

Standing on Melissa's doorstep waiting for an answer to her knock, Sarah almost had second thoughts. Too late! The door opened before she could make a run for it. A stranger's face peered at her. This woman was older than Melissa by several years, Sarah guessed. Her hair was almost white and pulled back severely from a wrinkled but friendly face into a tight bun.

The woman's blue eyes twinkled. "You must be Sarah. Melissa told me your name. I've often seen you go past the window."

Sarah smiled. If this was Gwen, she was far less intimidating than her sister. "That's right, and you must be Gwen."

"So you decided to join us? I'm so glad, we could do with some fresh blood." Gwen waved her in and pointed down the hallway. "They're all in the dining room. Come on, I'll introduce you."

Nervous when mixing with lots of new people, Sarah's apprehension must have shown, for Gwen added with a grin, "Don't worry, they're all very nice – never been known to attack a newcomer."

The dining room was crowded and hummed with conversation. Sarah's eyes scanned the room. Groups of women of varying ages were gathered in huddles; some round the dining table, others near the fireplace, and a couple of older women – one was Melissa – by the window. There was no one, apart from Melissa that she recognised.

Gwen's knuckles rapped on the door, getting everyone's attention. "This is Sarah, ladies. Do come and introduce yourselves. She's dying to meet you all."

There were titters of laughter, and Sarah forced a smile to her lips. She hated being the centre of attention. A drink was pressed into her hand by a woman who introduced herself as Sylvia.

"Try this. It's one of Melissa's homemade concoctions. Not bad, but it's got a bit of a kick."

Sarah sniffed the glass and took a cautious sip. It tasted quite nice, in fact. She wasn't sure what was in the drink, but after two glasses, her nerves had disappeared, and she was chatting and circulating round the room as if she was an old hand at socialising. Normally at social gatherings she found a cosy corner to hide in until she could make her excuses and leave.

Sarah had never known time to pass so quickly. Before she knew it, she was tottering back up the path to her front door. It took several attempts before her key found the keyhole, and she almost fell into Dave's arms as she staggered into the hall.

"I see you've been having a good time." He smirked. "You girls when you get together - I don't know." His eyes narrowed. "Though I hope it's not going to be a regular thing.

I'm not doing the washing-up every time you decide on a night out." Putting his arm round her shoulder, he guided her into the living room. "I'll make a cup of tea, shall I? I suppose I'd better. You look as if you could do with one." Grumbling, he went off to make the tea for a change, leaving Sarah slumped on the sofa. She shook her head. The room was spinning. Those drinks had been a lot stronger than she'd thought. Next time I'll be more careful, she told herself. Next time? She giggled, closed her eyes and before long was fast asleep.

A week had passed since her evening out, and Sarah still couldn't remember exactly what had happened. From the moment she'd entered the dining room it had all become a bit of a blur. But she must have made a good impression on her new acquaintances because several times when she'd been out at the shops a couple of ladies had waved and smiled at her. One had even told her that, as they had so much in common, they must arrange to meet up separately, and insisted on exchanging phone numbers. Sarah was finding it a bit bewildering.

It was in the deli again that she saw Katie. Rain had been pouring all morning, and Sarah had put off going out until quite late in the afternoon. By the time she reached the deli, she was absolutely drenched, despite her waxed jacket and umbrella – the sort of soaking one could only get on a wet Glasgow day. Ignoring the glare of the assistant behind the counter, Sarah padded over to an empty table, very aware of the trail of wet footprints being deposited in her wake. What did the woman expect? Sarah wasn't the only one who'd decided to find shelter. Surely, the owner couldn't complain if the coffee takings were up?

"Thought it was you." Katie's face peeped round the corner of the shelving housing the homemade breads. "Fancy some company?"

Sarah smiled. "Yeah. How are you?"

Two coffees and two pineapple tarts later – sometimes the lurid yellow cakes were the only thing that satisfied Sarah's craving for sugar – and Sarah and Katie had set the world to rights. Sarah checked her phone and decided she'd better make a move. She'd got a casserole planned – a sausage one, as it happened – and wanted to get it in the oven so she and Dave could eat by seven.

"Hang on a minute." Icy fingers gripped her hand. Her eyes shot up to meet Katie's dark green ones. If she didn't know better, she'd have thought her new friend looked angry. The impression was fleeting and disappeared in an instant. Now Katie was smiling. "Sorry, I know you're in a hurry, and we've spent a long time chatting, but…"

Sarah sat back down again. "What's the matter?"

"It's about Helen."

"The lady who used to live in my house? Have you found out where she is now?"

"That's just it. I had a phone call from her son at the weekend. He told me that she's had to be sectioned."

"What!" Sarah knew that sectioning someone meant that they were quite seriously ill and might harm themselves." "Oh dear, that's not good. Are you able to visit her?"

"No. Apparently she's not allowed visitors. It upsets her too much."

"That's dreadful. Poor lady."

Katie dabbed at her eyes. "Awful. It's even worse because…" She paused, her eyes shifting away from Sarah's. "I feel really guilty."

"Why's that?"

"Oh, before we went on holiday I'd asked her about trimming back the trees; they really have an effect on my garden, what with the leaves in autumn, the berries making such a mess when they fall, and I can't get anything to grow that side of the fence."

Sarah's stomach clenched. Katie was referring to the lovely rowan trees in her back garden. Helen, the previous occupant, must certainly have liked them, for there was a row planted along the back fence, as well as the one at the front gate. Several times Sarah had wondered whether Helen enjoyed making rowan jelly. There must have been tons of berries. Her mind came back to what Katie was saying. It sounded like she was being asked to do something about the trees.

"I think I upset her; she was rather obsessed with those rowans." Katie shook her head. "Said she'd sooner die than chop them down."

"Pardon?"

"I know. A bit extreme, I grant you. I suppose I should have seen her breakdown coming."

Sarah reached out across the table and patted Katie's hand. "You shouldn't blame yourself. It sounds like your friend already had a problem if she was obsessed with trees."

There was a loud sniff, and Katie dabbed at her eyes again. "I know, I know…"

Sarah decided to steer the conversation back to gardening. Perhaps if she offered to do something about the trees? Not chop them down, of course, but trimming them might help. "About the rowans…"

Katie's head shot up. "Yes?"

"We're going to be doing some work in the garden. Tidying it up and making a few changes, you know? I don't suppose it would hurt to thin them out a bit…" Sarah had barely got her words out before Katie grabbed her hand.

"That'd be fantastic. I'll let you have the name of a chap I know. He specialises in trees."

Before she knew it, Sarah was on her way home, in her pocket the name of the gardener that her friend had recommended. She didn't really want to do anything to the trees, but Katie had seemed so upset that the words had come out of her mouth without thinking, and it had snowballed from there. She hoped Katie wouldn't be too disappointed when she saw that the rowans were only trimmed and not lopped. Closing the front door behind her, Sarah shrugged her coat off her shoulders, threw the card with the gardener's address onto the hall table and went into the kitchen to start the dinner.

Three weeks later

The drive from Oban had been slow. A bit of an anti-climax after a lovely holiday when the sun had shone nearly every day. Now, the skies were grey, and rain threatened. Typical Glasgow weather, thought Sarah. If only the rain would hold off until they got home and had unpacked the car. She glanced at Dave in the passenger seat then turned up the radio to drown out the sound of his snores.

Twenty minutes later, Sarah slowed down for the corner and steered into their cul-de-sac. Dave was not pleased to be awakened and was muttering under his breath. She pulled on the handbrake and stared through the windscreen towards her home. Something was different.

"That's better." She knew Dave was smiling by his tone.

"What have you done?" For some reason Sarah's fingers wouldn't loosen their grip of the wheel. A good job really, otherwise they'd be round Dave's neck. She turned her head and saw the smug grin on his face. "How could you?" She spat out. It had been a long time since she'd felt this angry.

He shrugged. "I thought you'd be pleased. Besides, we missed all the mess and the noise. Doing it while we were away seemed like the perfect solution. Good job I found that card you left. He was the only chap who'd crack on with it while we were away."

Sarah got out of the car, slamming the door behind her and stalked up to the open gateway of their drive. The stump of the rowan tree stood by the gatepost like a rebuke. Her lovely tree...gone. The car horn tooted, making her turn to see Dave, who was now in the driver's seat, waiting impatiently for her to get out of the way so he could get the car on the drive. God, how she wanted to throttle him. Instead, she shifted and went to the front door. How daft to think a holiday might change things; he was still the same.

The next day, Dave was back at his office, and Sarah was clearing the breakfast things away before settling down to work at her computer, when the doorbell rang. She hurried to the front door, pulling off her washing-up gloves as she went and hoping it wasn't somebody who would take up too much time. She'd promised to write an article for her old boss, who still sent her the occasional piece of work, and the deadline was near. The dark silhouette of someone tall cast a shadow through the opaque glass of the front door. Suddenly it felt quite cold.

"I hope you don't mind?" Melissa grinned at her from the porch. "Thought I'd see how your holiday went. Did you have a good time?"

Melissa brushed passed her and was halfway down the hall before Sarah found her voice. "Er, no. I mean, I don't mind. Though I haven't got much time, to be honest."

"Is this your lounge?" Melissa was in the living room by the time Sarah closed the front door. She'd never seen a woman move so fast on stilettoes. By the time Sarah entered the living room, Melissa was perched on the sofa and gazing out at the garden through the patio window. "See you've had those trees taken down. I was always telling Helen to do that. They're not good for the garden."

Sarah's eyes followed Melissa's towards the stumps at the end of the lawn. Yes, Dave had also taken it into his head to get rid of those. She wondered if she could ever forgive him. Why did he just go ahead without checking with her?

Melissa's eyes glittered. "Why don't you put the kettle on, Sarah? I shouldn't wonder if Katie might be joining us. We're dying to hear about your holiday."

The doorbell rang.

"That'll be her now, I expect," said Melissa, crossing her legs and making herself comfortable. "Be a dear and let her in and then we can have a nice cosy chat."

One month later

Well, that had been one of the strangest days of her life, Sarah thought when she recalled that first visit from Melissa and Katie, a smile curling her lips. Very strange indeed. But what a difference it had made. She'd never have guessed that the pair were really the best of friends. They'd both been playing her.

She finished typing, shut down her computer, then checked her phone. Just enough time to get changed and join the girls over at Melissa and Gwen's house. Then of course there was the chat she needed to have with Dave.

Sarah swiped a lipstick over her mouth and checked the result in the bedroom mirror. Crimson really suited her. Why had she never tried it before? She glanced at her feet. Killer heels had never appealed, but these black patent stilettos made her feel great; she might even buy another pair in red.

"Don't forget to put the washing on, will you, while I'm out?" Sarah smiled sweetly. "You'll be able to get the ironing done in peace too. That'll be nice for you, won't it?"

Dave was standing near the bedroom door, his shoulders hunched. The apron stretched over his paunch made him look like an overweight waiter, with its pseudo bow tie and buttons down the front.

"Yes, love. No, I won't forget. Enjoy yourself," he answered, a hesitant look in his eye. "Is there anything else you want me to do, dear?"

"No, that's fine. Don't wait up." She gave her hair one last pat and swished past him.

Yes, that meeting with Melissa and Katie had changed her life. Who knew being a witch could be so empowering? Thank goodness for Dave and his overbearing masculine sense of superiority. If he hadn't arranged to have the rowan trees chopped down…

Sarah grinned as she trotted down the path, casting a derisory glance at the rowan tree stump as she passed.

―――――――――

*Some time ago, **Penny Hampson** decided to follow her passion for history by studying with the Open University. She graduated with honours and went on to complete a post-graduate degree.*

She then landed her dream role, working in an environment where she was surrounded by rare books and historical manuscripts. Flash forward nineteen years, and the opportunity came along to indulge her other main passion – writing. Encouraged by friends and family, three years later Penny published her debut novel, *A Gentleman's Promise*, a traditional Regency romance, shortly followed by more in the same genre. But never happy in a rut, Penny is now exploring suspense and the supernatural.

Penny lives with her family in Oxfordshire, and when she is not writing, she enjoys reading, walking, swimming, and the odd gin and tonic (not all at the same time).

She is the author of the full-length novel, *The Unquiet Spirit*.

Cats and Dogs

Val Penny

There are many ways this chain of events could have been stopped or changed so that I would not end up in this dark place. But hindsight is 20/20 vision. Vision, that's a laugh.

It was the end of yet another depressing weekend and when I got to work on Monday morning, I was not at all ready to start the day. Even my colleagues noticed, and they hardly paid me any attention.

"Eileen, you've been crying."

"No, I haven't, Joan."

"Then why is your nose red and your mascara running down your face? Have you been dumped again? "

"No! Why would you even think that?"

"You look like that every time it happens."

"What do you mean 'every time'? You make it sound like I get dumped every week."

"Perhaps not every week, but certainly most weekends. Wouldn't you agree, Derek?"

"If you haven't been dumped, why are you crying, Eileen?" Derek asked.

Anna glared at me. "Is it just your way of getting out of making the tea today?"

"Of course not. If you must know, I spent all weekend at the vet. Not that it did any good. My cat, Mrs Slocombe, died this morning at 3:22, and there was nothing I or the vet could do for her. She had kidney failure and I had to let her go, to save her from any pain." Tears began rolling down my cheeks again. and I couldn't stop crying. "Poor wee Mrs Slocombe. I had had her since she was a kitten, and now my best friend was gone. I feel so alone."

"And I feel so put upon because I'll have to make the tea.

You should get a dog. They are more robust." I heard Anna clatter the mugs together and stomp off in the direction of the kitchen.

"Don't be like that, Anna. You know Eileen is a mess right now. Just make the tea and I'll try to get her sorted so that she can actually do some work today."

Joan put her arm around my shoulder. She rocked me back and forward until my sobbing had stopped.

"Eileen, you need to pull yourself together. You know there are going to be redundancies. Don't make it easy for the bosses by being so hopeless. Look, my cousin's cat had kittens a couple of months ago. Why don't I see if you can have one?"

"I can't just replace Mrs Slocombe! She meant the world to me."

"Seriously, Eileen, you said that about Alan, and Bob, and even Colin. If you can change your men so easily, a cat should be no problem."

"If you don't want a new cat, why not get a puppy?" Anna plonked the tea onto my desk.

"I know I've been unlucky in love, but I don't want a bloody puppy! Will you two just leave me alone? Piss off, both of you." Of course, just at that point the boss marched into the office. He glowered at me. I felt my face go bright red.

"Eileen Shaw, my office, now," he said.

I heard Anna laugh and Joan sigh as I dragged myself through for another bollocking. I tried to explain how dreadful my weekend had been and that I had been up all night making the decision to have my cat put down. He did not look impressed. He stood up and strode from one side of the room to the other. He shouted at me, berated my excuse, and made it crystal clear that if I used bad language to my co-workers again, I would be dismissed.

So there I was on a Monday morning with no boyfriend, no cat, and in danger of losing my job. I was grateful when Joan took my arm at lunchtime and said she had an idea. She suggested we eat together in the canteen so that she could tell me all about it.

I can't pretend I was good company. I wasn't really even listening to what she said. I just drank my cup-a-soup, and chewed my slightly stale ham sandwich, and nodded.

"So that's settled. My cousin has one kitten left. He'll bring it in tomorrow after work. Bring your cat basket. And you'll give the other thing a try, won't you? I'll help you set it up." I heard her say.

"Sorry, what was that?"

"Oh, come on, Eileen. I'm not going through it all again. It's a new site. Surely we can manage to get even you a couple of dates. You need to get out of yourself and look forward, woman. I'll set up a profile for you tonight. Do you have a decent picture? Or better still, an indecent picture!"

I spent all evening looking for a photo that I would not mind getting passed around the office, because I knew that's what would happen. Another reason for poor little Eileen to be pitied or humiliated. However, I did remember to take the cat basket with me. Mrs Slocombe could never be replaced but as the tiny kitten needed a home, I couldn't reject her, and with her little black ears she looked every inch a Princess Leia. I had another cat. I wasn't alone in the world.

When I went home that night, I was armed with the profile Joan had made for me and a tiny new companion. I poured a glass of wine, ordered a Dominos pizza, and began to explore the new dating site while Princess Leia slept in the crook of my arm.

***

I have never really liked dogs, although I wouldn't be without my alsatian, Rory, now. I have been a cat person all my life. So, at that time, as I looked at the pictures on my screen, I swiped left at all the dog lovers. It was a good feeling and made me feel powerful. At last I was getting to reject people instead of the hurtful series of rejections I, myself had suffered recently.

And then I saw him. He was tall, with dark hair and the

73

deepest chocolatey dark brown eyes I had ever seen. His smile was warm and reached all the way to his eyes, even in his photo. He was casually dressed in a fashionable shirt and light chinos. His picture was taken by the seashore, facing the sea, and he had bare feet. I don't like feet. Men's feet especially are generally ugly appendages, but his were beautiful. He was sitting on a sand dune and I could see the Bass Rock in the distance behind him. That meant he didn't live far from me. The fact he preferred dogs to cats didn't matter this time. I swiped right.

To be honest, I didn't expect him to respond. I have never been beautiful. Oh, my figure is good enough. I try to keep fit. But my hair is mousey brown, and my eyes are a funny colour of violet. Also, on my civil service salary, I cannot afford to go to fancy stylists, nor can I afford to frequent beauty salons for facials, massages or to get my nails done regularly. I didn't hold out much hope of a reply.

Imagine my excitement when he swiped right too. I couldn't believe it. I did my happy dance around the living room until I was dizzy, and I cuddled Princess Leia tightly until she jumped down to hide under the chair.

His name was Frederick. I had never known anyone called Frederick before. Frederick, Frederick, Frederick. It was a new start for me. I could put Alan, Bob, and Colin behind me. I didn't need to think about those disastrous relationships anymore. I had Frederick now.

We started our relationship conventionally enough, if meeting on the internet is considered to be conventional at all, now. We exchanged messages through the dating site. That's the way they liked you to do it, for your own safety, and so they could charge you for the privilege.

At first, our messages were short. He told me he lived in North Berwick and I said I was in Edinburgh. We both commented on the fact we lived quite close to each other and agreed that long-distance relationships can be difficult to maintain. He shared a house with his cousin. I lived alone in a small flat in Tollcross. He thought I was lucky to have my own space, while I envied the fact that he had company. He replied with a laughing emoji and said I had obviously never met his cousin. He went on to say that his home was in a quiet part of town. I told him my little flat is in a busy area. He said he knew that because his last girlfriend was a woman who worked in a bank there.

Then our messages evolved and became more personal. He told me about that girlfriend, and that she dumped him just because she couldn't see him anymore. No proper excuse. I told him how Alan had left me for a woman old enough to be his mother, how Bob dumped me for a Spanish girl, and that I discovered had Colin two-timed me throughout our relationship. It was then that I explained to Frederick because of all this, I wanted, needed, to take things slowly this time.

Frederick was so kind, so understanding, and he agreed that it was no surprise I had lost all trust in men. He said it was not a problem. We would take things at my pace. He said he knew I would be worth waiting for. He could see it in my eyes, my beautiful, bright, shining violet eyes. He would wait, but he asked if we could message each other directly rather than through the dating site. This meant we could both cancel our memberships. It would be so much cheaper. He emphasised that he was certainly not interested in meeting anybody else and he hoped that I felt the same.

Did I want to date other people? No way. Frederick was the man for me. My colleagues in the office couldn't believe my luck.

"There must be a catch, Eileen. He's way out of your league!"

"Thanks Joan."

"He's married."

"No, he's not, Anna."

"He's out of work with piles of debt."

"He's an eye specialist: a professional man, Joan."

"So, what the hell does he see in you?"

"We have a lot in common, thank you very much, Derek."

I agreed with them that he was gorgeous, definitely a nine to my six, but everything was going so well. And anyway, I felt I was due a bit of luck in the love department.

"I can't see him staying interested in a boring little mouse like you with your creepy cat for company and your 1990s fashion sense," Derek said.

I ignored him. He was twice divorced and always smelt of beer. Derek was not the Adonis of the office that he liked to think he was.

Not long after that, Frederick and I exchanged mobile numbers. He texted me several times a day and always ended his message with a kiss and a smiley face. He sent me pictures of his 'just woken up face', It was so funny, not at all like his posed shot on the site. He sent photos of his dog lying across his legs, but his feet did not seem as pretty as I remembered. Oh well, my feet were nothing to write home about either. I sent him pictures of my cat curled up in the sun, me at my desk in the office and a selfie of me hiking in the Pentland Hills. He got worried about me hiking alone, said it could be dangerous especially if I stumbled or got lost. Nobody had ever bothered about me like that before, but Frederick really cared.

As our relationship grew, we chatted almost every evening, sometimes for hours. He laughed at my stories about what Princess Leia did and shared the antics of his dog. We were really getting to know each other, and I enjoyed having somebody to talk to when I came home from work, even if it was on the phone. On the evenings that he was out playing squash with his cousin or working late, I missed the sound of his voice.

Then one day he asked, "Do you really have violet eyes? I only ask because, thanks to coloured contact lenses anyone can have violet-coloured eyes these days. Of course, the actress, Elizabeth Taylor really did have violet eyes. The first tinted contact lenses weren't available until the 1980s, so everyone knew her eyes were real."

"Oh yes, my eyes really are that weird violet colour, Frederick. My Dad always said I had eyes like Elizabeth Taylor. My Mum just used to reply, 'If she doesn't get married that often, I'll be happy. We couldn't afford that many weddings, George.'"

Frederick laughed. "I hope you won't get married that often too. I am much too selfish to want that."

I didn't know what to say. What did he mean by that? Did he want to marry me?"

Then, when he continued to speak, his voice changed and sounded professional.

"The appearance of the iris, that's the coloured ring around the eye's black pupil, depends on how much of the natural pigment, melanin, it contains. The more melanin in your iris, the darker your eyes will look. You can't choose melanin levels; they are determined by your genes.

"For example, my irises are dark brown, so my eyes have more melanin than your eyes. Elizabeth Taylor's eyes had an extremely specific, and rare, amount of melanin, and, if your eyes really are violet like hers, they are equally rare. Of course, there are various shades of light eyes: blues, greens and greys, with many in-between. Violet may have been Taylor's typical pigmentation. It's possible to have that violet eye colour. It all depends on the amount of melanin, but I have never seen truly violet eyes."

"Well when you see mine, you will see truly violet eyes. I don't even like them. I wish I had brown eyes like yours"

"Don't wish for that. Brown eyes are extremely common. Your colour is much rarer and more beautiful." He paused and breathed in deeply. "Would you like to FaceTime with me, Eileen? Then I could see your pretty face and gaze into those beautiful violet eyes."

"That would be wonderful," I purred. "I can look at your handsome face and melt into those big brown eyes of yours. They are so warm and comforting, like melted chocolate."

"You are much too kind, darling. I have always preferred light-coloured eyes to my common old brown ones."

Darling. He said darling. He called me darling, and the thrill of that word made me tingle all over. I gasped and grinned down the phone. I was so excited. I could hardly breathe.

"Eileen, angel, are you still there? Has the line dropped?

Can you hear me?"

"Yes, Frederick. Yes, I can hear you. I'm sorry, Princess Leia got in the way," I lied. I couldn't tell him I'd had to catch my breath.

"Thank goodness, darling. I thought you might have had an accident. You are alright, aren't you?"

He did it again. Darling. Angel. He really cared. I flushed with excitement.

"If we were on FaceTime, I could see that you were alright, and I wouldn't worry. Shall we do it?"

I looked down at my old pyjamas and fluffy slippers and my heart missed a beat. I couldn't let my own dear Frederick see me looking like this.

"Maybe we could start tomorrow. I'm just in my pyjamas, and I look awful tonight."

"Darling Eileen, I'm looking forward to seeing you wearing a lot less than that. But tomorrow it is. Take care my angel, till tomorrow. Goodnight."

"Goodnight, Frederick."

I hung up and lay on the couch, staring at the ceiling, replaying his words over and over in my head. He called me darling.

***

When I went into work the next day, Derek was standing by my desk, putting a mug of tea onto my coaster.

"Good morning, Eileen. How is the great romance going?" He sneered at me as I reached up to put my coat on a hook.

"Fine, thank you, Derek. Not that it's any of your business."

"Ooh charming. I should put salt in your tea to see if that sweetens you up."

I ignored his snide comment and almost danced to my desk thinking, Frederick called me darling. I had hardly slept, repeating the word over and over again. His lovely warm voice echoing around my head. I knew I would not concentrate today. How could I? When Joan came into the office, she noticed right away that there was something different about me. She came over to my desk.

"Eileen, you look different this morning. You're wearing makeup, and you look really nice. Is that a new dress? I don't think I've seen it before."

I stood up and hustled Joan towards the ladies' loos. That way Derek could not come with us.

"Let me get my coat off, Eileen! For goodness sake, I only said you looked different. What's the big secret?"

I moved from foot to foot as Joan took off her jacket, glancing at me nervously, and then she followed me. She looked at me curiously.

"So what's going on, Eileen?"

"You'll never believe it. Frederick called me darling!"

"Never! Did he really?"

"Yes, he did. More than once, Joan. It was so romantic. I hardly slept. I kept thinking about his warm voice, loving words, and his beautiful big brown eyes. I think I'm in love."

"You haven't even met him!" Anna said, as she walked out of one of the cubicles. She washed her hands as she continued. "He might be a down-at-heel tramp or an axe murderer."

"Anna's right. You can't be in love with a man you've never met," she said. "Come on. Pull yourself together. We better get back to our desks and start work before Derek complains to the boss."

I followed her into the office. Now I was in a bad mood. I hadn't slept well, and she was telling me that my feelings for a Frederick were not real. How dare she? Just because Frederick and I had not met in person didn't mean that our feelings were not real. We spoke every night, we talked about everything. Nobody knew more about me than Frederick did, and I knew everything about him. And we had so much in common, I had told him I was an only child, so was he. My parents died in a house fire, He lost both of his to cancer. I was brought up by an old auntie, his aunt and uncle brought him up with his cousin. He and his cousin are still remarkably close and shared the old family home. We both

79

like animals. I have Princess Leia, my kitten, and he has a golden labrador called Harry.

While I sat there thinking about Frederick, I didn't get much work done, and I even forgot to get the teas at 10.30. Luckily, Derek was there to remind me. After that, I tried to put my office head on for the rest of the day. But as I left the office, Joan whispered to me.

"Remember, you cannot be in love with someone you have never met. It may be infatuation or lust, or perhaps at a combination of the two, but you do not love him."

She was simply wrong. Of course Frederick and I loved each other. He called me darling.

That evening, when we were talking on the phone, I told him what she had said. He was taken aback.

"What does she mean we can't love each other? What nonsense! Do you feel that way, Eileen, darling? I'm sure I don't."

"No, of course not. We know all about each other. We talk every evening. Nobody knows me better than you do."

"I feel the same way," he said. There was a pause. I looked at his handsome face on my screen. He seemed a bit different from the photos on the site, but that was probably the lighting. I felt so lucky to have met him. Then he said, "I think we should meet. Then we will know for sure if we are right for one another. What do you say, my darling? May I come up to Edinburgh next weekend and take you out for dinner? I like to stay at the Waldorf Astoria at the west end of Princes Street. Do you know it? Is it easy for you to get to, or should I get a taxi to pick you up?"

"Of course I know it. That was the old Caledonian Hilton. It is very fancy and terribly expensive. Are you sure, Frederick?"

"Certainly I am sure. I can gaze into your beautiful violet eyes and hope you will love me and that they, I mean you, will be mine. The Waldorf Astoria is my favourite hotel in the city. Do you like the menu at the Pompadour restaurant?"

"I don't know the menu."

"I will arrange for us to get a table overlooking the castle.

It's a lovely last view in the evening."

"My goodness, I have never been able to afford to eat anywhere that grand." I heard his warm laughter and I smiled nervously. "What should I wear?"

"I know that you will look lovely whatever you wear, Eileen. But perhaps you could wear a pretty red dress. That way, if the waiter spills the wine, you won't need to worry."

I remember thinking that if a waiter at a hotel like the Waldorf Astoria spilled the wine, he would probably have more to worry about than I would. However, Frederick clearly had far more experience of fine dining than I did, so I took his advice. Joan came shopping with me on Thursday evening. It was late-night shopping and we had plenty of time to find a suitable dress. We went into Debenhams, but I didn't see anything I liked. I decided to go to Jenners. Joan thought it would be far too expensive, but Frederick was taking me to dinner at the Waldorf Astoria, expensive seemed to fit the bill.

There were lots of different designers and concessions to choose from. Some of the prices were eye-wateringly high and there weren't many red dresses. Then I saw one. It was perfect, and it was in my size. The red velvet sat just off my shoulders. The cut flattered my figure and even made me look petite, which I am not. It was beautiful. It was also over two-hundred pounds. No way could I afford that, but Joan talked me into it.

"Come on Eileen," she said. "This is the first decent date you've had in years. You've gone out with more losers than everyone else in the office put together. Splash the cash, girl, and buy the pretty red dress." When I began to argue, she shouted, "Eileen, just bloody do it. I can't bear this one to go wrong because of a few pounds and a dress."

Of course she was right. I bought the dress. I knew it looked good on me and I felt good in it. Sooner than you can imagine, Saturday came round. I decided, that having spent so much on the dress, I might as well look the part. I made an appointment to get my hair done, my nails matched my dress and I even got a matching bag and shoes. Even though I say so myself, I looked fabulous. I had never seen myself looking so good before and, little did I know, I would not do so again.

***

Frederick and I had arranged to meet in the bar. I saw him at the far end of the room. He stood up as I walked in and came towards me, with a beaming smile on his face. He was shorter than he looked in his photo and seemed older than thirty. His teeth were not so white. Gosh I was thinking such unkind thoughts. I'm no oil painting.

"Eileen, darling." His voice was the same. You couldn't tell height from a photo and if I'd lost my parents as early as he had, I wouldn't have aged well either. I was ashamed of myself.

"Frederick, how lovely to see you."

He smiled warmly and gazed into my eyes. "They are truly violet."

"I told you that."

"Yes, you did, darling, and your dress is lovely, perfect for this evening. You look gorgeous." He took my hand and led me to our table. "I ordered champagne for us to enjoy before we go through to dinner. I hope that is not too presumptuous of me."

"No, not at all. I've never had real champagne. It's always been Asti Spumante or Cava."

"Well, I feel like this is a cause for celebration. I get to stare at my lovely girlfriend with her beautiful violet eyes all night." He pulled out my chair and I sat down. He treated me like a real lady. It was so romantic.

His girlfriend. He thinks I'm gorgeous. A celebration. Champagne. I was drunk with delight before I'd even sipped the champagne.

We chatted about the weather, his train journey from North Berwick, the décor in the bar and the deftness with which the barman made cocktails. We linked arms across the table and sipped champagne from the glass each other held. Then the head waiter came through to tell us our dinner table was ready. Frederick and I linked arms and followed him into the restaurant like a prince and princess. I felt as if I was walking on air. We were seated by the window with a beautiful view of the castle, as he had said. The sky was clear, and the moon rose above the turrets of the historic building. I will never forget that fabulous view. The evening was so perfect.

"Your menus, sir."

"The lady's is a guest menu?"

"Oh yes, sir."

I smiled and took the menu proffered by the waiter.

"Have anything you like, darling. This meal is entirely my treat. I want you to enjoy it."

"But Frederick, there are no prices on the menu," I whispered. "I don't want to choose something too expensive."

He smiled, the warm smile I had come to know so well as we facetimed. "Darling Eileen, yours is the guest menu. There are no prices so you will not feel inhibited from choosing your absolute favourite meal. Please, choose anything you like."

I smiled nervously.

The wine waiter came over to pour us another glass of champagne while Frederick led the conversation about the delicious items on the menu. A waitress brought us a bowl of olives to nibble and then a basket of breads was placed on the table. I am not keen on olives, so I picked a piece of the bread and ate that.

A different waiter came to take our order. Frederick chose the scallops followed by a rib-eye steak. I ordered the salmon mousse followed by the mushroom risotto.

"And we'll have the Chateau Ste Michelle Pinot Gris followed by the Argentinian Red Wine, the Susana Balbo Nosotros Malbec 2014 with the main course," he said.

"Excellent choices, sir."

Frederick had not asked my opinion on the wine and he ignored the waiter's comment and handed back the wine menu without looking at him.

"How do you know so much about wine?"

"My uncle was a vintner. I learned from him, and I started young." He smiled. You see, for seafood that's higher in oil like salmon, tuna and ocean trout you need a white wine that's richer in flavour. Chardonnay and Pinot Gris are perfect, as they have the requisite weight and power to withstand the stronger flavours of these types of fish. We are both having fish for our starters and I, personally, much prefer a Pinot Gris to a Chardonnay. I hope you agree, darling."

"I like Chardonnay. I've never tried the other one, but I'm sure it will be fine." I smiled at Frederick. He knew so much about so many things. I was beginning to feel shy. Maybe I would bore him. "Why did you choose a different wine for the main course?"

"I am having steak and your mushroom dish has a woody, meaty undernote, so rather than a Shiraz, I chose a Malbec. The Malbec contains tannins like a Shiraz does and is said to offer a great health boost. Its flavours usually revolve around a smoky flavour combined with pepper spice and black fruits but Shiraz is best paired with game meats like duck and veal, so I thought our meal would be better complimented by the Malbec, don't you agree, darling?"

"I don't often drink red wine. I did have Beaujolais Nouveau once. I didn't like it."

"I'm not surprised. It's a dreadful con the French perpetrate upon their British cousins. Ah, here comes the fish."

We ate our starters and watched the moon rise behind Edinburgh Castle. Frederick asked about Princess Leia and told me about a long walk he had had along the shore with Harry before leaving him in his cousin's care until he got home tomorrow.

My mousse was served with melba toast. It was had such a delicate flavour and the wine was delicious with it. The wine waiter came to refill our glasses. I tried to decline by putting my hand over the glass. The waiter looked at Frederick and raised his eyebrows.

"Eileen, darling, let him fill your glass. If you don't want any more, just don't drink it."

I blushed. "I'm sorry Frederick. I'm beginning to feel a little lightheaded."

"Don't worry, darling. Have another piece of bread and when your risotto gets here, you'll be fine. I must agree, I'm feeling lightheaded too. I'm so excited to be here with you. Perhaps we should ask the waiter for some ice water. Maybe that will cool us down. I have dreamt about this for so long, I just want everything to be perfect."

"Me too. And it is perfect. Maybe a glass of water is exactly what I need."

A waitress cleared away the empty plates of our starters. The wine waiter brought out the red wine and Frederick tasted it before approving it. My glass was poured first. The wine was a dark red and the odour was so strong that I didn't need to raise my glass to be aware of it. I didn't like the smell at all, and wasn't sure I wanted to drink any more, but Frederick clearly enjoyed the red wine and wanted me to savour it too.

It was then that I stood up. Frederick looked at me strangely.

"I must go to the ladies' room before our main course is served," I said.

***

I enjoyed my risotto, and Frederick tucked into his steak, heartily. He was right after all, the red wine did go well with the meal. To me it tasted a lot better than it smelled. The waiter offered us a dessert menu when he took the plates away.

"Would you like dessert, darling?"

"You know, I think I would."

I chose the chocolate cheesecake and a cappuccino. Frederick just had a double espresso.

"You'll never sleep after that," I giggled.

"I have no intention of sleeping, Eileen."

I giggled again and reached for the sugar to put some in

my coffee.

"Let me help you with that," Frederick said. "Isn't the moon beautiful now?"

I looked at the dark, clear sky. "It is lovely. The view, the meal, the company, this whole evening has been lovely."

"I'm so glad. And I think it will only get better."

I don't know if it happened then, or whether it had happened when I went to the ladies' room, but I do know that by the time I stood up, my legs would hardly carry me, and I felt very sleepy.

"I think you have had a little too much wine, Eileen."

I looked up at him and nodded. My mouth didn't work anymore.

Frederick called for the bill. I noticed he paid cash. "My fiancée has taken ill," I heard him say.

I remember wondering when I became his fiancée. Had he proposed? Had I accepted? How could I have forgotten that? Anna, Joan, and Derek would be surprised. I tried to smile, but the muscles in my face wouldn't move.

"Perhaps I should take you to rest in my room, darling. Let me help you to the elevator."

I couldn't answer, but saw the waiters looking at me with disgust. I felt so ashamed, but there was nothing I could do. Frederick supported me as we moved towards the elevators and pushed the button for us to go up. But we never made it to his room because when we got in, I saw him push the button to go down to the basement. Then he stopped the lift between floors. I was confused.

He laid me down and took a teaspoon and his steak knife out of his pocket.

"You have such beautiful eyes, Eileen."

I wanted to scream. I wanted to run. I couldn't move a muscle.

I felt the knife slide into my eye socket while the teaspoon held my eye in place. I think it was then I passed out.

***

When I came around, the elevator was moving again. Then it stopped and I heard the doors open, but my world was dark.

"God in Heaven, Meera," a man said. "Another one with the eyes removed."

"But this one is still alive, Hunter," the woman replied.

Val Penny is an American author living in SW Scotland. She has two adult daughters of whom she is justly proud and lives with her husband and two cats. She has a Law degree from Edinburgh University and her MSc from Napier University. She has had  many jobs including hairdresser, waitress, lawyer, banker, azalea farmer and lecturer.

However, she has not yet achieved either of her childhood dreams of being a ballerina or owning a candy store. Until those dreams come true, she has turned her hand to writing poetry, short stories and novels.

Her crime series, *The Edinburgh Crime Mysteries* is, of course, set in Edinburgh, Scotland.

Follow Val on Twitter @valeriepenny

A Distant Rumble of the World We Knew

Joanna Krystyna Radosz

The mirror is broken. I notice the fact as soon as I enter the room.

First I feel something is wrong, something has changed while we were away. Then I see the cracks, like a spider's web covering the upper half of the mirror in the hall. Its frame remains untouched and the glass seems damaged by something sharp and pointy, like a small stone. Obviously such a thing couldn't have been done accidentally.

Someone was here while we were away.

I look into the mirror and can't help but smile. I'm not afraid. I'm waiting.

Yet the surface remains calm, reflecting just my bony cheeks and tousled jet black hair.

Behind me, Fae takes a step forward and stumbles. She moans quietly, her voice echoing through the hall, still clearly audible. I manage to take my eyes off the reflection and look back at her. Fae gets her body together and stands up with her ears alarmed and eyes pointing at the cracks. I shrug. Slowly she shakes her head, sighs and walks back. The sunbeams, shining through the doorstep and half-closed door, light up her ginger hair. She is a true-blood Scottish beauty. Somewhat irrationally I think that no matter how hard I try, I would never be as much a Scot as Fae is.

I smile and return to the mirror. This time I finally walk up to it and lightly touch the cracks, trying to read from them what might have happened in the building during our absence.

"What do you think, Fae?" I ask. "Who was there? Any ideas?"

Fae remains silent. Only when I turn my head to her, I notice her flaring nostrils. Her ears are still stiff. She's watching.

"Someone's here?" I ask her, and then I ask again, this time the space around us. "Someone's here. Hey, anyone?"

My voice gets stuck in my throat. I wait five seconds, then another five. Finally I give up and follow Fae to our feast-to-be, the fox we managed to hunt.

Skinning the poor animal, I can't help but think about the cracks and what they possibly mean. Someone walked into our solitude and broke the mirror. Why? To make sure I would get the message? What kind of message?

Fae lies at my feet, ears relaxed, yet her nostrils are still moving. She sniffs around for danger or at least for anything unusual. She wasn't born to guard, yet for all these months she's guarded me and I've fed her, although I wasn't born to hunt, especially to hunt foxes.

I get rid of the fur as soon as possible so as not to look at the distinctive red colour, just like Fae's hair. In the past I saw foxes either when we were out to the woods or at very special nights when they came to our estate to rummage for food in the bins. Mum used to say that when they weren't afraid of people anymore, it was a bad sign.

Nobody believed her then. Yet even if someone had done, it wouldn't matter now. It wouldn't have changed anything in our lives.

I finish skinning the fox, cut off the fatty portions, and start preparing meat for smoking. Living here for... I don't know, half a year, nine months?... I've learnt to survive, not faking it as we did during the camps. Still, I'm not sure how much meat we need for a day, a week, a month. Anything we hunt I skin and prepare, and I hope it will be enough until we hunt again. My movements have become automatic, my mind free for other thoughts.

Or, rather, this *one* thought: who was it, who walked into the club building and broke the mirror? The neighbourhood emptied long time ago, right after Fae and I arrived in Armadale. We came just in time to see the caravans of people leaving the place in search for a better life. How ironic! That was exactly the reason we arrived . We were escaping a worse life for a better one. And yet, in this town of ghosts, someone real is here.

My heart misses a beat in a mix of fear and excitement.

"Calm down, Fay," I tell myself. "It could mean anything."

It doesn't help, though. For the rest of the day, several times I walk up to the mirror, touch the cracks, and look deeply into the surface hopful that I might see someone there.

But the evening comes and nothing changes. So we walk out through the back door, eating the meat, and doing the same thing we have been doing for the past I-don't-know-how-long.

We head to the stadium. Tonight nobody is there either. Yet it feels eerily cosy and home-like to sit on the bench in the middle of an empty stand and to look at the gravel track, imagining the rumble, the noise of engines, the cheering of the crowd. I hardly remember the speedway. Dad used to take me to Armadale for the Monarchs matches when I was little, before the pandemic outbreak and before the world we knew collapsed. After the club has closed, after the sport has become a distant memory, Dad went back to the great years of Edinburgh speedway many times. I didn't remember then what had been so special about the sport. I recall all these things as soon as I first see the stadium again and the hall of fame in the club building, and the cups behind the dusty glass. Nobody stole them because nobody cared. Cups were neither edible nor especially useful when fighting a disease.

The stadium is a symbol of the memory of those careless childhood years when one weekend I would go with Dad to the match to support the Monarchs and take selfies with riders, and the other – I'd take off with my mum to her another camp, learn how to light a fire, how to make a proper hut to endure the night, how to tie a knot…

Back then I never thought it all would be so useful – except how to make huts. But here we are, in a world where possessing the skills to light a fire, to tie a knot, to hunt a fox and to distinguish an edible plant from a poisonous one, is extremely valuable. This is a world where you'd better have a gundog beside you, a world where the only soothing stories left are the well-known one of the sporting heroes from the past, the ones who rode, who raced, the ones who fought.

My mum taught me to survive in this world. My dad taught me to recount stories so I'd never forget. To be a human is to know than just how to survive.

"They promised us, Fae." I speak into the void that once was a speedway stadium. "They promised us they'd take care of everything and find us. You remember, right?"

Fae, lying at my feet again, lifts her head and whimpers. Maybe she misses them too. Maybe she doesn't remember them anymore.

Tonight, lying beneath the battered blanket, I dream of the world I know from Dad's stories. I cheer on the unforgettable Miss Fay Taylour, my namesake, that courageous girl who raced with her rivals and with her times. I walk up to her just in time to see her fixing her face in a ladylike manner. Only a stain of dirt on Fay's neck betrays the rider in her. She smiles at me and says something. It's inaudible, and yet, I feel strangely relieved.

"Come to Armadale," I say. "We need to have you racing for us."

"Armadale?" Fay laughs. "Never heard of it."

Then I remember she raced long before Edinburgh speedway moved to Armadale. It was even before the Powderhall period. If I said Powderhall, she would think about the greyhound races.

"You mean Edinburgh, right?" she says suddenly and I shiver. "I'm going to go there soon."

I want to tell her not to be. I want to say that I left Edinburgh less than a year before, and that it was hell back then. Fortunately, Fae wakes me up and all the stories remain stuck, unspoken.

It is the night, still, and Fae becomes relaxed as soon as I wake, so we cuddle together and sleep again. If there is one thing I've learnt during the last few months, it is that the night is for sleeping. Nocturnal animals become aggressive only when startled. And what about the evil creatures of the night? Never met any of them. Maybe they, too, have been scared off by the pandemonium radiating from Edinburgh and Glasgow, embracing first all Scotland, then the rest of the UK. Maybe there are no creatures as evil as mankind itself.

So we sleep.

The next day the weather is clear and the air slightly humid, so I decide to go to the city. I'm sure there was a time when, if someone from Armadale decided to go 'to the city', they meant Edinburgh. But that time was long forgotten, and Edinburgh is twenty or so miles from here. Besides, I'm not completely sure whether the pandemic has already emptied the city, too, and scared the rebels off. Even if it was closer, I wouldn't risk going around those streets again, seeing the decaying bodies in front of the temporary hospitals. They would 'turn' virtually any building big and spacy enough. During our escape, I overheard someone saying that in Edinburgh only the ill and the rebels were left, and I was trying to avoid both of them. That was then, in March. I don't know whether it has changed at all.

No, it's definitely better this way, with a relatively short and peaceful walk along the road to Whiteside or Bathgate. The towns are mostly empty, but their shops remain full of food with long expiration dates, not just tins, but chocolate, crisps, energy drinks too. It's all the junk things we used to condemn when life was quite normal.

Actually, I don't know if I'm still scared. Maybe I'm so tired of living this way that I'm not afraid of anything. I want to have at least a piece of normal life, so I break into abandoned shops and steal the most useless food I am able to find. I can hunt, I can gather plants, and tell toxic from safe. I steal not out of physical hunger but out of mental one, a hunger for my former life.

Fae always joins me in any trip to the city. She counts on getting some treats. Lately we haven't been lucky because all the dog food had already gone from three shops we visited. I suppose some survivors decide to live on dog food rather than of learn how to hunt. Can't blame them, though. All I know is that I've learnt because my mother used to organize survival camps. If it hadn't been for her knowledge and skills, I wouldn't lead such a comfortable (all things considered) and safe life, now. But I'd eat dog food, too.

Instead, I steal and eat crisps and marshmallows, chocolate and gummies, drink energy drinks and coke, and recall the world I once knew. Somebody told me – maybe it was my mum herself – that surviving wasn't about the physical abilities but about the mental ones. Junk food is the closest thing to keeping my mental endurance in order.

As we walk down the empty alleys and streets, Fae remains calm and even happy, lurking, smelling, going for the small birds and insects. For the past few months I've been amazed by how quickly she has adapted to the new world. I remember that lively, crazy ginger puppy that would jump on every person she met during the walk. She loved the whole world, craved for other dogs and snacks, and lived according to the principle, 'the more people, the better'.

When we escaped from Edinburgh, at first Fae treated it as another adventure and one big walk. She would run up to the flowers and bushes, go for butterflies and bark at anything unusual. Sometimes she would stop and stare at distant figures, as if trying to recognize my parents. Sometimes she lay down and growled, as if thinking of them. But all in all, she has adjusted quickly from the big-city-life with a huge house, to our wanderers' existence, escaping through the woods and along the highways and, now, living at the empty speedway club building with me, but without my parents – *our* parents. I bet she doesn't remember any more that my dad used to call her *The Toller*, arguing that Fae and Fay are homonyms. She doesn't remember Mum either, that strange woman dressing as a fairy or in battered jeans and comfy t-shirt, who would call her 'sweet changeling'.

Sometimes I want to be like Fae and just forget. I want to live day by day and expect nothing, hope for nothing...

Yet I *do* hope. I feel it especially strongly some hours later as we are coming back home from the chemist shop, with my backpack loaded with cosmetics and whatever junk food I could find there. As soon as we leave Whiteside, my heart becomes heavy in my chest, beating faster and more desperately. Again, I think about the broken mirror and imagine about what we would find when we get back.

The building looms on the horizon, and Fae stops and sniffs around. My heart misses a beat.

"Honey, you feel something?" I ask with a raspy voice, pointlessly trying to hide all the hope. "Fae, you know that smell? Is it... theirs?"

For some reason I'm not sure myself, I don't want to remember my parents' names. I'm afraid she'd recognise them and start missing them all over again. It's enough that I dream of my parents, and think of them, and hope they'll come for us as they promised back in Edinburgh.

I try not to expect anything, but when Fae jumps and runs towards the club, I can't help it.

She stops outside the building, lifts her head, and whimpers.

"What did you smell?" I ask, as if she could tell me. "Fae, what's going on?"

She stares at me intently and I feel that if she could speak my language, she would say, "I'd like to know it as much as you do."

Fae enters the building, her nostrils still flaring and her ears still pointed. I come right beside her. She sniffs the dirty floor across the hall intensely, then moves forward to the hall of fame. She misses the mirror, but I don't. I stop and look into the surface.

It is as cracked and broken as before, but this time I see something else besides my pale, tired face. Someone is standing there, in the shadow. I see the silhouette of a short-haired woman, dressed in leather trousers and a jacket, straight out of the 1920s. And I recognise her.

I gather up my courage, but refrain from turning to face her, knowing I wouldn't see anyone if I did.

"Fay?" I say quietly. "What are you doing here?"

As expected, she doesn't reply. Yet she smiles, or so it seems.

"Was it you who broke the mirror?" I ask. "Why? You wanted the place for yourself? For God's sake, Fay, we need it! We'll leave soon, I promise!"

The shadow doesn't move and her face doesn't change. Somewhere in the distance I can hear the light patter of Fae's steps, but I can't move to look for her. I am unable to blink, either. If I blinked, Fay Taylour's silhouette would disappear.

"Are you mad at us?"

Fay slowly shakes her head.

"You want us to do something?"

Fay shakes her head again.

"Then why the hell are you here, breaking the mirror and making me believe that they will come?"

I can't explain why I'm shouting. The shadow disappears, just like that, without the smallest sound, as if she was never there, in the mirror. My dog bursts out into barking and runs towards me. Collapsing on my knees, I feel Fae's warm fur and her wet tongue even before I realise there are tears running down my face.

"It was a ghost, doggy dog," I murmur into her ginger hair, letting Fae lick away my sadness. "Just a stupid ghost. It wasn't them, you know? Maybe it will never be them."

I'm not afraid of Fay Taylour's ghost. I'm only disappointed, since I hoped the mystery of the broken mirror would point to something else. I can't give up hope that my parents will return for us as they promised when we parted.

I remember that evening so well. My mum had just come home from another camp. This time I hadn't accompanied her, and my dad returned from the conference. It was a sunny, beautiful Sunday, the first one that year, but the sun seemed eclipsed by yet more protests and riots. The Isles Government had announced they would cease NHS support for Scotland despite the pandemic. People went out on the streets, shouting and damaging property. From our flat just outside the centre we could hear shop windows rattling and cracking, people yelling, people coughing. Some of them fell down the streets and died right away, their bodies remaining there forever. Some carried on and moved forward to Princes Street, as if they hoped someone would listen to them out there.

"We have to run," my dad said. "It's getting dangerous out there. Soon all the city will die either of the disease or in the protests."

The Disease. We never called it anything else. At first it seemed like just another flu, but then it mutated. It became even more contagious, invasive, lethal. Or maybe it seemed so because the healthcare was already ruined and there was literally no one who could take care of all the infected ones. And surely it didn't help to extinguish the pandemic. It coincided with mass protests against the imperialist Sassenachs and their tendency to decide our lives.

"I won't go anywhere," my mum protested. "This is my place. I will stand and fight for it."

"We should fight for our lives in the first place," Dad said. "Aileen, it's not feasible for us to stay here, to wait for something, or someone, to kill us. And no, we won't move out of Scotland."

Mum was as Scottish as Fae. She organised survival camps, and managed folklore trips in search for the lost and forgotten soul of Scotland. She was truly her nation's daughter. Dad was more pragmatic. In fact, his naming the dog Fae was the only reference to the folklore he ever did.

"What's the alternative?" Mum asked, dryly. Dad started explaining how we would go to the abandoned building, Edinburgh Monarchs speedway club, and stay there until the situation calmed down. Meanwhile he and Mum had to go to Inverness for my sister and to check whether there it would be a good place to live. Then we would decide together whether we should all move to Inverness, or stay in Armadale, in the club building, and wait until everything had ended.

"If something goes wrong or we cannot get in touch anymore, stay in Armadale and wait for us, Fay," Dad told me, holding my arms. He looked utterly desperate. "Please, promise me you'll wait."

"I will, Dad," I said without hesitation. My parents then gave me the dress that was meant for my birthday. I never loved dresses, but had fallen in love with this one as soon as I saw it in the window of mum's favourite boutique. It was off-the-shoulder and grey, and I thought that it made me look like quite a lady. The dress was meant to distract me from the hell outside, and remind me that there was a future.

I can't remember where I put it. Anyway, I still believe they'll return for me and Fae.

Buried in hope like a warm blanket, I come out of the building and go straight to the stadium. As soon as the afternoon starts turning into evening, I can see the ghosts again. This time, though, they don't belong to daring Miss Taylour, they're the figures of Edinburgh's speedway past. I'd seen them before. In twilight, they had been riding on the ruined track, as if dancing, parading from the 1920s, the first days of speedway in the city. There was Drew McQueen, that brave boy who had made thirty-thousand people freeze almost to death on New Year's Eve just to see him race, and poor Peter Craven, whose life had been taken too early on that September evening when he tried to avoid crashing into his opponent and crashed into a fence instead.

I know these stories from my dad and so here they are, vividly played right in front of me. It's just like Armadale took all the spirit of Edinburgh speedway, its past and its memories, and poured them onto the abandoned track, replaying it over and over again for just two spectators, two survivors – one girl and one dog. Perhaps we were just too stupid to escape whilst we still had time.

It might sound strange, seeing the ghosts in the empty town, and not feeling scared. But let me tell you a secret. When I was a little girl, I used to have a story book. I don't remember the stories, but what I *do* remember, still, are the pictures. One was of a forest, a dense and dark forest, with a small clearing in the middle. On the clearing, by a bonfire, sat a boy and a girl, watching, with a mixture of fear and wonder, as a ghost danced around them, flashing between the branches and gleaming white against the dark background. The ghost was almost translucent and yet had distinct features.

I loved that picture, but was scared of it at the same time. There was something about the ghost that made me uncomfortable back then, even before I was diagnosed. It felt off, dangerous, terrifying. Yet the glistening figure, both strange and eerily familiar, became carved into my mind and stayed there forever, for longer than the names of any people I once dared to call my friends.

I recall it now. I can feel the stiff paper beneath my fingertips. I feel like I am a child again. Except I'm not. And the forest, the bonfire from time to time, the ghost – all of this is real. I try to remember, if I ever made a wish to meet that translucent being from the bedtime story.

Be careful what you wish for, huh?

I spend the next few days lying in my bed with Fae beside me. None of the mundane things in life have been cancelled, including my period. Fortunately we have enough food and water that I don't need to leave. From time to time I unwrap the blankets and walk unsteadily around the place to see if the distillers work properly and, whenever needed, to empty them. The weather has turned cold enough so that the small den just away from the building has become a natural fridge. There I keep meat and grill it over the fire in the evenings. The place feels abandoned, as if there is no one in the whole world but me and Fae.

Never mind, I think, whenever I'm able to think from behind the curtain of pain. We manage together. And when I say it aloud, Fae agrees with a yawn, before coming back to our bed.

I'm extremely grateful to my mum for teaching me to survive, and for teaching that there's nothing like a warm blanket, or five of them!

On the third day I'm wide awake long before the sun rises. Feeling strange excitement, I creep quietly out of the bed, so as not to wake Fae, and go out to the track. The dawn is just breaking and the ghosts are moving in the dim light. I watch them for a while, uncertain what they are doing, before I realise that I know the scene far too well, although I am too young to remember it myself. Dad told me many times about a rainy October day in the early 1990s, when there was a testimonial to be held in Powderhall for a local rider called Michael Coles. It was, no surprise, rained-off. But what was so special about the meeting was that before the crowd left, every single person there gave a standing ovation. It was Coles' wedding later that day. When Dad told me about the big event, where riders and fans got together to celebrate the star's greatest day. Now I felt like I was there as well.

So here I am, the whole place to myself. The stands don't seem empty anymore. They are full of people and although I can't hear them, I imagine they're cheering and shouting, and wishing all the best to the newlyweds. I can see Michael himself, standing in the centre of the withered grass oval in the middle of the track. He grants a broad smile to the crowd, bows, and waves his hand. It may not be Powderhall, but the ghosts feel here at home.

I close my eyes dreamfully, trying to catch a glimpse of the ghosts' joy, but suddenly an eerie silence fills my ears. As soon as I stop seeing them, my mind stops imagining the sound. There is nothing but the vacuum I find myself in.

I shudder.

Strangely, the excitement doesn't leave me for the whole day. When we hunt for yet another fox (sometimes I feel like there is nothing in the Scottish woods but foxes), when I sun-dry the meat, when I empty the distillers and pour the water to the bottle deep inside the den, finally, when we go for a walk to the park. It is nearby, as empty as the rest of Armadale, but wandering around it makes us both feel so… normal, like nothing ever happened. It is just another autumn day, too cold for some to have a proper walk, but not too cold for a girl and her dog. We play hide and seek, I toss Fae some sticks, and pet her in the grass. She lies down, paws upwards, wagging her tail.

It passes for normal. I need such moments as much as I need crisps and chocolate. I need to feel there's more to life than just surviving it.

On our way home, Fae barks excitedly at every tree and every empty lane. I dance and jump when no one is watching. Dodging the holes in the path, we hide from foxes and boars (until The Disease, I didn't know that there were boars near Edinburgh). Finally we reach our clearing, and the stadium looms in front of us.

Suddenly Fae stops, raises her ears, and stares intently into the distance. Something is there, out of my reach. I stop halfway through a pirouette, lose my balance and nearly fall on the ground. Regaining control over my body, I fix my eyes on Fae and wait.

She begins to bark. And then she starts to run ahead, as if someone dear awaits her in the building.

My heart jumps. Trying not to run, not to get excited again, I follow her. Fae storms into the building, looks around, goes in and out of each room, one after the other, nearly tipping over a single cup on a small table. Eventually she runs back out and up to the track, barking with such excitement that I can't help but hope she isn't wrong and there *is* something to be excited about.

Abruptly I see him, beard as ginger as Fae's fur, inseparable hat on his head, bag over the shoulder. He sits on the stand, but as soon as he hears the barking, he turns around with a smile on his face. My head bursts with a mix of joy and disappointment.

"Fergus!" I exclaim. "You? Here? How come?!"

Meet Fergus McAvoy. Back in the old life, Fergus was my father's best student, then a great colleague. He would often come to our house to talk about the history of sports in Edinburgh, or to give my father another battered book that he'd found in a secondhand bookshop somewhere on the Isles. He was a self-proclaimed traveller/researcher/sports fan/rebel. And he was the only one of Dad's colleagues who never called me *Miss Fay* or *Miss Atkins* (my proper surname was Adair-Atkins, which they never seemed to notice).

And he was so Scottish that my mum fell in love with him at first sight.

I'm not sure about his Scottish-ness now. It is strange and even uncomfortable to see him in trousers instead of his beloved kilt.

"Fay! Sweetie Fay!" He almost sings my name now. I run to him, but Fae is first to meet him and licks his face frantically. "I finally found you!"

I stop immediately. My heart pounds in my chest with a series of thunderclaps.

"Oh, so you were looking for me?"

It takes him a moment to answer, since Fae begs for his attention. The moment seems an eternity for me.

I imagine him saying that he met my parents and they sent him for me to Armadale. I want him to say it.

"Surely," he tells me finally, petting Fae, who jumps around him with a puppy-like excitement. "Back in Edinburgh, your father told me you're going to Armadale. Somehow, I hoped I'd find you here. An sae here ye ur."

"So here I am," I echo, staring blankly at the ghosts on the track behind him. "You met my father? When? Fergus, is he all right? What's with my mum?"

I can't hold my temper any longer. Fergus grabs my shoulders.

"Up tae thon time, Fay. I don't know what's going on with them. I haven't seen them since March."

Since March. Since the time we parted.

My heart falls.

"Oh, I thought…"

"Sit down, Fay," he tells me in a calm voice. "Come 'ere. Sit beside me."

I do as he wants, too stunned to respond properly.

"I've been watching you for some time, girl," he continues, placing his hand on my shoulder. It seems weird and alarming. Yet I'm sure that if something was wrong, Fae would help me instead of fawning over Fergus.

"You were the one who broke the mirror?" I interrupt. He smiles regretfully. Still, I sense something insincere about this smile. I try not to stick to the thought. It may be just my own disappointment, nothing to do with Fergus.

"Aye, Fay. I'm sorry. I didn't do it on purpose. Hit wis juist a accident."

"It was five days ago. Why didn't you show yourself then?"

Fergus looks away, pretending to be absorbed with Fae, who plays with his shoelaces.

"I wasn't sure how you would take me. I heard you shooting." We both laugh politely. The situation gets more uncomfortable than my life after Edinburgh has ever been. "Seriously now, sweet Fay. I wasn't entirely sure how you'd react to what I've got to tell you. But I watched you, I thought about it, and eventually I decided you're the perfect person."

"The perfect person for what?" I ask, still looking at the track. It itches me to tell him to look back, since there are people in leather suits racing against one another. Still, I'm afraid that if I did, it would turn out my dad told him about my diagnosis. The wrong one, actually. If I really was schizophrenic, I would never survive after the end of the world.

I'm not schizophrenic. Under no circumstances is seeing ghosts an illness.

Fae breaks the silence, whimpering and demanding more petting from Fergus. He does as she wishes and waits another eternity before raising his eyes on me.

"The perfect person to come with us to Edinburgh and start all over again."

"Come to Edinburgh? Why? Who is 'us'? And what do you want to start?"

"Fay, Fay, Fay, please. One question at a time, okay?" he says in a low, warm voice. "You remember what I did back in the auld times?"

"Sure." I don't know what he's going to say. I'm getting nervous, and my hands start sweating. "You were a researcher in the Institute for the History of Scotland, a sports fan, a traveller…"

"There was more than that," he interrupts me before I can add a rebel to the list. "I was calling for the independence of our nation. When my compatriots protested, I stood with them. When the usurpers tried to make us forget about our roots, I stood against them. I know your family, Fay. Your father might have underestimated the power of Scottish spirit, but your mother got it well."

I want to demand him to stop talking like my parents were already dead. They aren't, I know they're not.

But I don't say a word about them. I am speechless. And in the corner of my mind there is a thought, absurd now, how, ironically, he stops mixing English and Scots the moment he starts talking about independence.

"The Scottish spirit's strang," I agree wearily. "But don't you think right now there's no difference between the Scottish, the Welsh, the English? We're all in the same shit." He opens his mouth to speak again, but I'm quick. "I know what you want to tell me. Something about the best time to say goodbye to the Sassenach invaders. And a year ago I'd have agreed. Now I think we need someone who is eager to help. But let's put this question aside. It's a tricky one, isn't it? Are you sure the pandemic is over? Are you sure it's safe to come back to Edinburgh?"

"No less safe than before, for sure. All the infected ones either recovered or died. All the occupants ran. Ma fowks say that Edinburgh is the best city to live in now. Although, I must say, quite... empty an' lyfless. But it's temporary."

"If you say so..." I'm still not convinced, but that's not the most important thing at the moment. "I'd love to return to Edinburgh, then, as soon as my parents come back for me."

Suddenly his face changes. He frowns and looks at me with a piercing gaze, as if I did something really inappropriate, like fooling around at his mother's funeral.

"Don't delude yourself, Fay. If they didn't come back yet, they won't," he says and then looks away. "The world you knew is long gone, and your parents are surely no exception. Dale wi' it."

Fae barks warily, as if she understood the heresy behind

103

his words.

"You should come back to Edinburgh with me," Fergus continues. "Now that all the Sassenachs are gone, we can rebuild it our way. We can bring back the monasteries, the Hope Mansion, all the city we once lost… Co' an jine us, Fay."

And I am the one deluding myself? I think. Surely, I believe that the protesters who survived can restore old Edinburgh – but whom for? The ghosts that no one can see, except me and Fae?

I look back and notice a shadow, barely visible in the corner of the track. I can't tell whether it is Peter Craven or Michael Coles. All I knew is that Fae and I are not alone.

"No", I reply finally. "My parents told me to wait, so I will wait for them."

Not that I have many other things to do.

"Fay, sweet Fay." Fergus shakes his head. "You won't survive in this…"

"I've already survived almost a year," I remind him harshly. "Don't underestimate me."

"Winter is coming," he says, making it a bit louder, that distant rumble of the world we once knew. "You don't know what it's like, to endure the winter out in the wild. You won't make it alone."

I don't answer. I know better.

The next day Fergus is gone. It is as if he was never here at all, more elusive than ethereal. I find my grey off-shoulder dress, put it on and take Fae for a walk to the nearby park. This time we don't need food or supplies. I am simply fed up with ghosts of the past and in the desperate need of a change.

Morning air is chill, bringing the first breath of the upcoming frosts. Yet, it's going to be a sunny day. Suddenly, first sunbeams defeat the clouds and light up the trees until they become as green as ever. We walk down what remains of the paths, like strolling in the park. Except the park is a mess, and we both, despite my clothes, are an utter mess, too.

Still, I keep waiting for the distant rumble of the old world to come. That's all I can do.

Joanna Krystyna Radosz is a Polish writer, translator, journalist and researcher (PhD student in Russian studies). By 2021 she has published four books, all in Polish, and several short stories in anthologies and magazines, including speculative fiction queer story A November Without Dreams (Listopad bez snów) in Rainbow and Fantastic (Tęczowe i fantastyczne) collection. She loves speedway, Russian culture, traveling and learning new languages. A Distant Rumble of the World We Knew is her debut in English.

Follow Joanna on Instagram @jkradosz

Free Reel

Edward Yeoman

"Johnathan? Johnathan Jude?" This must be the journalist who wants to interview me.

"Hi, yes. Pleased to meet you…?"

"David McGreggor, Edinburgh Daily Tribune."

I know what's on his mind; it's always the same when the press wants a chat with me. With Johnathan Jude of Free Reel, the glorified free cèilidh band. Then again, I always play along. It's not as if we're making enough money that a few free drinks wouldn't go amiss.

That's why, as a matter of routine, I insist on these interviews taking place in a bar; the journalist always feels obliged to buy me a couple of beers. As the band's name implies, in the past we played a lot of free gigs. Our main outlet for years were the free festivals – acoustic raves, if you will. Being free, nobody used to have any money to pay us. We would just pitch up on the arranged day, play, sell a few tapes, pass a bucket, and slip-off to the dole office to sign on as unemployed. Well, that was life on the banks of the Clyde in 1981.

"Call me Johno, David. Everybody does. Mine's a pint."

He goes to the bar and returns with a pint of dark brown ale and a half of pale, insipid-looking lager.

"I'm working, so I have to be careful," he explains.

My reputation as being a bit of a pisshead would have nothing to do with it. Mind you, with what happened *that* night, who wouldn't be a little *disturbed*? I know we were all changed by it! Then that was what this interview was going to be all about. It is what they are all about.

"OK, Johno, do you mind if I tape this chat?"

"Not at all, if it will stop you putting words in my mouth." I take a long, deep tug on the beer.

He fiddles with a recorder for a few moments. Then, setting it down on the table between us, he starts.

"Perhaps it would be good for you to introduce yourself."

"Yeah, Ok then, I'm Johnathan Jude, singer and guitarist with Scotland's finest free cèilidh band, Free Reel."

"I notice that you describe yourself as singer and guitarist, omitting that you are the main songwriter for the band, Johno."

I definitely know where this is going now, the same place as so many other interviews over the past dozen years since that night. No, that is just since the song was recorded. It must be at least fifteen summers since that night. I point to my empty glass. The journalist signals to the bar.

"I told the barman to keep them coming. Why didn't you mention song writing?"

He has me there. I am the main songwriter in the group, having written eleven of the twenty original songs we put out on the three albums we had been contracted to do. That was in the days of the CD, real albums. The rest of the tunes had been traditional songs. Popular reels and jigs, done in our unique way.

The first CD had done moderately well; the second pretty poorly. The third only got released because there was enough material left over from the first two that meant it was cheaper to put it out than buy us out of the contract. Still, they own the rights to the original recordings, so they hadn't made a loss. Especially as over the years we have continued to work hard and remained popular.

"We hardly did any original material." I keep trying to deflect the questions. I would rather not go where all the interviewers want to go. "We started off just doing rockier versions of Jimmy Shand material and stuff they used to do on telly on Hogmanay. Punk cèilidh we called it, until we discovered that crap on TV was the vanilla and what we were doing was more like the real cèilidh. The early days were really wild!"

My second beer arrives. David, the journo, is still on his first half of lager. Not that I care. He wants us to go to that night and that place. I don't. Even a decade and a half later, I'm not keen to revisit that night without the protective screen I have built around it. So, I just keep talking.

"Everybody knows that we started off doing the Free Festival circuit that ran all summer long back in the day. No money but free beer, free drugs, free sex. Lots of free sex! It was pretty wild. We realised we needed to get a wee bit more savvy about things, noticing that the promoters were getting paid; getting money for various things from food concessions to getting incentivised to play certain CDs between the live performances. We started selling tapes and passing a hat round 'for petrol money'. We were finally making a few bob to supplement our unemployment benefit.

"Then the big day came. We got paid to headline some rich kid's do in the woods, or so we thought. It turned out it was a birthday party for some guy who was running a successful printed T-Shirt business. When we got there, he had an offer for us: we could have the fifty quid we'd been offered or... He had some girls' crop-tops that hadn't sold well. Hardly surprising! 'I get 'em out for FREE' was not the sort of slogan a good Glasgow lass would wear to the boozer on a Friday night; even if it was true about most of them."

I pause while David splutters into his lager.

"He offered to modify them for us," I continue. "And while we were on stage doing our first set, he got the word REEL printed onto them. So, we got a hundred and fifty 'I get 'em out for FREE REEL' crop tops. We managed to sell quite a few during the break, including to this woman with a massive pair of jugs. She whipped off her old shirt and put it on in front of everybody. Whether it was down to the size of her boobs or the shortness of the top, but every time she moved, she flashed her nipples to all and sundry. That attracted more than the odd glance. So, part way through the second set I decide to give the tops a quick plug while we were getting running repairs done to the bass. Suddenly she was up on the stage showing what she had got – and the crop top. That went down well with the guys in the crowd!

"The bass all sorted, we got into the next number, and there she is. Just behind me, leaping up and down shaking it all about in time to the music. At the end of the song the lads in the crowd started chanting, 'Get 'em out! Get 'em out!' She comes over to the microphone and bawls into it, "Ah wull if youse dae it an a'!", and as we start the next song she does and so do most of the audience. Of course, we get her to join us for the rest of the summer, and we made a fortune with those tops!"

Suddenly I realise I'm out of story. He's going to ask about that night, I know it. I sink the rest of my pint and signal for a refill, anything to delay that question.

"Free Reel are still out there, performing. Apart from the occasional prestige gig, you appear to spend most weekends playing for an audience who get in for free. How does that work?"

Crafty bugger, he has heard from somebody who has talked to me before. Unlike the last twa' who came straight out with it. I panicked that night and just ran off. That journo might still be in that bar, waiting for me to come out of the gents.

"We still do all the old stuff like CDs, tapes, posters and t-shirts." I see him smile at the vision I had planted in his mind of Sookie swinging her jugs on stage with us. The memory still makes me smile too. She's a mother of three, with a bottle-a-day habit, living in Govan now. Life can be shit like that.

"Besides all that conventional stuff we have a booming download market. The record company might own the original recordings of our stuff, but we do live versions and what the big labels call re-mixes. If you go to one of our gigs and shout out something funny or rude, you can buy and download the concert complete with your witty barb to play to your mates." I'm running out of things to say again. I need something to divert the conversation. "At any rate none of us are signing on anymore."

That's the end of that part of the story. Where to next? That chilly early September evening?

"What does it feel like when you are on stage in front of a thousand or more revellers who are having a great time listening to you playing and singing?"

That comes as a surprise, not the question I was expecting at all. I fumble for an answer. "Magical, I suppose. We start the evening driving our enthusiasm for the music into the crowd and gradually bit by bit it comes back to you. Then it grows and expands, and there is a huge ball of excitement. We are at one side of it, the crowd is at the other. Where the energies from both sides meet, they reinforce each other, powering your spirit higher, spiralling up into the sky and it goes on and on, until at the point exhaustion, the show is over and everything dissipates."

"Your song, *Dance of the Dead*, you play that one every time I have seen you, yet you don't like talking about it. Why is that?"

There! He has asked the question, except he hasn't, not quite. I can answer this one, so I do, in a roundabout way.

"Can you imagine going to a Deep Purple concert and them not doing *Smoke on the Water*?"

"Fair point. It's a key part of their set, one of the songs that everyone knows them by."

"Exactly, David! Go into any guitar shop on a Saturday afternoon and you'll hear it, 'dum dum duuum, dum dum tee dum'! It's the second quickest way of getting thrown out of my local guitar emporium."

"The second? What gets you thrown out quicker?" That little deflection seems to have worked

I'll go with it.

"Actually, it is the third, tucked in closely behind dropping a Gibson onto something but way behind the fastest way out. Any idea what that is yet?"

"I'm not going to try to guess."

"Get me another pint, and I'll tell you!" The man with the expense account waves at the barman, who nods back and starts filling another glass.

"Come on then, Johno, what gets you thrown out of a music shop faster than damaging an expensive guitar?"

"Oh, you probably won't have damaged the Gibbo much, but you'll have smashed whatever it fell onto. They are bleedin' heavy!" I laugh, but I can see from his expression that he is getting cheesed off with this diversion. Time to end it. "Starting to play the intro to *Stairway to Heaven* – the staff hate hearing that played badly. Do you play at all?"

"I always wondered why I wasn't allowed to buy a proper guitar." He sneered. "You were telling me about why you play *Dance of the Dead* before we got side-tracked." He takes a long, slow, sip of his drink.

"We were. Like I said, Deep Purple have to play *Smoke*. The audience demands it. We do *Dance* because if we didn't, we would have to learn something new to fill a fifteen-minute-long hole in our set." No, he is not buying that one. "And there would be hell to pay."

"That is not the only similarity between the two songs, is it? They both tell a story of an event in the band's history."

"Yes, and I bet if you ask Ian Gillan, the Deep Purple singer, to explain what the song was about, he'd laugh in your face and tell you the words explain it!"

"And you normally say much the same things about *Dance of the Dead*, and then you storm out of the interview."

"Yeah."

"Joni Mitchell, in her song *Woodstock*, wrote about bombers turning into butterflies, which sounds a little 'trippy' to me. Is *Dance of the Dead* a song about a bad drug trip?"

"A bad trip? Yeah, but no drugs involved." I am on the point of telling him the story. Should I inflict him with it?

"No drugs? Really?" He fails to keep his disbelief out of his voice.

I silently answer my internal question. Yes, he has asked for it.

"Have you got an hour to spare? No further use for your soul?"

The journalist glances at his watch. "Take all the time you need!"

111

I take this as a positive response to both questions.

"The third of September 1988. We were booked to play a late night cèilidh rave party in an ancient wooded area a wee bit to the south of Dunbar. It was going to be our last outdoor event of the year. Let's face it, September is pushing it a bit this far north."

I remember it as having been a cold night. The instruments kept going out of tune because of the falling temperature. We finally got on stage just before ten, and the audience were keen to get dancing to warm themselves up. We were just as cold, and it took a couple of numbers to get the fingers working. Once things had started, it soon came together, and the energies started to flow. That's why there weren't any drugs. That energy is such a buzz; you are so high on that feeling you don't need any other stimulants.

The drugs come after the buzz has gone, an attempt to recapture that high energy state, the one in which you experience transmigration to different plane of existence. If you have ever been there, ridden the perfect wave, clipped all the curbs through a complex set of bends, or known that the ball is in the goal as it left your boot, it will make sense. If you haven't, I'm sorry for you and my inability to communicate the feeling. Come to one of our gigs and get lost in the music, it might help!

"We played the first set then took a short break. We were running late, and like I said, it was freezing cold. Rather than hang around, we got back on stage pretty quickly and started the second half of our show."

"That's all in the first verse of the song."

"Do you want the story or not?" I raise my empty glass; the barman gives me the thumbs-up. This has to be my last. I fell asleep on my doorstep last time I had a five-pint night.

"Sorry, please tell the story in your own way."

"Thank you." My pint has arrived. I thank the barman, but it effectively shuts the journo up at the same time. I take a small sip. "You might want another drink too," I suggested to David. He orders another lager.

"We were halfway through the first number when they

112

appeared.

"I mean they appeared. They didn't arrive. I looked down for a chord change, and when I looked up, there they were. Eight of them. Bikers. Hell's Angels, I thought. Bearded, long-haired, unkempt, that was the typical appearance of a biker gang member at that time. They were dressed in studded and padded sleeveless leather jackets, and metal helmets that might just be legal. Their faces were covered in grime, and there was a wild look in their eyes. I was scared shitless."

"That certainly sounds like a crowd of trouble causers."

"Yeah, well, we had all seen them, and the music faltered for a few seconds, but the guidance 'play through trouble' kicked in. If a fight starts, the best thing for the band to do is keep playing, hoping the trouble passes before everyone notices and takes sides." I reach for my glass and stroke the rim. From here on there is no point in drinking; it isn't going to change anything.

"We got back into the groove of the Duke of Atholl's Reel, so the audience didn't immediately notice the new arrivals. They had, however, noticed the missed beats, and it took a few bars for them before they picked up the rhythm and resumed the dance, bouncing and skipping around. After a few moments, the eight strangers formed up as a set and started to dance. It wasn't like any of the variations of dance we had ever seen. Even back then we got all sorts of groups turning up at our gigs, some of them really dedicated dancers. We knew most of the takes on the basic reel the Duke of Atholl allowed. This wasn't any of them."

The journo nodded; he must have recognised this much from the song.

"Whatever steps they were doing, they were well into it, arms and legs flailing about, heads banging back and forth. They were giving it huge. I was starting to worry about them crashing into the other dancers. Except they didn't, not once. The rest of the crowd seemed totally oblivious of their presence in their midst.

"We reached the end of that dance and launched into a jig.

113

The strange thing was the energy levels were starting to flag. The audience were not quite as 'bouncy' as usual. We put it down to the cold. However, the Hells Angels were still giving it their all, swinging round and round, crashing into each other as they danced back and forth."

It was getting late. It might have been a party in the woods, but the promotor had a licence for the event. We had to finish at midnight. We stopped playing just a few minutes before the witching hour for a different reason. The same thing that caused Sookie to trade-in dancing with Free Reel for a life of urban uniformity.

"The band's energy was flagging still further, and if the official end of the show hadn't been in sight; we might have wound up the set earlier. That might have prevented it. Then hindsight is always perfect vision." I take a swig of my beer. I am still trying to delay the end of the tale. One final deflection. "You must have listened to the song more than once. What does it tell you happened next?" I ask the journo.

"That is the mystery, why so many people have tried to find out what you really meant by 'the dancing dead are dead, the dancing dead-man lost his head, man. The dancing dead are dead again, dead dancing feel no pain'. Not the sort of words you find in many jigs." He fixes me with a stare. "They sound like the ramblings of a very stoned man!"

That does it… He is going to get the full story, with all the consequences. The ones that mean we do *Dance of the Dead* every gig. The price that is so high Sookie never dances anymore. I wonder how they will manifest themselves to him. I'll find out soon.

"It was a very nasty trip; one that was taken straight, sober and on a low." I hear the bar door opening, and I look up and see someone heading out into the night. I sense something cold slipping into the warm fug of the room. It's too late to turn back.

"I was telling you about the night of the third of September 1988. Do you know the significance of that date?"

"Not in any important way that I can think of. Is it significant then?"

"We were just outside Dunbar…"

"No, still nothing."

"The anniversary of the Second Battle of Dunbar."

"No, history is not my strong point."

"1650, a large Scottish army assembled to support Charles the Second as rightful King of Britain was routed by the bastard Cromwell's English army."

"This is important because?"

"That night in 1988 marked the three hundred and thirty-eighth anniversary of the defeat, as Malachy, our drummer and an amateur numerologist, pointed out after the event. It was the double thirteen squared date: 2×13^2 – a rather unfortunate number."

"Thirteen's unlucky for some." The journalist takes another sip of his lager.

The cold presence I feel in the room comes closer.

"Yes, particularly unlucky if you were one of a group of eight survivors of that Scottish army trying to slip away through the woods looking to reach safety."

"Oh?"

"Yes, as they started to relax, congratulating each other on living to fight another day, they walked into an English ambush. A single salvo of shots from two dozen muskets, and they all fell dying. We saw them falling. We heard their screams of agony. We saw the shot passing through them, tearing their bodies apart. The eight Hells Angels, who we had watched dancing with such reckless abandon, fell screaming for someone to take vengeance against the English."

"But that was nearly four hundred years ago. A great story for a song, so why the reluctance to tell anyone?"

"Remember that energy I talked about the audience generating? The enthusiasm the band puts into driving the music that the audience picks up, amplifies and radiates back to the performers, that drives the musicians and in return the audience even higher?"

"I remember."

"Well, the Dead Dancers are drawing on that energy. We

assume they will one day use it to wreak their vengeance on the English."

"So why do you play the song all the time?"

"If we ever fail to play the song, they manifest in the audience and absorb all the energy. The entire night is ruined. If we play the song, they merely absorb the energy created during 'their' dance."

"Oh!"

"Yes, very Oh! Every gig we have to watch them being slaughtered, every single time the same pain, mutilation and screams. It is like having the same waking nightmare every time we play."

"Then why have you carried on?"

"We haven't all. Sookie couldn't take it anymore and quit. It wasn't enough. Every time she tries to dance, the Dead turn up and take all the energy from the room. So, Sookie never dances anymore." The normally rowdy crowd clustered around the pool table are intently watching a dull match with sullen eyes. I can feel the cold presence gathering from all corners of the room and coming closer to our table. "Some of the guys in the band have tried playing in other bands. Can you imagine being part of a thrash-rock concert when all of the head-banging excitement is suddenly sucked out of the hall? It happened when Robbie stood in on bass in his brother's band. It took him a while, but he spotted the Dancers in the crowd. The quilted leathers stood out once he started looking."

"That sounds scary!"

"Now, you are about to find out all about it too!"

"How do you mean?" He sounds frit. Mind, he has good reason to sound terrified.

"Well, David," I lower my voice and lean closer to him. "It seems to me as if it works like this. The Dead will only take energy from the dancers while we are playing *Dance of the Dead*. Except, if we try to omit it from our set, then they appear to get angry with us and absorb all the energy generated. It is like they gain something from us telling their story besides the energy we create."

I pause and look up, "Now that you know the full sorry saga, I expect they will want you to write it."

I look at the eight leather clad, cold-eyed figures who stand silently around our table. They must be visible to my journalist friend, judging by the sudden pallor replacing the colour in his complexion. He turns from figure to figure, his eyes like saucers with terror as he stares at their faces.

"Vengeance will be ours!" A voice nobody else appears to hear sounds in my head. "You have delivered us a mighty weapon, Johnathan. We will have our revenge on the English now!"

I am certain they will. After all, the pen is mightier than the sword.

*Being different, **Edward Yeoman** is the real name of the author better known as Ted Bun.*

Ted Bun writes stories with a very specific theme. When he started writing material which did not involve people running around naked, he wanted to mark the difference. He had this name, which had only been used for articles in medical journals, lying around; it seemed a shame to waste it.

Edward was born in London lived most of his life in the south of England. The expression "Edward of all trades, master of none," could have been created for him. However, the diversity of experience is starting to pay off now.

After a lifetime of not knowing what to do, he decided to do something new. He decided to retire, found L'Olivette, his little paradise in the South of France, and started dreaming up stories.

117

During the long evenings of the winter months, a novella started to take shape, "The Uncovered Policeman." A light, cosy mystery romance with a cast of pleasant happy people, with quirky characters. It was first published on Valentine's Day 2016.

Since then, Ted Bun has published over twenty novellas and many short stories.

Edward Yeoman has published several short stories and one novel "The Last Day of June." Being different, he can't decide what genre that book belongs in; any suggestions would be most welcome!

Follow Edward's Blog - www.tvhost.co.uk

The Road to Mallaig

Denise Bloom

My mother and father met on a blind date, on the post office steps, in the city of Edinburgh. My dad had been stationed in Scotland in 1950. My mother had been sent from Bradford, West Yorkshire to help set up the telephone exchange and to train new telephonists. After they were married, and because they were both romantics, every holiday was spent in Scotland. The ritual was that we went to the post office steps and stood, while my mother and father looked into each other's eyes. We then had to have two minutes' silence. That was my father's sense of humour. My brother Andrew and I squirmed as they kissed each other. When I was thirteen it was not cool to see your parents showing affection. From Edinburgh we went to Uncle Alec's in Hamilton. He was not our real Uncle, but someone my dad had been in the Army with, and they had remained good friends ever since. We would stay for a couple of nights, which were filled with laughter and tears, and stories from their army days when they hunted seals and whales around the Orkneys and Shetland Isles while delivering supplies to army camps throughout the area. From there it was up to Fort William and then onto Mallaig, the Bahamas of Scotland. The west coast was like a tropical oasis. It had white sands and blue lagoons, the sea warm from the gulf stream. The summers always seemed to be long and sunny. We were not rich, although I thought we were. We had holidays every year, my friends and our neighbours did not seem to go anywhere. However, there was not the luxury of a hotel or boarding house. Our holidays were always camping, and wild camping at that; no fancy shower blocks or mini golf. It was a farmer's field with water from the nearby stream.

It was late summer of sixty-five, we had been to the Isle of Skye for the day across on the ferry, then back to our camp in Mallaig. We always stayed at Arisaig Croft. The farmer and his wife were friendly, and we would be invited up to the farm on some evenings for a drink and a story. The gathered party would be other campers or people from neighbouring crofts, all gathered to tell tales of the legends of the Highlands or of further afield. My father was always a good storyteller, tall tales peppered with reality. As children we would be asked to contribute stories of our own. Each narrator would get a round of applause and cheers. It was magical. On that day, we were the only tent in the farmer's field until about eight o'clock in the evening. A green A35 van pulled into the field, Mr Mackay the farmer showing them where they could park. Andrew and I lay on the tartan rug watching them unpack the van. There were three people, two men and a woman. I could not tell how old they were, though one of the men seemed much older. I thought that it could have been a father and his adult son and daughter.

"It's her boyfriend, the younger one," said Andrew.

"It might be her husband," I butted in. "Maybe the older man is their carer," I added.

"What's a carer?" My brother was only ten years old, he had not experienced the world as much as I had.

"Someone who looks after someone else if they aren't able to look after themselves, dummy."

"Oh, don't call me that." He leant over to give me a whack. My mother interrupted what was going to be a scuffle.

"Go take the kettle and get some water from the stream." We both ran down the field trying to get to the water first. I won, as usual, and pushed my brother into the stream. The water bubbled over the stones. The setting was perfect. I could feel the warm breeze on my cheeks and taste the sea on my tongue.

"Look, Jennifer. The seals." Andrew pointed out to the sea.

I could see the six pairs of eyes looking at the two of us, bobbing up and down with the tide. You could have mistaken them for humans and remembered my dad's tales of fishermen believing they were mermaids. The smell of bacon drifted down the field. The Munster family (the name we had given them) was cooking their supper. It reminded me that I was still hungry. Tea had been hours ago, and I was a growing girl. My mum opened a packet of Grey Dunn's wafers and we had cups of hot chocolate, then all to bed. Our tent was modern and divided up into sections. Andrew and I had a blow-up Lilo in one section and my mum and dad on the roll-up bed in the other part. Within a few minutes there was silence from my brother and my parents. I could hear an owl. Lifting the edge of the blue canvas, I tried to catch a glimpse of the bird. There was no sign of the owl, but I was able to see the Munsters' tent lit up by a paraffin lamp. A full moon shone onto the tent where three humped shadows all grouped together. I wondered if they were saying their prayers. Then one of the shadows grew larger, engulfing the other two, until there was just one shadow, tall and thin. It was rocking from side to side. I looked at my brother who was fast asleep with his thumb stuck in his mouth.

The tall slim shadow began moving around the tent. It rose upwards then collapsed into a ball. Where had the other two gone? I scraped my nail down my arm. Yes, I was awake, this was not a dream. The soft sound of the waves kissing the shore calmed my nerves. Looking out again, the lamp was still burning, but the shadows had gone. I pulled on the tent peg and crawled under the canvas. The grass was wet, though there had not been any rain. There was still a faint odour of bacon, from the direction of the Munsters' tent. My pyjamas kept the gentle breeze from causing a chill. With each cast of wind, it grew colder until I was shivering. I had to reach the Munsters' tent. The thought of seeing what had happened to the shadows spurred me on. What was I going to say if someone saw me? Then, as I got closer, I thought I could pretend to be sleepwalking. My mother always called me Sarah Heartburn, whoever she was, some other drama queen.

The tent flaps were open, but there wasn't anyone inside. The lamp swung from the top rod of the tent, creaking with every move, swinging quickly now with the gaining force of the wind. I strained to see any sign of life on the shore beneath the field. The seals had come onto the beach to sleep, their bodies swaying from side to side to find a comfortable spot. Then I saw a shape, dark and fluid. It did not have a body or a face, but it was alive, and it was not a seal. The moon came from behind a cloud and I saw the dark shape rise. It was a column of dark matter that was now ten feet tall. The movement of the shape made it look as though it was dancing with the rhythm from the incoming tide. Could it have been a seal, or a monster? I was transfixed. My toes almost frozen together, my hands turning blue. On the wind there was another sound, a screaming in such a high pitch that I had to cover my ears. The noise stopped as suddenly as it started, and the column collapsed. The black shape created another form, like a priest in a flowing robe, a hood over his face. He was looking at me. I turned and started to run back to our tent. The groaning monster was following me, I had to get to safety. This fiend was going to devour me. I lifted the side of the tent and crawled under the canvas, quickly fastening it as well as I could, and pushing the tent peg back in place. I laid still, trying not to breathe. My knees knocked together as my legs shook uncontrollably. My brother had not noticed my absence and was curled up in the foetal position, still sucking his thumb. There was now a threshing sound just outside the tent.

"Mum, Dad, wake up. Help." Andrew turned over.

"Wake up, wake up, please." I shook him with both hands, but it was a waste of time.

There wasn't a sound from my mother or father. The wall of the tent began to shake. My screams were wasted on my family members. They were asleep or something more sinister. The tent peg was pulled out by an invisible hand and the bottom of the tent wall started to rise. My screaming stopped. Although my mouth was still open, I could not raise a sound. A black fog seeped slowly into the bedroom space.

It was moving with the intention of suffocating me, I was sure. In less than five minutes I was part of that black matter. It was moist like fog and I felt tiny electrical shocks. They made my skin tingle. It moved again and Andrew was its victim. It covered every part of him, like a swarm of bees moving across, feeling every part of his body. The swarm then lifted his arms and legs, and he was floating gently above the ground. This entity was taking my brother. I tried to pull him back, but his body was going through the gap at the bottom of the tent.

"Wake up, Andy," I shouted as loudly as I could.

"Mum, Dad, wake up please. They're taking Andrew." There wasn't any movement from my parents. The canvas fell back in to place as Andrew was dragged to the shore. I clambered over the sand dunes and rye grass. There was a trough in the sand as his body was pulled towards the sea. The seals, disturbed, began making squealing noises and paddled their way into the ocean. The thrashing of the seals did not deter from the mist that carried my brother away.

"Let him go. Let him go." I made grabs at my brother's body, trying to save him from his watery end. The fog became one with the water, from mist to liquid. My brother's body floated at first, then disappeared beneath the waves. The seals joined him in his watery grave. The sky was green and shimmering, the silence like a graveyard.

Morning came, bringing the new day, warm with the sound of gulls screeching above. I was lying on the white powder beach curled into a ball. I stretched, every bone in my body aching.

"Jennifer, Andrew," my mother shouted from the front of the tent. How was I going to explain what had happened to Andrew? Maybe it had all been a dream.

"Where's Andrew?" my mother asked. I tried to tell her that something had taken him into the water, but she had stopped listening to me and was screaming at the top of her voice.

"Andrew." A police constable from Mallaig arrived first, then more. The farmer had telephoned neighbours, and there was a search of the area. I was questioned by numerous officers, but what could I tell them that they would believe? The Munsters' tent had gone. My mother asked if they had something to do with Andrew's disappearance. I nodded and pointed to the sea.

"They took him to the water."

"Are you sure, Jennifer? Did you hear the van go?" I shook my head as I hadn't heard anything after Andrew disappeared into the sea.

I walked up to where the Munsters' tent had been pitched. The grass had not been flattened and there were no tyre marks. It was as if they had not been there at all. My mother and father said they had not noticed much about the family, only that there were three people. I couldn't understand how they hadn't registered any more details; the make of the van, the father having grey hair and a beard. The girl had long blonde hair and large eyes; the boy was pale-skinned with a birthmark on his cheek. The police asked the farmer and his wife, and they said they did have a family in, but they didn't stop the night. Mr MacKay had heard them go about two o'clock in the morning. This gave my mother hope that Andrew was with someone, that he had not been drowned.

"Jennifer, tell me again what you saw." The policeman was hoping I would change my story, whilst my mother and father stood close by and listened intently. I had a sneaking suspicion that my mother had thought I had drowned my poor brother. I gave the descriptions of the Munsters, but insisted it was not them that had taken Andrew; it had been the fog. Nobody believed me and, in the end, I refused to answer any more questions. The lifeboat sailing up and down the coast looking for a body found nothing. It was thought that the Munster family had taken Andrew. There had been a kidnapping seven years before. The child had never been found. After a week, with no sign of Andrew, we reluctantly had to return home to Yorkshire. The nightmare did not stop there. Every school holiday we would take the road to Mallaig. We stayed at Arisaig farm. I was terrified by each journey, expecting the fog to appear again. We walked the hills and the shore looking for some evidence of what had happened to my brother. The disappearance was never spoken about at home as it would upset my mother. It could only be discussed in Scotland as that was where my parents thought Andrew still was.

Our tent had now been replaced by a small caravan. The memory of his disappearance was never far from our minds. The terrible event shaped the rest of my life. It had instilled a fear in my parents that I too would come to a grisly end, therefore I was not allowed out of their sight. This, I suppose, benefited me as I turned to my studies and attained good enough grades to go to Edinburgh University to study Medicine. When I moved to student accommodation my parents both wept as they felt they would lose another child. However, I had to grow up sometime. I couldn't be thirteen forever. They continued their pilgrimage every few months to Mallaig, often visiting me on their journey up. In October '74 I'd been in Edinburgh for three years. I was at my part-time job in a coffee shop near Waverley Station. A policeman entered and asked if I was Jennifer Jackson.

"Yes. What's wrong?" The officer looked at the floor.

"There has been an accident near Mallaig."

"My parents are on holiday. Are they alright?" He didn't answer me straight away and couldn't look directly at me.

"I'm very sorry." I felt my knees buckle, and I dropped to the floor. The officer and my manager helped me to a chair. It just could not be true.

"How do you know its them?" I asked.

"The car registration and documents were in the car. You will have to identify the bodies unless you have another relative that could do it?"

"There isn't anyone." I could barely speak. My throat felt as though a stone was lodged in it.

"I can arrange transport for you."

"No, I have my own car." I didn't want to be stranded in the middle of nowhere. A picture of my dad came into my head.

"You don't want to be reliant on anyone," he said as he

handed me the keys to a beautiful red mini.

My lovely mother and father were now in a morgue in Fort William. Nobody knew what had happened. The farmer thought they had gone into Fort William for some shopping. No other car was at the scene. Their vehicle was on its roof. I hated myself for not ringing everyday as I always promised, for not spending more time with them. Too late now; they were gone, and I was alone.

I set off the following morning with sandwiches to eat on the way. It would take me about four and a half hours if the traffic was good. As I passed through the city, the scenery changed. It was a road I had travelled so many times over the years. The heather-clad moors rose at either side of the road, guiding me to my destination. I wanted to stop and get a breath of fresh air, but I needed to get to Fort William. I passed an occasional car, but mostly drove alone on the winding road. I turned the radio up full belt and opened my window.

Fort William was busy in the late afternoon. The police station was signposted, so I presented myself at the front desk. The policeman asked me the necessary questions. His manner became noticeably different when he realised I was the child of the poor couple killed on the Mallaig Road.

"I'm sorry for your loss Miss. I'll get someone to take over here and I'll show you the way to the morgue. It's at the rear of this building."

Entering the morgue gave me a shiver through my body. There was a slight smell of disinfectant. The room had been prepared for my arrival. My parents lay side by side, with crisp white sheets covering their bodies. There wasn't a mark on their faces. They just looked asleep. My mum's face was devoid of make-up; she would have hated being without her lipstick. My dad just looked sad.

I confirmed that they were my parents.

"Do you have a funeral director travelling from West Yorkshire?"

"No, I'm going to ask a local firm. I haven't any other family and this is where my mother and father wanted to be."

I told him the story of my missing brother, and he said he understood, and that he remembered the case. I accepted his sentiments.

"Can I have a copy of the report please? I want to know the details. I think it may help to understand what had happened." He nodded and went to a drawer pulling out an envelope.

"This is the report from the crash site and photographs. I'm sure its ok to give them to you."

I took the envelope and sat. The photographs were not noticeably clear. There was a dark tyre mark across the road as though they had tried to avoid hitting something. The policeman said a possible reason for the accident was a deer wandering on the road and my father swerving to avoid it. There wasn't any evidence of another vehicle.

The constable gave me a brown box that held the contents of the car. I thought it could wait until I got to Mallaig before I went through it. I would organise the funeral next day. I had rung through to Arisaig Croft where Mrs Mackay insisted I stayed saying it wouldn't be right for me to sleep in my parents' caravan. I wanted to be close to all the family, and that farm had become a second home. Mr and Mrs MacKay made me welcome. The farmer's wife who had been like an auntie hugged me, and it was then that I allowed the tears to flow.

"There, there. Now go on up to your room." She dried my tears with her apron. It was like silk and smelled of the sea.

My room was at the front of the croft. It was light and airy and had a wonderful view of the shoreline. However, it was not wonderful to me. It was a picture of my darkest nightmare. The clear waters and white beach were a graveyard. I opened the box of effects the police had given me. There were several maps that had areas marked out. These had been our bibles over the years, my parents crossing off every hill and beach in their search for Andrew. There was a coin bag with a small amount of money in it. Looking at my mum's handbag brought a tear to my eye. My dad's wallet had a hundred pounds in it. I lifted out a brown

127

bag. It was quite heavy. Inside were dozens of seashells. I was curious as to why they would have so many in the car. The shells were all different sizes and colours. I automatically put the small conch shell to my ear. I could hear the sea as though it was telling me a story. The whooshing noise took me to Mallaig beach, to the white sands, watching the seals. Mum and dad must have collected them on their quest to find Andrew, all in vain. Mrs MacKay called me to supper.

"You will be ready for some food, Jennifer. Come and sit down with us." After an enormous meal of lamb stew, I said I needed a walk.

"Be careful, Jennifer." She shot a glance at Mr MacKay. I put my coat on as the temperature had dropped.

"Here, Jennifer. Take this." Mrs MacKay wrapped a hand-knitted scarf around my neck. She kissed me lovingly on my forehead.

I walked down the field over the stream and onto the beach. It was a sight to behold. I felt so small. The vast sky was peppered by stars, with the green hue of the Mirrie dancers rippling across the sea. It was a reflection of the night Andrew had been taken. A full moon was set centre-stage. Beneath my feet the sand was like icing sugar as I walked along the shore. I could see the familiar sets of eyes in the sea watching my every move. A mother and her pup slipped into the water to avoid me. I thought of my family who were all gone. What would happen to me? With a heavy heart I turned back towards the farm. There was only one tent in the field, too late in the year for most holidaymakers. My parents' caravan was parked in its usual place. I tried the door and it was unlocked, just like them to be so trusting. The torch was on its hook by the sink. The beam of light lit up the table where a cereal box still stood. I looked through the cupboards, but found nothing to indicate they had found what they were constantly looking for. There was a slight breeze and the door of the caravan banged annoyingly on the side. You could smell the sea inside the room. It was then I noticed more seashells, on the table, on the sink, on the seating. They had been busy. I picked up a spiral shell; it was a beautiful pink one that was almost like enamel. I took one last look around and saw a book with the picture of a seal on the front. The legends of the Selkie. I put it in my pocket to read later.

The paraffin lamp in the tent had been turned up and the light made strange shadows across the canvas. A chill ran down my spine and I immediately turned my head back to the sea. There was a column of water growing up to the sky. The column swayed in the breeze, then crashing to the shore. This did not feel right. I stumbled quickly across the pebbles that surrounded the caravan, then onto the grass. My breath was laboured as I fought to climb the incline back to the farmhouse. A slight moan came from something behind me. I had heard the noise before; it was the night of Andrew's disappearance. It had gathered speed. It was not now liquid but a gas like fog. The grass became slippy and the ground came up to meet me. I turned onto my back and screamed. I pushed with all my might until I was upright and clambered towards the farmhouse. If I could just get to the door, I would be safe.

"Help, Mrs MacKay. Mr MacKay, please help me." The door opened and the light shone down the path. Before me were two people that first I recognised but, as their bodies swayed, their facial features ran together until all that was left was a dark substance. The clothes they wore were now in a pool of water discarded on the path.

What was happening? I ran back towards the caravan. This must be a nightmare. The handle to the caravan was slimy and difficult to open. Eventually the door yielded, and I was able to lock it behind me. The mist gathered outside and swarmed across the little caravan which was gently rocking at first, then harder and faster until it tipped onto its side. I was trapped. The steel frame groaned as it bent and warped until the plastic windows popped out. The mist curling and filling every crevice of the room. My screams went unheard and I was alone with the monster. Raised up from the wrecked vehicle, I was slowly manoeuvred towards the sea. The sound of the sea was growing closer. Then the shrieking began, and it was one of triumph. The cold water licked my skin, thankful for its gift. I am to die. Nothing can save me. What had I done in my short life for it to end in such a way? My life played before me and I remembered with horror the days of my childhood, my father telling his tales of the seals, the Selkies. The mythical beings had taken my brother. The unexplained accident of my mother and father. The shells in the car. The water covers my face I can no longer breathe, my thoughts registering the truth. The Selkies are here. A life for a life; revenge for my father's stories. All part of the legend.

Denise Bloom was born and brought up in Bradford West Yorkshire and now lives in the South West of France. She has an Honours Degree in Social Sciences. Always interested in writing she wrote short stories within a creative writing group.  *After encouragement from others she went on to publish her book, The Ladies of Whitechapel. The book is four stories with a common thread. Each story is the life of a woman that lived in 1888. When not writing Denise enjoys reading (usually history), painting, and volunteering for a cancer support charity.*

Follow Denise on Twitter @DLBloom_16

Repeating History

Jennifer C. Wilson

Castle Baideal, 1545

It's a strange feeling, the moment you decide to convince your husband to murder you.

Lady Catherine McLeod knew something was wrong. To the outside world, she claimed tiredness, worry over her nephew, embroilment in some courtly scandal, and the uncomfortable month-long heatwave Scotland had been experiencing until recently. But deep down, there was something much worse afoot.

She sat, fingers entwined in her long blonde hair, watching Angus, Lord of Castle Baideal. He was a bully, a coward, a thief. He was her husband.

Earlier, she'd witnessed him send two innocent men to their deaths. Granted, he spared them execution, but by throwing them into the dungeon, he might as well have hanged them there and then. They wouldn't last a week in that rat-infested hell. Now he was enjoying the fear, the averted eyes of servants, the nervous glances of tenants. He enjoyed seeing the men suffer, enjoyed the terror he caused on 'his' island, tucked away off the west coast, in the heart of the Hebrides. Here, McLeod ruled, and if something didn't please him, the causes of his displeasure were swiftly dispatched.

To the outside world there was limited knowledge of his true nature. To his clan, and neighbours, Angus defended his land, supported his monarch, kept the peace.

Catherine knew the truth, and suspected her time was

running out.

Another year had passed, the sixth since their marriage, but there was no child, no heir. A man like Angus would never tolerate such a failure. He wanted a son to follow him, and daughters to marry off.

With her dowry long-spent, Catherine had become a burden, and was no longer considered a prize. She needed to act, soon.

Word spread fast in the Western Isles. Most knew the tale of Lady's Rock, which sat in the shadow of Duart Castle. Another Lady Catherine, another cruel husband. That one had abandoned his wife on the rock, watched the waters rise, and awoke the next morning, full of despair as he delivered the news to her brother. He hadn't reckoned on local fishermen rescuing the lady, delivering her safely to said brother, who calmly welcomed the husband, his sister watching on, safe. And so, he was dealt with. Not that day; the brother was more subtle than that, but later, in an anonymous room in Edinburgh, he was dealt with. Brother and sister carried on their lives, happily and in peace.

Duart Castle wasn't the only stronghold with such a rock.

Catching the attention of the one man in the castle she knew was entirely loyal to her, Catherine smiled. In a moment, Duncan was there, refilling her cup with their finest wine. She didn't want to think how it came to be in her husband's cellar.

"Meet me in the solar at sunset."

Duncan raised his eyebrows, but nodded, his dark brown eyes filled with curiosity and concern.

A plan had been forming in Catherine's mind. She was unnerved by the glances between her husband and the women who visited the castle, and suspected it wouldn't be long until Angus found a way to be rid of her. He couldn't be allowed to devise any plan of his own though; Catherine wouldn't survive if Angus decided to strangle her one night, or to throw her from the battlements, blaming it on poor weather. No, he needed guidance.

Catherine was already planning her tranquil life, back in her childhood home, as she told Duncan her plan.

"You want him to kill you?"

"In a way. I want him to try and kill me, and to think he has been successful."

The young man's eyes narrowed, as he ran his fingers through his hair. "What if he *is* successful?"

"But that's where you come in. Borrow your brother's boat. Bring him with you if you're truly worried."

"I… I don't know. That rock's treacherous. You might slip before I reach you, while he's still in sight. How do you know he'll leave, and not stay to make sure you drown?"

It was a good point, but Catherine knew Angus. "Because he is ruthless, and cruel, but essentially a coward. He'll want to be far away from this, once set." She reached for Duncan's hand, squeezing his fingers tight. "It will work, I promise, but I need your help."

Catherine wasn't trying to manipulate Duncan, but she knew his affection for her was winning the battle with logic and reason. He would help her; he just needed convincing it would work out well for them both. That they could find happiness, together, anywhere but at Baideal.

"Watch, wait, then come out as the waters rise. We'll travel to the mainland, to David. He'll take us in, and neither of us need ever worry about Angus, or Castle Baideal, again. We'll be free."

It was enough.

Over the next few days, the plan would never be far from Catherine's mind. She watched her husband, monitoring his every move, ensuring she hadn't misread anything. No, she was sure. His attitude had changed; he was being almost kindly towards her, at least to the casual observer. They would have seen him escorting her to dinner, or them practising archery together in the inner bailey. They wouldn't have felt his iron grip on her hand, forcing her to grit her teeth to avoid showing pain, or the look he gave her, moments before hitting the dead centre of the target, his eyes cold and empty.

Her heart raced with fear each time they were alone, but thankfully, with Duncan as an ally, this was becoming rarer and rarer. Somehow, he managed to construe a genuine, if complicated, reason for somebody to disturb them, to get Angus to check something, or to tell Lady Catherine some urgent news. He couldn't do it forever, but they had their date set now: just five more days, and, according to Duncan's brother, the tides would be perfect. All she had to do now was get the idea into Angus' head...

She made her first move that evening, after they retired to their chamber, which overlooked the bay, and the outcrop of stone on which she placed all her hopes.

"I still find it fascinating, watching that rock come and go, every day," she murmured, just loud enough for Angus to hear.

"What?" He grunted.

"The rock. Our rock," she said, louder. "I just enjoy seeing the waters rise and fall. Duncan did explain how the tides work, but I still don't entirely understand."

Angus smirked. "You don't need to understand it. Why would you? It's of no concern to you, or even me. We have people who deal with that for us."

"Duncan says the next time it is completely covered will be in five days. I think it's magical that people can know these things."

"He's from a family of fishermen, of course he knows. And we pay him to tell us when we need to know too. Magic! Don't talk such nonsense, woman."

Catherine forced a weak smile, and turned away from the window, noticing, to her delight, that Angus didn't follow her, not straight away. For a few long moments he looked out into the fading light.

On the second day, knowing Angus was watching, Catherine stood on the battlements, looking out again over the rock.

On the third day, she found Angus on the shoreline. He was staring across the waters. At dinner, she spoke of Lady Catherine Campbell, and Inveraray Castle. Had Angus ever visited, Duncan enquired, innocently, as talk turned to the infamous story.

On the fourth day, she saw her husband talking to local fishermen, handing over a bag of coins.

On the fifth day, Catherine woke with excitement and dread. Had she planned things sufficiently? What if Duncan was wrong? What if they'd muddled their timings? What if he didn't reach her in time? What if Angus stayed? No, she mustn't allow herself to think like that. In a matter of hours she would be safely away from Angus, away from Castle Baideal, and under her brother's protection. And back with Margaret. At the thought of her sister, Catherine felt her resolve harden. The poor girl was never seen in public, hidden away through her family's shame at her infirmity. Being back at Blackreef would give Catherine time to be with her, help her. Yes, everything just had to go to plan.

***

Catherine wasn't alone in her worries. So concerned was Duncan about acting naturally, he forgot what normal days looked like. Whenever Catherine was out of his sight, he felt his panic rising. He hadn't confided in anyone, on Catherine's wishes, but now he was regretting everything. The whole scheme was ridiculous. He was reading so much into everything Angus did. When the man threw a pewter cup at his own nephew, Alistair, Duncan jumped as though he had been struck himself. As the younger McLeod stalked out of the room, he paused.

"You're jumpy today. Got yourself in a twist over a girl?"

Duncan forced a laugh at Alistair's words. They had formed a friendship of sorts, arriving at the castle at around the same time, albeit in very different positions. "Ah, I couldn't tell you if I wanted to, Ally," he said, sure his words were jumbled. How did spies or criminals act like this all the time, and never get caught? He'd been doing it less than a week, and he was a wreck.

"Well, I wish you joy of it, and her, and hope you get out of this blasted place as soon as you can."

The man's words surprised Duncan. He knew Angus and

Ally weren't close, but as his uncle's current heir, Ally, had little choice but to stay, and put up with whatever was thrown at him; literally, in today's case. Perhaps Catherine wasn't the only one that would have been happier if Angus wasn't around. But it was too late to change their minds and plan now. The highest waters were due that evening, in only a few hours' time, just after darkness fell over the island. He was going to have to be ready.

***

Undressing as darkness fell, Catherine selected the under-gown she had been preparing. Each day she had stitched another jewel into the material. She refused to leave them to whichever young thing Angus decided to replace her with. Now she pulled it on, glad of the cold night, and the excuse of a second, warmer gown over the top, although not the thick, woollen one she would usually have selected. If it got wet, it might prove impossible to stand in, and that was a risk she couldn't afford.

There was a full moon, Catherine noticed, as Angus entered their bedchamber, calm and controlled. This was it.

When she looked back on that night, all Catherine remembered was the cold.

The sense of her blood turning to ice in her veins as Angus threw a heavy cloak at her. The rush of cold air as he pushed her out through the postern gate to the shoreline. The shock of the freezing water as he shoved her towards the boat tied to the jetty. The wind whipping around her, chilling her to the bone. And the brutal, harsh cold of the rock, as Angus forced her back out of the boat.

Scrabbling for purchase in her thin-soled shoes, Catherine finally managed to lower herself safely to the flattest, highest park of the exposed stone. She watched her husband, wide-eyed, staring back at her through the moonlight.

"You won't get away with this," she shouted, feeling she needed to say 'something', or he would think her too compliant.

"But I already have. After all, who knows you're anywhere other than safely in your bed? No, it'll be sad, but in the morning, I'll find you gone, and there'll be talk of somebody hearing a scream and a splash, and it will all be over."

"And you'll replace me?"

He shrugged, then without another word, to Catherine's relief, pushed the boat off and rowed away.

Now all she had to do was wait for Duncan.

***

The boat was heavier than Duncan remembered. He'd lost count of how many times he'd borrowed the small craft from his brothers, the whole family happiest on the water in one way or another, but tonight, in the darkness, it felt as though the strength had drained from his arms. He had to hurry, or it would be Angus whose plan succeeded, not Catherine. Duncan couldn't allow that.

A noise behind him on the shingled beach, in a cove hidden from the castle, jolted Duncan, and he lost his grip on the boat, almost falling to the ground.

"Duncan? Is that you?"

Ally. Panic flooded through Duncan. Yes, the man hated McLeod, but would he go against his uncle? There was no choice. "Aye, it's me, and I cannot tell you what I'm doing, or why, but please, help me."

Ally must have sensed Duncan's urgency and, without question, joined his friend. Through their combined efforts, they got the boat onto the water, Ally jumping in before Duncan could stop him.

"Are we off to find your girl?"

"In a way. Whatever happens in the next hour, I don't care what you do to me when we get back, but let her escape to safety. Promise me?"

Even in the half-darkness, Duncan saw confusion cross Ally's face, but he nodded anyway, and Duncan pushed on, keeping his eye on the dark patch of sea in which he knew the rocky outcrop lay.

As they approached, the sound of waves breaking gave

him hope; it was still above water for now then, and if Catherine had been able to hold her position, their plan might just have worked. He hadn't seen or heard any other boats as they pushed on, but finally, he heard it.

"Duncan? I'm here!"

She was alive! Fresh energy rushed through him, and suddenly it was though the day was new, his arms fresh and strong, slicing through the water with ease. Ally rose unsteadily as the boat began to slow.

"Your girl's on the rock?"

"She's on the rock, but she's not my girl," replied Duncan, though it pained him to admit the latter. "Here, hold us steady," he added, handing over the oars.

He was close now; there was the white of Catherine's gown, the shape of her against the moonlight, and finally, the shine of light in her eyes as they bumped up against the bulk of stone. There was no need for words as he reached forward, and lifted her into the boat.

The same couldn't be said for Ally. "Catherine? What the hell are you doing? You could have died!"

***

Catherine couldn't help but laugh at her nephew's words. Yes, she could have died, and to the outside world, she had. Now, huddled in the bottom of the boat, it took her a moment to realise there was no reason for Ally to be there. Were they betrayed? Was she about to be handed back to Angus? No, that couldn't be right. Ally was helping, she thought, as he handed her his cloak, and pulled her towards him.

"Are you hurt?"

She shook her head. As Duncan rowed them to shore, the madness of their scheme tumbled out. Hearing him explain all to Ally, even as the plan was still technically underway, it sounded more like a story than truth. Had she really just convinced her husband to murder her? The numbness in her hands and feet told her she had, but there was a warmth in her heart that she hadn't felt for years, as Duncan kept them on a true course to the mainland.

As dawn broke, Duncan began preparing for their journey to Oban, and her brother's rooms. It didn't take much to win Ally's silence.

In Oban, Catherine took a deep breath before knocking on David's door, surprised when her brother himself opened it.

"Catherine?"

"He tried to kill me. I escaped."

"What?" David grabbed Catherine's wrist and pulled her inside, glancing up and down the street before closing the door, as though afraid of something. To Catherine's relief, he didn't see Duncan hiding around the corner.

The thud of the door shutting behind her jolted Catherine to her senses. David wasn't acting as she expected. "What's going on?"

"Where's Angus?"

"He, well, I don't know. At home, I should imagine, waiting to be told of my demise no doubt, so he can rush to you. Then you can accuse him of what he tried to do."

"What?" David repeated.

Catherine drew her brother to sit by the fireplace and told him everything, of the cruelty, the fear, and her plan to free herself. At the moment she expected the sympathy to flow, for him to pull her into his arms and tell her that Angus wouldn't get away with it, David's face darkened.

"You've. Done. What?"

"I escaped, David. I thought you would be happy."

"Happy? That you've made a fool of Angus McLeod? Possibly brought down the wrath of that entire bloody island on my head?"

"But what he did? How he treated me?" Catherine heard the panic and anger rising in her voice. Why was he acting like this? Her own flesh and blood, acting as though she was in the wrong.

"It's McLeod, you stupid girl! Angus McLeod!"

"But you've twice his land, what does he matter to you?"

David was up on his feet now, pacing the small room. "Twice the land, but half the wealth. It's dead, Catherine. Dead. Our lands have nothing left. Our alliance with McLeod was all that kept us safe from the creditors. As soon as the world knows you've died, and that's over and dealt with, they'll come for us. We'll lose it all. The MacGregors will be wiped out of this area."

"But I haven't died, that's the point. And when the world discovers what Angus McLeod really is, he'll be ruined."

He laughed, a cruel, hollow laugh that Catherine had only heard from Angus before. "Nobody is going to find out. No, if McLeod thinks you're dead, that's what you'll be."

For a moment, Catherine thought he was actually going to kill her, and instinctively pushed herself back into the chair, shrinking away from him. "Dead?"

"Yes, to everyone else! You've brought this on yourself."

"But, but I wanted to escape. You should be defending me." She paused. "Where will I go?"

"You'll stay with Margaret."

Blackreef Castle. It was half her plan, returning to their childhood home, with her sister, with David. But not like this.

"I'll be a prisoner," she whispered.

"You chose this." He moved towards the door. "I have things to do. Stay here, out of sight. No doubt McLeod will be at Blackreef soon, with the news. We must be ready."

With David gone, Catherine's mind was a whir. This was not the reunion she had planned. How had she got everything so wrong? Duncan. There was still Duncan. If there was anything the last day had proved, it was that Catherine could rely on Duncan. Straightening her shawl, she hurried to the door, only to find it locked. Her new prison sentence had already begun.

***

Duncan watched David leave, turning the key. Keeping Catherine safe, or prisoner, he wasn't sure, but something about the man's demeanour told him not to approach. Whatever was happening, or not happening, he needed to be patient. If Catherine was safe, then barging in could make things worse, and if she was held against her will, the last thing either needed was David turning against them. He might be as bad as McLeod for all Duncan knew, whatever his sister thought.

It took two days of sitting in taverns, waiting for news, but finally he heard Ally had arrived in town. By then, David had whisked Catherine away back to Blackreef, under cover of darkness, only spotted by Duncan by chance, as he paced his rented room in the inn opposite. He had never seen Catherine looking so dejected, even when Angus had been at his worst. Back then there was always an air of defiance about her, but that was gone now.

"Angus is putting on a great show of sorrow," reported Ally, as the two men sat over a mug of ale.

"Will he travel to Blackreef?"

Ally nodded. "He's dealing with some business in town, then heading up later today. How will MacGregor react?"

"No idea. I didn't dare approach him. I'm wondering what to do next."

"How do you mean?"

"Well, has McLeod noticed I'm gone? Will he suspect anything? I know I shouldn't be selfish. I should focus on helping Catherine, but I don't want to cross McLeod."

"Look, Angus thinks Catherine's dead, that he killed her – he has no reason to suspect you of anything. Come back with me. I'll say we were sorting some business together."

"We?" Duncan noticed the casual way Ally used the phrase. "What do you mean?"

"Don't make me out to be a saint. But Catherine was my uncle's wife, and a good woman. And if David doesn't reveal her, that reduces the chance of Angus leaving an heir. No heir, gets me the McLeod wealth, and Baideal. It's in my interest that Angus continues to believe he was successful. The fact that doing so happens to help a lady I care for, and a good friend, is a happy accident."

Duncan laughed. "Well, if you're helping, I don't care about your motives. So yes, I'll come back with you. Tell whatever lie you like, if it comes up."

By the time their ales were finished, a plan was agreed on.

***

David MacGregor welcomed the McLeod household to Blackreef Castle with the finest food and wine. Standing behind Ally, Duncan couldn't help but look around, wondering where poor Catherine was. He had hoped she would be present as events unfolded, but if she was, she was well hidden.

"MacGregor, I bring terrible news," Angus began, arms spread wide. "There's... there's been an accident," he continued, the break in his voice adding authenticity to his show of sadness. "Catherine, poor Catherine, fell from the battlements. I'm so sorry to tell you, David, we believe she drowned. We found her cloak on the shoreline." Angus hung his head.

David froze for a moment, then slumped into his chair. "She's dead?"

Duncan swallowed the lump in his throat. Both men were acting out a ridiculous play, but even knowing it to be false, he felt his heart constrict.

Angus was nodding. "I'm sorry, brother. I know you love your sister; I wanted to tell you myself. We are devastated." He gestured to the men behind him. A demonstration of strength, in case any were needed, to show David why not causing trouble was his best course of action. Accidents happened, after all.

Duncan watched David take in the scene, as though wondering how best to handle it. A minute nod of his head, and he seemed to have decided.

"We were brothers through Catherine, McLeod, and I hope that continues, whatever the future holds."

It wasn't until he felt Ally's hand on his shoulder that Duncan realised he had taken half a step forward.

"Not now, not here. We'll think of something."

That 'we' again, but this time, it calmed Duncan; now Ally knew of the deceptions, how low both men were willing to stoop, they could work something out.

Back at Castle Baideal, they watched as McLeod flexed his muscles even more than before. Without realising it, Catherine had been a calming influence, and with her gone, nothing could stop the man. In the space of a month, he launched raids on two nearby islands, carrying off half their livestock whilst holding the women of the land hostage, knives at their throats. A sense of fear pervaded the castle, the household divided into those who sensed an opportunity from these new activities, and supported them, and those repulsed by the monster McLeod was turning into, but too scared to either confront him or leave.

News from Ally one morning changed everything.

"He's remarrying?" Duncan spluttered the ale he'd been drinking when Ally charged in, not bothering to knock.

Ally nodded. "He just told me. You should have seen his sneer. He knows it moves me away from his money, the bastard, and enjoyed telling me so." He dropped heavily onto Duncan's bed. "I won't have it."

"What do you intend to do?"

"The same as Catherine."

Duncan narrowed his eyes. "Fake a death?"

"No. Learn from history. She took Duart, I'm taking Dunstaffnage."

"You'll have to enlighten me."

"John Stewart of Lorn, decades back, cut down by a rival's supporters on the way to his wedding. Mind, he survived to take his vows. Angus won't be so lucky."

"You're going to kill him on the way to his wedding?" Duncan couldn't believe what he was hearing. So far, there had been nothing illegal in his actions. Deceptive and dangerous, yes, but not illegal.

"Yes, we are. It has to be done, Duncan. The man's a menace. Besides, I know who he plans to wed. Campbell's sister, young Moira. She's a sweet thing, wouldn't hurt anyone, and wouldn't last a season as his wife." Anger darkened Ally's face, and Duncan sensed there was more than mere chivalry behind his friend's proposed actions.

"You'll have my support, on one condition," Duncan said

quietly.

"I already anticipated that, my friend. When Angus is gone, and Baideal's mine, we'll rescue Catherine."

Duncan's head snapped up. Were his growing feelings for her that obvious? Ally's grin showed they must be. "Then you have my sword."

They didn't have long to wait, just one more month of Angus' cruelty. Moira's arrival did nothing to temper him, but how could it, when she was just a girl, compared to the measured, controlled experience of Catherine? She sat beside her future husband at dinner each evening, eyes wide, but mouth firmly closed.

Men were thrown into the castle's cellars for the smallest of crimes, families made homeless for being a day behind with payments, and merchants' bills being torn up in their faces. Nobody dared confront him. David MacGregor himself suffered, when two of his men were sent home bloodied and bruised having delivered a demand for some of Lady Catherine's possessions to be returned.

"How can he act like this? McLeod's abusing his sister in death just as much as he did in life!" Duncan threw off his sword belt, as he and Ally retreated to Ally's chamber. Standing at the window, he couldn't help but look out at the rock which started all of this. "If Catherine had lived, in Angus' eyes, do you think we would be in this position?"

"No," replied Ally, bluntly. "Chances are he'd have killed her for real. His way. At least you know Catherine's safe, albeit miserable. Here, she was miserable, and in danger. But it does show one thing; MacGregor clearly isn't going to move against my uncle. We go ahead."

Checking the door, Ally outlined their plan, to attack between castle and chapel. Only a few short minutes' walk, but sufficiently open. Unbeknownst to Duncan, Ally wasn't doing this alone.

"We have fifteen men."

"Fifteen? Is that enough?"

"It is, when witnesses will only say there were three of us."

Duncan shook his head. "Your confidence terrifies me, but tell me what I'm to do."

The morning of the wedding was suitably foreboding, with a heavy mist, and the threat of a storm. The weight of the air seemed to dampen everyone's spirits, with nobody in the mood for a celebration, and many guests put off attending by the predicted weather. It was just what Duncan and Ally had hoped for. Their fifteen men were drawn from the household itself, and Ally's friends, keen to help the young man win the McLeod inheritance. So many different motives, thought Duncan; he hoped they could all pull together. He watched as royal blue caps danced in the crowd, their means to find each other in the confusion which was bound to arise. Ally was the only one not wearing the same, not taking any active part, for fear of being tainted, and unable to claim his title and wealth.

Duncan felt the weight of his knife, hidden deep in his pocket. If he was honest, he hoped one of the others would reach McLeod first, freeing him from driving the blade home himself. It was one thing to wish somebody dead, even to plot it, but to use his own knife, see the blood on his own hands? Duncan wasn't sure he had the nerve.

Just before noon, the wedding party left the great doors of Castle Baideal, and crossed the grassed area towards the woods where the small chapel stood. The girl looked terrified, as Angus gripped her hand. The ringing of the castle's bell, intended to signify celebration at the wedding, was the signal they awaited. As the joyful peals rang out, one glance was all it took, and the blue-caps closed in.

In the crush, to his horror, Duncan found himself immediately behind McLeod, the blue-caps occupied in a combined effort of keeping the man's guards away, and moving in themselves, blades drawn, scarves pulled up around their faces.

Then he saw Moira's face.

The fear was still there, but behind that, a glimmer of hope. Did she think they were rescuing her? Had Ally made some sort of promise, that all would be well? Or was it simply that these men, whoever they were, were removing the risk of marrying Angus McLeod? In a heartbeat, Duncan realised that was just as important as avenging Catherine. By killing McLeod, he was protecting Moira, saving her from the same fate Catherine was subjected to.

His doubts faded away as he thrust his blade home.

He wasn't alone. As he watched the light fade in McLeod's eyes, Duncan counted at least five other knives in the body. In the confusion, the blue-caps dropped back to the shore, where their feigned escape route waited.

The plan was simple; three men, hitherto uninvolved, would row across to the mainland. If they were lucky they would time their arrival to align perfectly with the arrival of the storm, then smash the boat on rocks just outside Oban, leaving evidence of the murder behind. The actual killers now changed quickly from their bloodstained clothes, washed their hands, and threw everything into the boat. As their accomplices set off, the now former blue-caps returned to the castle, shouting that the killers escaped.

Ally played his own role to perfection.

"After them! Now – they will not get away with this! Duncan – you're with me." His yelled instructions had added emphasis, as he cradled his uncle's body. Then, gently, he lay the corpse down, and called to the terrified priest. "Please, see that my uncle is taken home. He should be accorded dignity, whatever these foul enemies would do."

In the ensuing movement of people, the fifteen blended in perfectly with the rest of the household. Duncan called that his boat was ready. Leaving the priest in charge, Ally called more instructions over his shoulder, as they ran to the shore.

As they reached the boat, Ally's feigned panic turned to laughter. "We made it! We've actually made it!"

"Stay calm my friend. We're not there yet." Duncan steadied the boat and cautioned Ally. "If anything happens to the men in the first boat, we will still be lost. We mustn't lose focus now."

The weather was closing in as they each pulled an oar to keep the boat moving, but eventually the harbour of Oban was within sight, tucked safely behind its island barrier.

"There!" Ally saw it first; the wrecked boat, smashed on the rocks beneath Dunollie Castle.

As they carefully tied their own boat alongside, as planned, a witness rushed forward, to tell of three men, cast overboard in the poor weather, their boat was dashed by the tide. Two other men stood beside him, nodding, ignoring the obvious fact that Duncan and Ally's boat had easily survived the journey with only two men, whilst this bigger boat, with three, had not. But there was nobody around to contradict them.

"What do we do now?" asked Duncan.

"We wait. We cannot return at once. And I need to speak to the right people, ensure my claim to the inheritance is accepted. I might as well do that immediately. If anyone questions the speed of my decision, then my reasons are based out of concern that whoever did this to my uncle, might try and do the same to me."

"So the sooner you have control of the McLeod wealth and men, the sooner you are able to defend the castle, and yourself?" Duncan followed the sensible logic which had formed in Ally's mind.

"Exactly. And don't worry." He clapped Duncan's shoulders. "I haven't forgotten my promise. Once I'm secure, we travel to Blackreef."

***

News of Angus McLeod's demise travelled quickly, and although there was shock that somebody stood against him, and so violently, there was no sorrow. David MacGregor told Catherine the news as they broke their fast, no emotion in his words.

"Dead?"

"Aye."

"So what happens now?" She could hardly look her brother in the eye. Her life was comfortable, and she no longer woke every morning full of fear, but she was still a prisoner, allowed no further than the castle's grounds.

"Nothing happens. You're still dead. Although, I might contact that nephew of his. He might see fit to return whatever is left of your belongings. Rumour is he'll marry young Moira Campbell, some nonsense about honouring his uncle's wishes. Ridiculous."

Catherine's heart lurched at the mention of Ally. One of only four people who knew the truth, was it truly coincidence he was now in charge of the Baideal McLeods? Might he be somehow working with Duncan? All she could do was wait, and hope.

It took another month for Ally to be accepted into his new role at the head of the Baideal McLeods. All the while, Catherine ensured she was never far from her brother's office when any messengers arrived. His second appeal for her belongings to be returned had been greeted with politeness, but nothing more. Ally would, apparently, deal with such matters shortly, but was firstly focusing on restoring aspects of his uncle's estate sorely diminished through neglect.

Catherine guessed what that meant. Ally's friends were being released from the cellar prison, and he would be doing all he could to bring to the tenants to his side, preventing any risk of rebellion. Folk were less likely to be suspicious about how easily he was fitting into place if they were benefitting from it. And people *were* benefitting. That was clear from the gossip visitors brought with them. There wasn't the same sense of dread when people mentioned having to deal with McLeod of Baideal.

"He's coming to visit. Today." David's words came without warning.

"Who is?"

"McLeod."

The name still gave Catherine pause, as she reminded herself that the name now referred to her nephew, not her hated husband. "Will you welcome him?"

Her brother nodded. "Does he know about you?"

"I only told Duncan of my plan." It was the truth. Duncan told Ally, not her.

148

"Keep it that way."

Despite David's warning, Catherine couldn't help but linger at the back of the hall as Ally walked in. Hidden in the shadows, her head lowered, she doubted he'd notice her, until she realised his eyes were scanning the room. Was he looking for her?

"MacGregor," he greeted her brother warmly, clasping his hand as his welcome was returned. "It is good to visit. I know you and my uncle were close. I hope to continue the friendship."

"I see no reason why that shouldn't be the case. Please." David gestured to the array of refreshments set out in readiness.

"Soon. I came to discuss a deal, and I'd like to do so before we eat or drink."

There was something in his voice, thought Catherine. She had seen him arrive, and there were more men in his entourage than were needed. What was he up to? Her nerves increased as she saw another man slip into the hall from a side-door, clearly unobserved by her brother. Duncan. Where had he been? The quickening of her heart at seeing him again, and the fear that something may still happen to him, scared her.

"I came to return the remainder of Lady Catherine's belongings," Ally continued, after exchanging a quick glance with Duncan, both shaking their heads, so subtly that others most likely missed it. Catherine didn't.

"I am pleased to hear that. They included a number of family pieces; when I marry, I would wish to pass them onto my wife."

"No, I'm sorry. You misunderstand me. I came to return Lady Catherine's jewels to Lady Catherine." Ally paused. "If you could call for her to join us?"

"How dare you insult me so! My sister is dead." David's hand moved to where the hilt of his sword would be, if he had been wearing his sword-belt, but, as though realising he was unarmed, instead, he gripped the material of his jacket.

"Except, she isn't. I know she came here, MacGregor, and

I know that if she really is dead, then there's only you who could be blamed for it now. I'll ask again, please, call for her to join us."

"I'm here." The words escaped her before Catherine even realised what she was doing, walking towards Ally in a daze. "I'm safe."

There was a gasp amongst McLeod's men, as though they hadn't quite believed what Ally said, thinking it an odd ruse. But now they saw their former mistress alive and well, shock rippled through the group. There was only one reaction Catherine cared about.

Without even looking at Ally or David, Duncan rushed forward, and swept Catherine into his arms, pulling her close, their lips meeting for the first time. She didn't have to think, as her body responded instinctively, clutching at him as though she was back on the rock, and she realised that again she had been desperately waiting for Duncan's arrival.

Ally's gentle cough disturbed their reunion. "I wish to offer you a choice, Lady Catherine. Stay here, or return with Duncan and myself to Baideal. And believe me, it *is* a choice. I wasn't lying when I said I came to return your belongings. They are here," he gestured to two large chests being carried by his men.

Catherine looked at the furious confusion on her brother's face and knew there was only one answer she could give. If she was to be dead anywhere, she would rather be dead where she might stand a chance of happiness. But she wouldn't be returning alone.

"I shall come with you. I don't have a problem with being the second Lady of Baideal, and I'm sure I can find a friend in Moira. But I want to bring Margaret with me."

***

Even as she accepted Duncan's hand to step out of the boat and onto the jetty below Castle Baideal, Catherine was sure there would be a last-moment disaster, that, perhaps, Angus wasn't truly dead, or her brother would change his mind and chase after her, forcing her back to Blackreef.

Worst of all, it might all be a strange trick, and life back on this island would be nothing but a living nightmare.

She was shown to her chamber, no longer that of the laird and his lady, but that was fitting, and it was a title she was happy to leave behind. Her new room was smaller, but comfortable, and close to Margaret's. Duncan smiled, as he instructed servants to deposit clothes-chests, and for Margaret to be settled by her assigned maid.

"She'll be alright here?" he asked, shyly joining Catherine. Despite their passionate reunion at Blackreef, there had been no chance for private conversation, Ally having decided they pack and leave before David changed his mind. There was something wrong, but she couldn't work out what.

"She'll be alright wherever she has freedom. Here she can join us for meals, walk along the shore, and not worry about being mocked. Ally's promised me that."

Duncan stared out of the window, tying and untying knots in the cord of his shirt.

"Duncan?"

"It's all a mess." Sighing, he turned. "I wanted to ask you to marry me. You must know how I feel, and I hoped you might say yes. But you're still dead. If only your stupid bloody brother had been brave enough, everything could have been different."

She hung her head, but couldn't help smiling. "That's what's been troubling you. You want to marry me?"

"Yes. No. Not the wanting to bit, the fact that I couldn't help you as much as I wanted. I should have confronted David, made him expose Angus as a murderer. It's ruined everything."

Catherine stared at him, as the realisation hit her in a rush. "They never found my body, Duncan. Nobody found my body!"

"Well, no, of course not. There wasn't a body to find. What are you saying?"

"Can it be this easy? Only a few months have passed. What's to say by some miracle, I washed up ashore, found shelter with a crofter, unable to remember anything? But then I remembered, and I came back."

Duncan was staring again at Catherine now. "Nobody would believe it. Would they?"

"Would it matter? It changes nothing. Angus is still dead, Ally is still laird, still married to Moira. My being dead or alive changes nothing. Only to us."

She watched, delighted, as a smile brightened Duncan's face, mirroring her own.

It's a strange feeling, the moment you decide to come back from the dead.

———————————

Jennifer C. Wilson has been stalking dead monarchs since she was a child. It started with Mary, Queen of Scots, then moved onto Richard III. At least now it results in a story!

Wandering around historical sites has inspired virtually all her novels and stories to date, including the *Kindred Spirits* series, following the 'lives' of some very interesting ghostly communities, and published by Darkstroke. Her historical romances (no ghosts so far) are published through Ocelot Press.

She has a potentially unhealthy number of notebooks in her possession.

Visit Jennifer's website -
jennifercwilsonwriter.wordpress.com/

Out of Darkness

Brodie Simpson

Chapter One
Perceived Light

"There can be no new start. I mean, there was the time before and the time after, and no time to adjust to the change, but a new start implies I want to disregard everything from before, doesn't it?"

The stuffy room was silent apart from the ticking of an antique clock on the windowsill.

"Do you *want* to disregard everything from before?" he asked.

She shifted uncomfortably in the armchair thinking surely to God he could afford a comfier chair for his guests.

"No, it's not that simple, is it, because before is what I had but lost." Anger energised her voice. "It's irrelevant anyway. I feel like we've been down this road a million times before."

It was frustrating, the silence in the small room. She could feel his eyes on her, quietly judging her every spoken word, and what was time now anyway? It was just nothingness, space, shit.

"I think it's important you see the value in revisiting *before* as many times as you *need* to. It's uncomfortable, I know, but what you're still feeling is relevant at this particular moment. Listen to your inner voice, feel your body and what it's telling you."

She took a sip from the glass of water on the small table next to her. It would have been much better chilled, but room temperature would have to do. She'd been going there for two months. Why did it feel like years? She didn't know how many more times she could face him and his bloody obvious statements.

"Do you really think I can ignore what my body is telling me? Is it possible? It screams at me every day from the moment I'm conscious, right up to the point sleep takes me, and boy do I love that moment. A deeper darkness. You know, when I was a girl, I used to be terrified of the dark. I couldn't even sleep without a small light on in my room until I was, well, I must've been well into my teens. But now it's hard to explain, the pull toward intense comforting darkness is like a warm embrace to me."

His chair creaked as he leaned forward. She could always tell when he moved that little bit closer; she would smell his aftershave, usually followed by some attempt at textbook compassion.

"It's ok to *feel* the pain and engage with it." Bing, she was right.

"It's ok to acknowledge our helplessness. It's only through acknowledging the pain that we gather the strength to move on through the 'after'. I remember you telling me early on, during one of our first sessions, that you didn't believe in an 'after', that your life ended that day, but look, look how far you've come since then. Every day is a new opportunity to heal."

The thing that really pissed her off was he was right. He may have sounded like a walking self- help manual, but the little shit was right.

She nodded.

Time was difficult for her, just knowing what time it was or how much time had passed.

Before, everything revolved around time, getting to the fitness class, making sure she was back at her desk on time after lunch, picking up Sophie from the nursery. But since 'before' ended, and 'after' started, time had become shapeless. Time was like how she used to feel about the ozone layer. It existed, but it was more a concept that a tangible thing.

"I'd like to try something new at our next session, but only if you feel comfortable with it."

His voice was like one of those Radio 4 presenters. She

bloody hated Radio 4.

"We've only got a few minutes left today, but what I propose for next week is that we try some hypnosis. I know, it sounds a bit odd, but I really think it would help you lance the boil, as it were. I can see you're moving forward, but this could really be a useful tool. We could maybe try and penetrate the pain at a deeper level."

"Is that a normal thing to try in my position?" she asked

"Everyone moves at different speeds. Hypnotism isn't for everyone. In fact, I have to warn you that it doesn't work in all cases. But if you're open to it, well, I think it can have real benefits."

"So you've done it before?"

"Oh yes. Numerous times."

She could tell he had a self-satisfied smile on his face.

"Ok. I'm willing to give it a go. But I want you to promise that if I don't like it or I want to stop, you'll follow my wishes."

"Of course. Your wellbeing is my responsibility."

"Do I have to do anything to prepare?"

His chair creaked. He'd obviously leaned back into it.

"If you could get here ten minutes earlier than normal it'll give us some time to prepare. There really is nothing to worry about. Ok, that's time."

That's time. *You can say that again,* she thought.

"Thank you Doctor. I'll see you next Wednesday, same time. I mean ten minutes earlier."

She lifted her body out of the chair and steadied herself. There was a knock on the door and a woman entered. She approached the chair and held out an arm.

"Hello Cathy. Thanks for waiting outside as usual."

Cathy nodded and led her sister toward the door.

"I'll see you both again next week."

"Goodbye," said Cathy as she exited the room, her sister clamped to her arm.

Alone again in his room, Dr Ooesterhouse restarted his laptop. He had an hour free before his next patient. Plenty of time. He turned to his laptop, unzipped his trousers, pulled out his cock and readied himself for the veritable buffet of pornography that awaited him.

Chapter Two
Before

"Come on, *Sleepyhead*. We're going to be late!"

Sophie ran down the stairs in her stockinged feet and grabbed her trainers. Monday mornings were the worst. It was always harder getting herself and Sophie up after a weekend of fun and games.

"Soph, Mrs B won't be happy if you miss the morning song, will she?"

"I'm going as fast as I can, Mum. I've a lot to pack in my rucksack."

"What do you mean? I packed your bag last night. You've just got your lunch to add."

"Don't you understand? I promised Emily I'd show her my Disney Princess Jasmine. If I don't take it she'll hate me!" she shouted.

She can be such a little bugger, thought Julie.

"Ok, just hurry up. And Soph, you don't have to shout!"

Ten minutes later they were in the old Volvo and on the way to Lucky Cove Primary School. It was a bright summer morning. The roads were busy, but they were making good time.

"Is it this weekend I'm staying with Daddy?" asked Sophie.

"Yes, I'll drop you there on Friday after school. Are you looking forward to seeing Magnus?" Magnus was an extremely hairy sheepdog.

"I looove Magnus," purred Sophie.

Julie wanted to, but refused to, ask if she loved her dad.

"What the fuck!?" shouted Julie, slamming on the brakes as a figure walked in front of the car.

Sophie screamed, and bumped her head on the back of Julie's headrest.

"Are you ok, Soph?" Julie's voice broke with shock.

"Yeah, I'm fine."

They'd just turned onto Wheedled Bend, next to the cove. There was no other traffic around, and nobody much took this route anymore.

The figure stood stock-still, almost touching the front bumper of the car.

Julie unfastened her seatbelt and stepped out.

"Sophie, stay there."

"Seriously, what the fuck, man?!" she whispered with as little noise as possible to avoid Sophie hearing.

The figure just stood there. Julie couldn't see a face. A hoodie was pulled tight, long hair cascading out of it, like some yeti.

She stepped closer, slowly, and started to feel both exposed and apprehensive.

"Look, no harm done, mate. But I've got my little girl in there. You need to be a bit more aware of things, ok? Just be careful. Are you ok?"

It all happened so quickly. He went from catatonic to electrified in the blink of an eye. Julie didn't see it coming. She couldn't move. There was no time, and no reason, for it to happen the way it did.

Liquid hit her face, 'splashed' would be a better description. Only it wasn't water. She screamed in pain, feeling an agony impossible to comprehend. Julie could hear the awful sound, but it took a few seconds to realise it was her own voice. Her face felt on fire, melting. She was scared to touch it.

Suddenly she became aware of a different sound, a second scream coming from the car. Sophie.

Julie tried to speak, but her lips weren't working. Her body hit the tarmac with an agonising thump. Everything was dissolving into pain and numbness, consciousness was leaving her, and her mind unable to comprehend the horror of her situation. All she could see was Sophie's face, and then darkness.

Six months later

"It's ok, Sophie. We'll find Princess Jasmine later. We need to go. We'll be late."

Sophie bounded down the stairs, her rucksack leaping up and down on her back.

"Sophie what do you have in there? There'd better be room for your sandwiches."

"It's so heavy, Mum. I didn't realise how heavy it would be."

"What do you mean? What have you packed? You've not taken all your schoolbooks with you? Only take the ones you need for today. Which ones did Mrs B ask you to bring?"

"But I've not packed any books, Mummy."

Julie was running out of patience.

"Look, give me the bag, Soph. I'll sort it out."

Sophie sighed and reluctantly handed it over.

Julie undid the golden buckles and lifted up the flap before looking inside. A scream ripped through her body as she saw the dog's severed head filling the inside of Sophie's bag.

"It's ok, Mummy. I told Emily I'd show her Magnus. He's such a pretty boy."

Julie sat bolt upright in bed, sweat layered her body. She was shaking. Another nightmare. She wondered how many more versions of that morning her subconscious could create.

It had been six months since 'before', six months since the incident, six months since she had been blinded and lost Sophie. As the weeks had passed, she'd started to question her sanity. How could a life change so much?

After 'before', she'd had life-saving surgery, but not sight-saving. The world had become terrifying. Without her vision she was lost. She was unable to trust her other senses to keep her safe.

Following extensive rounds of surgery, she was reliant on a heady mixture of medication but remembered the song by The Verve.

Cathy had been her rock, as she'd always been. She was a good big sister. She had dealt with the media interest, and had shielded her from everyone and everything.

It was Cathy who'd broken the news about Sophie.

Julie had thought things couldn't get worse, but she'd been wrong. Sophie's broken body had been found in a shallow grave in Didhaven Woods, a short drive from the cove. Cathy had struggled to tell her the details, not because she didn't know them, but because she didn't want to.

Sophie had been strangled but not sexually abused. For some reason this made things a little better, why she wasn't sure. Cathy said Julie would be moving in with her for the near future at least. Julie hadn't even been able to attend her daughter's funeral.

She thought that 'before' and 'after' would be the bookends of her life, as sleep took her again.

Chapter Three
After

"It's good to see you again, Julie." Doctor Ooesterhouse squirmed a little at his use of language.

"Well, it's good to hear you, doc," she replied.

Cathy had walked her into the room and left her to sit down. It was only in the past few weeks that Julie had gained the confidence to walk unattended. But she wasn't quite ready to go solo yet.

"Maybe we should start as we normally do, with you telling me about how the past week has been," suggested the doc.

"Ok, well the nightmares are back. You know, the ones about that morning."

"Yes. Are they the same, or have they changed?" he asked.

"They've evolved somewhat. The basic scenario is the same, but the details change."

He moved forward in his chair.

"Well, I had one last night. I woke up Cathy. I was screaming so much."

"Carry on. You're in a safe space."

She thought that he could be so condescending sometimes.

"Well it started the same as always. Sophie is getting ready for school and…."

Doctor Ooesterhouse was listening intensely. He'd chosen to wear his skinny jeans today, 'work casual', they called it. He was getting a little bit bored hearing about the nightmares. They were almost always the same and *blah blah blah*. But she had fantastic tits.

Every session he would decide to push things a little further. Today he decided not to wear any underwear. It was a small change. But just a simple deviation from the norm was giving him enormous pleasure.

".....open the flap of her rucksack and it was my head inside it...."

The doc regained his composure.

"And how did you feel immediately after this dream?"

"How do you think I felt? They say that dreams are formed from events in your life. Why would I dream my dead daughter has my severed head in her schoolbag?"

"Well I can understand how shocking that must have been for you," he said.

He could feel himself starting to get erect. It was pleasant, and he wondered if blind women gave better blow jobs because their other senses were heightened.

"Are we going to try the hypnosis today as planned?" she asked.

"Yes, yes of course, if you're sure you want to try. It's entirely up to you."

Julie was conflicted. She could see the benefits her sessions with the doc were having, but she was sceptical about hypnosis. She'd read accounts of dodgy hypnotists who'd make you bark like a dog or cluck like a chicken, but she trusted the doc and knew that although he could be a bit soft and hippy, he was excellent at his job.

"I'm definitely willing to try it today. How do we begin?"

Doctor Ooesterhouse imagined himself standing naked and erect in front of her whilst she was hypnotised. It would be magnificent.

"Good, good. Well the first thing to do would be for you to lie down on the couch, and I will take you through a guided meditation, after which you will hopefully fall into a hypnotised state, and we can try and address the deeper recesses of your trauma."

An hour later, Julie was fully removed from her hypnotic state. It had been a complete success.

"How was that for you?"

"It was weird. I mean, I could hear your voice, but I wasn't in the room. I was back, back in the past."

She could hear his chair creak as he leaned closer.

"And do you remember any of the things you told me?"

"Yes. Again, it's weird because it was like I was in two worlds. Or maybe it's better to say in two different times, past and present."

The doc chuckled. "Yes. It's funny how it works. I remember my first experience of being hypnotised. I felt elevated from myself."

"Yes, that's a very good way to put it," Julie said. "But I'm not sure I got any deeper, or revealed any new truths."

"That's ok, Julie. Today was the first step. We now know you are receptive to hypnotic therapy and, if you're willing, I suggest we go deeper next week."

Julie agreed and before she knew it Cathy was there guiding her out of the room.

When the door was closed, Doctor Ooesterhouse swiped through the photos he'd taken during the hypnosis. They were wonderful, her face, the hidden scars were quite beautiful, and she looked at peace, serene, like a statue.

He pulled out his hard dick and started. He knew he had another patient in fifteen minutes, but the urge to satisfy himself was too strong. Next time he would go further. Maybe she would be grateful if he offered to fuck her. It wasn't long before he was wiping his screen clean with one of those handy wet wipes he kept in a drawer.

Chapter Four
Before

Timing is everything in this line of work. Not that I've ever done this before. Although I have fantasised about it. I've watched them many times now, always taking the same route, always rushing towards Lucky Cove. It's the girl I have a problem with. It makes me feel uneasy, but it has to be done.

I am nervous though. It reminds me of how I used to feel before kick-off, walking onto that pitch, the fans screaming at you, good and bad stuff, only words, but pressure, you know?

Not long now. Tomorrow it'll be over, and I'll move on.

Three miles away

"Soph, where are all your dresses?"

"I've got them all here. I don't know which one to wear."

"Christ, Sophie. It's only a birthday party. Emily won't mind what you're wearing."

"Mummy, please don't swear. I don't like it."

Julie muttered under her breath. Sometimes she could kill the little bitch.

"I'm leaving in ten minutes whether you're ready or not. I'll just have to eat all of Emily's cake and play with her toys."

"Ok. I'm ready," shouted Sophie.

Five miles away

"God. You feel so good inside me." Arching her back she pulled him in closer. She rolled him onto his back and got on top. She liked to be in control, bossing it.

"Yeah that's good. You feel good, baby," he groaned.

"I'm going to cum…"

Her body shook as she climaxed, her head flopping down to meet his chest.

"That was amazing, baby. You're amazing."

Two miles back

Julie had dropped Sophie at her friend's party and was heading to the supermarket for some supplies. She parked up, grabbed a trolley, and entered. It was pretty quiet for a Sunday afternoon. She hated crowds.

"Fucking bitch." She turned to find Simon Kington standing behind her, his face a contorted snarl.

"Simon," she said, calmly.

"You've got some nerve showing your face in this neck of the woods," he said.

"Stop being a prick. I can shop where I like."

Although calm on the outside, Julie was shaken, and made an attempt to move away as quickly as she could. She really didn't need this today.

"How can you look at yourself in the mirror?"

"Maybe it's because I'm beautiful." She smirked back at him.

"Beauty's only skin deep though, ain't it?" he said.

Three miles from there

"It's just not right, is it? I mean, look it's just wrong," she said.

He pulled on his jeans and a jumper and ran his hands through his hair.

"You're preaching to the fucking choir."

"I'm just fuckin' saying what's right and what's wrong."

He stared at her in silence for a beat.

"All I'm saying is timing is everything."

"So you're playing for time are you? Is that it? You weak as shit now that you've cum inside me?"

He held up his hands.

"Listen, babe. I'm not the enemy here. I'm just the poor sod who's lucky enough to be peppering that fine ass of yours."

This comment seemed to relax her, and a broad smile washed over her face.

"Now you're talking, babe. Why don't you get those trousers off again and remind me about that peppering you've been doing?"

Nowhere

"Let heaven and hell have their fight, and let the dice fall where they will. Let no man or woman ever doubt that vengeance comes when the time is right and not a minute before or after."

The next day

I wake like Lazarus back from the dead, knowing this is the day. Sometimes I think I'm a work of fiction, but then I understand nobody has such a sick mind. In a few hours I will change someone's life forever, and not just theirs. I will bring more pain into a world already overflowing with shit. It must be done, before the sun sets. On this day, things will change forever.

Chapter Five
After

Dr Ooesterhouse was pleased. Every pen in his pot worked. He'd used each of them just to make sure. He hated used pens. It was ten minutes before Julie would arrive for her second hypnosis session, and he had hardly slept the night before. Excitement had coursed through him, images of what might happen kept him awake.

He held up the piece of paper he'd tested his pens on. He'd created the perfect reproduction of the image in his mind. He was no Picasso, but he was pleased with what he saw. The drawing was of Julie's scarred face, her mouth open in supplication, awaiting the entry of his manhood, and he'd drawn it in all its magnificence. He found that if he folded the paper quickly and put it at a certain angle, his manhood would penetrate her mouth over and over in rapid succession. He chuckled to himself. *This was what life was all about!*

His phone buzzed, and Molly, his receptionist, told him Cathy and Julie had arrived. He folded the paper and put it in his drawer. He would return to it later.

Twenty minutes later Julie was deep into a hypnotic state. She had gone under much more quickly this time. Perhaps knowing it had been a success the first time made her more receptive, the doc thought.

"And tell me, what do you see in the tunnel?"

Julie scrunched up her face. "It's hard to make out. There are two people - a man and a woman."

"And what are they doing?"

"It looks like they are arguing. She is striking out at him with something. A stick, or pipe of some kind. It's horrible. I don't want to look…"

"I know it's upsetting, but try to stay with it. Can you get closer?"

"I don't want to, but I'll try."

"Do you know how old you are?"

"I think I'm the same age as now, or close, but it's all distorted. I can't focus."

Julie was getting agitated, and despite enjoying the session, Doctor Ooesterhouse decided to draw the hypnosis to a close.

Ten minutes later she was sipping her glass of room temperature water.

"I found that very frightening," she said.

The doc tapped his pen irritatingly on the wooden arm of his chair.

"Sometimes, when we go deep within ourselves, we are confronted by truths that are hard to stare down. This is the tough aspect of hypnosis, and why it's not for everyone. Do you think you'd like to try again next week?"

"I'm not sure. Can I call you early next week and confirm? I just feel a little rattled at the moment."

"Of course."

Alone in his office again, Ooesterhouse reflected on the session. It had not gone as he had fantasised it would. He'd imagined taking out his penis and advancing silently toward her, perhaps to within a foot or so and then, not stroking it, but maybe gently prodding for a bit. In his dream, the prodding had been accompanied by the theme to *St Elmo's Fire*. He wasn't sure what the connection was, but dreams were funny things.

Not to worry. Hopefully she would agree to another hypnosis session next week and he would set his plan in motion. That's it, he thought. Motion. He would be a man in motion. Connections were everywhere!

Chapter Six
Somewhere in between

Mrs B says sometimes that it is good to write stuff down so that we don't get stuck in life. I don't really know what she means, but I'll try. I think I might die. There, I said it, I think part of me wants to die, I know it's bad to think like this, but it's true. Mrs B tells us she understands things are not always fair, but how can she know about me? She is only at school. She's not at my house.

I hate Mrs B. Why won't she help me?

She told me yesterday that things will be better. It won't be long now, and I trust her, but she also told me I must be brave. Am I brave? Can someone be brave and still die? Please, someone help me. Please someone hear me.

Chapter Seven – Before

Sophie screaming.
Julie screaming.
Cathy screaming.

"Get out of here, you fucking bastard. You disgust me!"
"Jim, just leave," shouts Cathy.
"Sir, you need to come with me now. I won't ask again."
Sophie's father is arrested.
"Why are you doing this, Julie? Its fucking lies! Cathy, you have to stop this!"
"Just go, you fucking creep," screams Cathy.
"Daddy, Daddy, come back!"
Jim stares at Sophie, his eyes red.

Chapter Eight
Before before

"Shh, Soph. Shh. It's just me. I thought you might not be able to sleep with the storm outside, so I thought I'd stay in your bed for a while. Is that ok?"

Sophie nods. This isn't the first time she 'needed' protection from a storm.

An hour later she is alone again. She's wet her pj's, again a normal reaction to the fear and pain. She keeps asking herself when this all will end.

Chapter Nine
After

I woke up this morning and asked myself again, was it the right thing to do? As God was my witness, I thought it was, but doubt poked at my brain and I guess at my soul too.

It's been seven months since that day and there has been no peace. Perhaps there never will be. I got dressed and went for a run. There was a light drizzle that felt pleasant against my skin. I can feel my body getting stronger, and I'm able to push myself to complete greater distances. It's amazing what we can do when we push ourselves.

When I got home I was greeted with a welcome smile and a steaming cup of coffee. I am fortunate in so many ways. Living in two places, leading two lives, is starting to take a toll on me though. One of these lives must come to an end soon, the how and when still not clear, but it's coming ever closer. I'm tied to the track and the train approaches at speed.

Tonight I'll drink and fuck the pain away.

Chapter Ten
A little before

"We've talked about it, babe. I know it's terrifying, but it's got to the point that, well, fuck it, what can we do? We're dealing with a fucking monster here, a monster that needs to be stopped."

They sit in the corner of the Country Cove Inn, a warm

fire next to them.

"Talking about it and doing it are two different things. I fuckin' hate the monster."

They sit in silence for a bit, alone in their thoughts.

"Will you talk to her? We need to make her understand."

"Yeah, we've already talked and she is desperate for it to end. We just need to be strong, just a few more days."

Three miles away in the future

In his office, Dr Ooesterhouse checks his email. Good, he thinks, Julie has agreed to one more hypnosis treatment. He knows this may be his last chance to complete his fantasy. Of course he understands that because she is blind, he could have carried out the plan anytime, but the additional layer of protection provided by hypnosis makes him feel safer.

It always feels good to be naked in his office. Molly has gone home and he is alone. He has been fantasising lately about how it would feel if he were blind. He closes his eyes and gets out of his chair. Slowly he makes his way around the room. He stumbles as his leg hits the edge of the leather couch.

For a moment he stops, then launches himself onto it. He is fully erect and starts humping the cushions. It feels good to him. He's always enjoyed humping inanimate objects. Only last year he had an extremely erotic experience with a futon at a convention in Helsinki.

"Fuck," he gasps as he cums over one of the cushions. "Fuck. Molly will kill me. That's another one ruined!"

Chapter Eleven
Some time before

"Thank God they released you."

"The bitch decided to change her story, said that she exaggerated things. They still won't let me go anywhere near Sophie, and I'll probably still go on the register, despite having done nothing."

"Oh, Jim. I'm so sorry you've had to go through this. I

wish we'd moved things along faster, before this happened, but, well we didn't know for sure until just before the arrest. I'm so fucking angry, Jim. I don't know if I can keep it together."

"You have to. She can't know that anything's wrong. Look, we stick to the plan."

Chapter Twelve
The time it happened

Julie and Sophie will be driving past anytime now. It's ridiculously hot in the hoodie, but it will be worth the discomfort if everything works out.

There it is, the Volvo coming round the bend. It's now or never!

Stepping out in front of the car as it screeches to a halt, the fear is palpable. Julie gets out of the driver's side and approaches.

"Seriously, what the fuck man?!" Julie spits.

The time has almost arrived. The windscreen is misted up so Sophie is only a vague shape in the back the car.

"Look, no harm done, but I've got my little girl in there. You need to be a bit more aware of things mate, ok? Just be careful. Are you ok?"

The bottle of acid sprays its contents all over Julie's face. She screams and falls to the ground.

Sophie is screaming. There is no time to waste. Nothing can be changed now.

Cathy pulls down her hood and removes the cheap black wig. She's panting, desperately trying to ignore her sisters screams. She knows it's a quiet road, but that the chances of someone appearing in the next few minutes are quite high.

"Sophie, its ok. its ok. It's Auntie Cathy. Remember what we talked about?"

Sophie nods as she shivers. "Yes," she says in a small voice.

"We have to go now. Do you understand? Your dad has packed your stuff and he'll be here any second."

Moments later a blue mini rips round the corner and Jim

leaps out. "It's ok, Soph. Daddy's here." He glances to where Julie lies. It looks like she's passed out.

They get in the Mini and drive for a long time.

Chapter Thirteen
A long time after

Ten years later and many miles away

"Come on, Soph. We don't want to be late. We've got a long drive ahead of us."

Jim and Cathy were taking Sophie to her university accommodation in Aberdeen. She was going to study English. They were so proud of her and everything she'd achieved after such a traumatic start to her life. They headed toward Perth, taking the scenic route to the Granite City.

"I don't know if I ever said thank you to you guys. You know, for everything you did, everything you risked for me."

Cathy looked at her. "You know when we found out what your mother was doing to you, at first, well, I couldn't believe it, my own sister abusing her own daughter. Your father was the one who started to put the pieces together. The hell he went through. It took real courage for him to approach me and voice his concerns. I'm sorry to say I slapped him pretty hard in the face when he first spoke to me about it. But once I heard him out, I had no doubts. In fact it made me reflect on some strange behaviour I'd noticed, but not made a connection."

"It's ok if you don't want to talk about it, Cath," said Sophie.

"No, it's just, it was a nightmare, you know? We were going to go to the police, but then your mum caught wind of what your dad had planned, and she made all those false allegations. After your dad was arrested, we knew we couldn't trust the police or social services. We had to deal with things in our own way. You were so young, Soph, and we were terrified that this would scar you for life, our actions. But what could we do?"

Cathy burst into tears.

"It's ok, love," said Jim. "Look, Soph. I know we can't change the past. Your mum was a monster who abused you for a long time. I feel sick that I didn't see it earlier, but she couldn't hurt you anymore because she thought you were dead."

"Yes, that was rather clever of you, Cath, telling her I'd died."

"You know, Soph, none of it was easy. For a long time she lived with me, and I had to pretend I loved her. It made me sick. If it hadn't been for you and your dad back home at the farmhouse, I don't know how I would have survived."

"Well, I'm glad she's dead," said Sophie.

"I hate to speak ill of anyone, especially my sister, but she was an evil woman," said Cathy, still crying.

"But it's just so weird how she died," said Sophie.

Chapter Fourteen
After

Julie hated the smell of the room. For some reason, the musty atmosphere seemed more intense today.

Doctor Ooesterhouse counted her down until she was in a deep trance.

"I'm back in the tunnel. I can see the same people again, and I'm scared to go closer."

The doc was losing patience. "Try and stay with it, remember you are observing from a place of safety."

He slowly undid his belt buckle and lowered his trousers.

"They've started to move away. I see something else. it's like a moving flower…"

He took off his socks and slowly started to remove his shirt.

"Yes, that's it, Julie. Focus on the flower. Describe its petals for me…"

Julie was starting to feel sick. Her head was throbbing. She could feel an unpleasant burning sensation behind her eyes.

"Doctor, I feel weird.."

Fully naked and erect, Doctor Ooesterhouse felt magnificent. He slowly moved toward the couch where Julie lay. His fantasy was coming true at last.

"That's ok, Julie. Listen to my voice. I am a safe harbour. Nothing can harm you."

He was a foot or so away from her when, without warning, she sat bolt upright.

"I can see, I can se….."

She screamed at sight of the naked doctor, and bit his manhood hard. He screamed in agony.

"Stop. Stop! Let go!"

She wouldn't, or couldn't, release him. It was like her jaw was locked, or she was still in a trance. Without thinking, he reached out and grabbed the antique Charles Dickens paperweight on his side table and started thrashing wildly at her head.

"You bitch. Let go, you cunt."

He wasn't sure how many times he hit her, but the last thing he remembered before passing out was her lying on top of him on the carpet, her mouth still attached to his penis.

Brodie Simpson *is a Scottish writer originally from the North of Scotland but now living within words. He's written short stories and novels as well as collaborating with other writers. Brodie enjoys writing fiction (a variety of genres) as well as*  *dipping a stray toe into non-fiction when the mood takes him. An avid reader, Brodie continues to observe his "to read" list with a growing dread that there are not enough years left.*

Follow Brodie on Twitter @Brodiewriter

Unicorn Close

Alan Taylor

On the eighteenth of November 1781, the day before the end of the world, Malcolm MacLeod awoke to the sound of rain and the smell of other people's shit.

He had never found November a pleasant month in which to live, viewing it as somewhat of a disappointment insofar as months were concerned. He found the days oppressive and grey, the winds too noisy and disturbing with the resultant rattling of the casement windows proving particularly irksome. The light that did manage to creep into the tenement was dull and brief, and shorter days lay ahead. But December was more cheerful. The approaching solstice brought with it the promise of Hogmanay, and the secret kiss that Mistress McKain from Mary King's Close had promised him would be his under the mistletoe at Deacon Mather's party. Six weeks away. Five more weeks of ever-shorter days.

He slipped out of bed so as not to disturb Mhairi, and gave her a peck on the cheek. Her skin felt so cold to his lips, and he thought once again about calling for a doctor to take a look at her. But she disliked doctors, and always mocked them. They were men stealing credit for the work of women, she said. Taking old remedies and claiming that they were better now. Scientific. Still it was better to steal from women than to burn them as witches, she said. Malcolm knew better than to argue with her when she was talking about women, so he just nodded and agreed with her. She was right, as she often was. It was one of the things he had once found endearing about her. Less so now.

He decided to let her lie asleep for a while, to rest and

recover her strength. Even before she fell ill, she had been working long hours, sewing dresses for the fancy ladies' maids down at the palace. Her sickness was probably just exhaustion. Rest would be her best cure.

He spent the morning reading through the papers in the box that he had brought home from work, taking notes in his finest copperplate. He was focused on the fine details of the case, a lengthy dispute between Baron Norton and the George Heriot's Hospital concerning the land to the north-east of the junction where the road to Restalrig met the Easter Road to Leith. The documents were mainly charts and maps, mixed with depositions determining the rights to grazing and rights of way, many of which predated the construction of houses on the site, and contradicted each other. He lost himself in the detail of the work, marvelling at the way in which the same papers could be used to justify the claims of both parties, so much so that he let the fire go out.

What made it worse was that Mhairi had been unable to buy fresh coal for a few days, so they had none in left in the bunker, and only a couple of lumps left in the scuttle. As she was still sleeping, Malcolm took it upon himself to go out to get some. It being Sunday, he would not be able buy any himself, so he decided that popping down the street to see his friend Callum Simpson was the best course. He could borrow some coal and probably cadge a glass of wine too. Just a small one, to keep him going.

He checked in on Mhairi, who was still sleeping peacefully, even though it was well into the afternoon. She had barely touched her cup of tea. Better that than a fever, though. Then he headed out into the common stair, picking up the coal bucket and locking the door behind him before heading down to the close and out into the late afternoon rain.

Unicorn Close was little more than a side-alley that cut off from the west side of Semple's Close and ran down towards the valley where the Nor' Loch had been before they drained it. Entry was by means of a narrow covered passage that ran between two tall tenement blocks, and looked more like a laneway through to a back yard than a street in its own right. There was no sign over the arch at the entrance, no official name or signifier that it was anything more than a stray thread tied to the side of the main close. Some mapmakers included it, others chose not to. The nearest thing to a street sign was the carved bust of a chained unicorn, glaring down from the keystone of the entry arch.

Despite its inauspicious appearance, the close was well-known, indeed notorious, for three things. It was often held to be the shortest close in Edinburgh, the narrowest and the most haunted.

Malcolm would have added 'smelliest' to that list, particularly since the draining of the Loch meant that waste had nowhere sanitary to end up, despite the best efforts of the youngsters who would shovel it onto carts for a farthing. He was sure it was not healthy for there to be so much shit in the street. It gave him headaches, and goodness alone knew what effect it was having on Mhairi.

The narrowness of the close would only make matters worse, he reasoned. At ground level, it was barely wider than some of the wealthier men who made their home there, and you had to step into a doorway if you wanted to let someone pass you. More often than not, that meant a foot landing in the gutter too. What was more, the street seemed to grow narrower, the higher up the building you went - so much so that from some of the upper windows you could easily step across the close into someone else's home. Malcolm and Mhairi kept their window closed and bolted.

Unicorn Close was always quiet, but today it was deserted. Malcolm put that down to it being Sunday - most people would be at church, he suspected. And those that were not receiving the wisdom of the Lord would be staying at home like himself and Mhairi, hiding from the prying eyes of judgmental neighbours. Still, he found it unnaturally silent, and he made his way down the street as quickly and quietly as he could manage.

Callum lived three doors down, in Rutherford's Land. However, while Malcolm and Mhairi lived on the second

175

floor of their tenement building, Callum was wealthy enough to be able to afford a place on the top floor of his, which meant that Malcolm had to climb up six flights of stairs to reach the front door. Although Malcolm thought that he was reasonably fit for a man of thirty, he found that the climb tired him out more than he would have liked and left him with a worse headache than usual. As a result, he paused at the top of the stair to collect his thoughts and get his breath back before knocking. No reply.

He knocked again, less tentatively this time. Feeling the door move slightly, he gave it a cautious push, and was surprised to find it unlocked. Callum was a conscientious man, often to the point of appearing paranoid, and would not typically leave his door unlocked, despite the inaccessibility of his home.

The living room was as dimly lit as Malcolm's own. There was clearly nobody at home.

"Hello?" Malcolm said to the darkness.

He did not expect a reply but held his breath for a few seconds in any case. And when no reply came, he said "Hello?" again before he entered.

Malcolm knew that Callum habitually kept a candle on a holder by the door. It was there in its usual place, although lying on its side. He picked it up and lit it, and waited a moment for his eyes to become accustomed to the new light. Outside, the wind was whipping up, and there was a rumble of thunder somewhere far off. The window blew open and Malcolm cupped a hand around the flame to keep it from going out. Callum was most decidedly not the sort of man to leave a window open.

Indeed, if there was a word that Malcolm would use to describe Callum, it was 'methodical'. It applied to his approach in the courts, but it also characterised the way he dealt with everything in his life. His home was always tidy and ordered, with everything in a certain place. He would never leave a window unlatched, or a door unlocked. As Malcolm looked around the room, he found other things that were out of place: small things, like a drawer that had been improperly closed, or a chair not pushed into its place at the table. The bedroom told a different story. The bedroom was a mess.

Although this was the first time that Malcolm had seen Callum's bedroom, he quickly dismissed the thought that the man's fastidiousness in his public life hid something this chaotic in private. The bed was properly made, but strewn with clothes, pulled from the wardrobe and drawers seemingly without thought or reason. The wardrobe door stood open and one drawer had been pulled fully from the chest and left leaning upside-down against the side of the bed. Someone had been here. Someone had been through Callum's possessions, presumably looking for something.

Malcolm supposed that whatever the intruder had been looking for, they had found it in the bedroom, given that the other room was relatively untouched. Callum's prized books remained on their shelves. Both of his bottles of claret were still in place. Malcolm took one, and filled his bucket with coal, then paused to leave a note for Callum. He found a sheet of paper in Callum's writing desk that appeared to be some sort of official-looking letter but was conveniently empty on the reverse. Malcolm used the blank side and kept his note brief, letting Callum know what he had taken and explaining that he had found the place in its shambolic state. He left the note on the table, resolving to return in the morning, and if there was still no sign of his friend at that point, to notify the city guard.

The street was still deserted as he returned, and the rain was getting heavier. He hunched over as he walked, leaning forward to keep the coal as dry as he could manage. The bucket was heavy, and he was grateful for living on a relatively low floor as his shoulder was aching when he got home.

Mhairi was awake, sneezing again. He lit the fire and the stove, putting the pot of leftover soup on to warm and poured himself a glass of wine. Mhairi called for him, her voice weak, whiny and irritating. He downed his wine and poured himself another glass before going through to see her.

"How are you feeling, my love?"

"Oh," she replied. "Not too bad. I might get up later."

He sat on the bed beside her and took her hand between his. It was cold and pale, and she looked more frail than he had ever seen her. When he had fallen in love with her, she had been so utterly alive and full of spirit. She had caught his eye as she climbed out of Greyfriars Churchyard with some bread stolen from the harvest offering. She had seen him too and waved as she jumped from the top of the wall. Although she had landed clumsily , she had turned it into a roll and ended up sitting on the grass near to him, with the bread intact and a slight graze on her knee as the only souvenir of the mishap. They had shared the bread that day, as well as a surreptitious kiss that they had never told anyone about. Shortly after, they had started courting, then after he had taken the clerk's job at the solicitor's firm, they had married.

They had talked of starting a family of their own one day, but they were never blessed with the gift of children. Malcolm blamed Mhairi, although he always denied it, and he could see that she blamed him in equal measure. He was unsurprised that they had drifted apart, that she had started taking in sewing and encouraging him to work long hours, that his eye had started wandering.

But now she was ill, and that changed everything. Maybe she was even dying. When he looked into her eyes, he caught glimpses of the rebellious tomboy stealing bread from the church. Then he looked at her frail body, listened to her clutching for breath and found himself thinking that maybe today she would finally let go and release him. "That would be great," he said, forcing a smile.

She moved in the bed, trying to shuffle herself into a more upright position, and Malcolm tried to adjust her pillow to make her more comfortable.

"You've been out," she said.

"Aye," he replied. "It's quiet, even for a Sunday. And I think there's a storm coming."

Mhairi tried to laugh, and it seemed to shake through her. She was so fragile. It would be so easy just to help her on her way to the next life, he thought. It was far from the first time he had thought it.

"Don't you remember?" she asked as she managed to get her breath back. "It's been on the front page of *The Courant* for days. And a man came to the door to tell us just yesterday while you were at work. I nearly ended myself getting to the door to greet him. Tell me you remember, Mal."

Malcolm was confused. His headache was worse than it had been, and the claret was not helping. Yet there was something familiar about what she said, but what precisely she was getting at eluded him. Whenever he tried to focus, to remember, he just found himself thinking of details of property deeds, of boundary disputes, and the Easter Road to Leith.

"Tell me you remember," she repeated after what felt to Malcolm like an eternity.

"I… I don't," he admitted.

When Mhairi spoke again, her voice was gentle, as though talking to the child she had never known.

"Oh Malcolm," she said. "I do worry about you so. Your memory… it's so erratic. It comes and goes. Sometimes you remember things, and sometimes you just forget them completely."

"Does it?"

She sighed deeply, and her body shook again.

"You know you do, my love. We've had this conversation before. So many times before."

"We have?"

"The soup's boiling over."

Malcolm swore. He had forgotten about the soup. He jumped up and pulled the pot from the stove top, just before it boiled over. Carefully, he poured a bowl for Mhairi then cut her a hunk of bread from the loaf. He cast his eye around the room for a copy of the morning's *Courant*, but he had used the last of it to start the fire.

"So," he said as he put Mhairi's soup down on the nightstand beside her. "Remind me. Remind your poor forgetful husband of just what he has forgotten."

179

The look in her eyes was one of compassion and pity, the same emotions that he felt towards her. Each viewed the other through veneer upon veneer, as though the people that they were now wore the patina of experience, of failing health, of disappointment. He trusted her - he loved her, but only because somewhere deep beneath the surface she was still the girl who had fallen for him.

"I don't know how you could forget, Malcolm my love. It's been all over the newspapers. They say the plague is back."

The plague?

He confusion must have been obvious, because Mhairi gave one of her deep sighs and began to explain to him. She told him it was like the plague in the old times, a hundred years ago or more. It started with fever and chills, then weakness and pain. Then bleeding. Finally, as you lay dying, your fingers and toes started to blacken and lose feeling. Malcolm hardly heard her words though. He was thinking of her fever, and after it had broken, how clammy she had become, how weak she was. He looked at her hand, held tight in his own. Was the end of her finger looking a little darker than usual? Did she have the plague? Did *he*?

The more she spoke about the plague, the more everything made sense to him. Mhairi had been sick for weeks. He must have known about the plague, and probably even made a connection to her. But he had been so busy with work and caring for her that he had lost track of what went on beyond the walls of their home. Of course the street was empty, Mhairi explained. Everyone was staying at home, in quarantine. As for Callum, he had a place in the country, didn't he? He had probably gone there, in a hurry too, if the state of his rooms was anything to go by.

As she spoke, Malcolm felt his confusion fade. Mhairi was right - she usually was. Even in her sickbed, she was still the calm and rational one, and the more she spoke about the plague the more it made sense.

"I still don't understand," he said at last. "How could I forget something so important?"

"Oh, you silly, sweet man," she replied. "In times of calamity or catastrophe our minds can sometimes play tricks on us. You have your work to worry about. And your headaches. And taking care of me. That's enough for any man to remember. You shouldn't feel guilty for forgetting."

He knew that she was right. This part of their conversation was familiar. He had forgotten things before, but she had always been there to remember for him. They were better together than they would have been if they were apart. And although she told him not to feel guilty, he did. Guilty for forgetting things, guilty for doubting their love and for his feelings of lust for other women. He resolved then that he would not kiss Mistress McKain as he had intended. He would stay at home with his loving wife, who would be well again by then. He would care for her through her sickness.

He looked at her hand again, so tiny in his own. She definitely had the plague, he thought. He probably had it too by now. They might not even live until Christmas. She was asleep again, a loving smile on her lips.

She had barely touched her soup. He poured it back into the pot.

He closed the bedroom door and reached for the wine again. The pounding in his head felt more intense than ever before, and he found his thoughts merging into each other. Thoughts of Mhairi, the plague, his case, Callum. He tried to focus on each in turn, but the others slipped in and out of his consciousness, overlapping and overlaying each other. And there was a new thought in there, gradually emerging from the mix of memories and worries. Chains.

The storm broke overhead and the rain started. It came in waves, light then heavy, drumming against the roof, echoing down the stairwell. It was coming almost straight down, stabbing down into the narrow street, pelting off the cobbles. Malcolm was glad - it might shift some of the built-up effluent from the gutter and clear the air. God knew it needed to be cleared. Another glass of wine. Might as well finish the bottle after that.

The sound of the rain wrapped itself around him,

enclosing him in a soft deep dark murmuring drumbeat that drove thoughts from his head. As he dozed off in his armchair, the empty wineglass slipping from his hand to the cushion beside him, he was led into dreams by the memory of a unicorn.

When they were courting, Malcolm and Mhairi had joked about running away to the country and finding unicorns. It was the main reason they had ended up moving to Unicorn Close. They liked the idea of being watched over and protected by their national animal. The unicorn, after all, had been the symbol of Scotland for centuries, proudly rampant supporting the shield on the royal coat of arms. As a boy, Malcolm had thought it stupid to have a national animal that didn't exist. But as he had grown older, he had found it first charming, and then reassuring. His national animal was so cunning that it had never even been seen. So elusive that it could never be caught, and even its image had to be chained. What country would not want to be protected by an animal with a built-in sword?

The unicorn carving over the entry to the close was one of the oldest images of a unicorn, apparently. Some of the residents claimed that it was *the* oldest, and furthermore that it was originally carved and placed there because King Alexander the Fierce saw a unicorn there. Whatever the truth of the matter, the unicorn was decidedly unique. While they were typically depicted in chains, but nonetheless proud and regal, this one was unchained, wild, defiant and angry.

And that night, that last night, Malcolm dreamed of an unchained unicorn, trotting up the close. It did not pause or look back. It simply left.

On the nineteenth of November 1781, the day that the world ended, Malcolm MacLeod awoke to silence, fresh air, a clear head, and the certainty that his wife was dead.

He could not be absolutely sure why it was that his headache had abated, but his immediate thought was that it was due to the storm. The stench from the street had diminished greatly, and the air smelled almost fresh.

With lucidity, though, came memory. He remembered his last fight with Mhairi. It had started as an argument over money, but she had mocked his ability to provide and had impugned his masculinity, saying that if he could not give her a child, she would find a man who could. He had struck her, and she had scratched his face. And then... then the memory started to blur. He remembered grabbing her by the wrists, pushing her back into a corner, placing his hand over her nose and mouth. He remembered how it felt when she stopped struggling. The relief, and then the panic. And then the calm. He remembered deciding that he would tell their neighbours that she was sick. He had thought that would give him time to work out what to do next.

Deciding on that little lie had made him feel so much better. He had practised it, standing in front of the looking-glass, saying the words to himself over and over until it sounded so convincing that it simply had to be true. Perhaps he was influenced by the fumes from the street, or perhaps he'd driven himself insane, but it was easier to believe his lie than to face the truth.

It had been four days.

He had done nothing about her body for four days.

He stood at the bedroom door holding the handle for a full minute before realising that he would never be able to open it, to face what he had done.

He had only one option. Flight.

It took him just a few minutes to rummage through the dresser for money and papers. His clothes were in the bedroom. He could manage without them. He stuffed bread in the pockets of his overcoat and took a final look around the dingy room. He tried to remember an occasion when he and Mhairi had been happy there but found nothing. He pushed the armchair over before he left. Maybe when the city guard came to investigate, as they eventually would, they would think there had been an intruder, a struggle.

Malcolm did not lock the door as he left.

The close was as empty as it had been the day before, and the buildings were silent. That would be because of the plague, he thought. That was a good thing, because everyone would be staying indoors, shuttered up, and nobody would see him leave and he could make a clean escape and that made absolutely no sense any longer because the only person who had told him about the plague was Mhairi and she was dead because he had killed her, oh god, he had killed her so she couldn't have said anything so it must have been a spectre or his own imagination in his state of temporary lunacy or a hallucination, the plague was just a dream, a fantasy that he must have concocted, so where the hell was everyone?

"Hello!" he shouted, aware of his voice cracking. No reply.

Where was everyone?

It worried him, confused him. It was a mystery, but he knew that it made no difference: he still had to leave.

The top of the street was the narrowest part and took a sharp turn into the covered passage that led out into Semple's Close. That passageway was blocked by stones, as though the far end of the building had collapsed. In the shadows, Malcolm could see the eye of the carved unicorn, looking out accusingly from the pile of rubble. He was reminded of his dream from the night before, but then recalled something else.

He had seen a unicorn crest the day before. When he had written his note for Callum, he had used the reverse of an official document, headed with the royal crest. He had only skimmed it briefly, but had failed to appreciate its significance.

He heard a deep, rhythmic pounding noise, although he could not say if it was real or imagined. Words came to him, flashes of memory stabbing into his brain. *Construction of the Earthen Mound, Demolition of Close, Mandatory Evacuation.*

He started to run for the bottom of the Close as the hammering intensified, and stones started to fall from the top storeys of the buildings on either side of him. The tenements leaned ever closer together, blotting out the feeble light and tumbling down to wrap him in their cold embrace.

Alan Taylor *works with numbers during the day and words in his spare time. Born in Edinburgh, he has lived and worked in Hong Kong, Dublin and London, and is currently quite happily back in Edinburgh, where he lives with his husband. He dabbles in photography, cooking and planning global domination (badly).*

His writing is mainly short stories – he likes to write SFF, sometimes in other people's universes, but increasingly he likes to explore the alternative paths that history never took.

He can be found on twitter as **@alan_is_writing**, even when he isn't writing, and he occasionally blogs at **alaniswriting.wordpress.com.**

The Devil's Business

Patrick Welsh

One of the first things I learned from living in St Andrews was that there wasn't much else to do there besides drink. At least, not if you wanted to make any friends.

I learned this the hard way during Freshers' Week, and ran out of things to do whilst sober. On the first day I'd unpacked, done the meet-and-greet in the hall of residence, and had dinner with hundreds of strangers where the main topics of discussion were Λ-Level grades and speculation on what went into the curried pasta bake. After that came a pub crawl, where I stayed sober, and watched two lads arguing in the Students' Union about who had the next go on an arcade machine. The next day, I went out to explore the town, looked around the little shops, chuckled at the street sign for 'Granny Clark's Wynd'. But it didn't take long for me to learn that St Andrews was really just three streets, and had more pubs than the local economy justified. So I'd run into some of the people in my hall, and they'd gone on a pub crawl. On Monday I matriculated, got my library pass, and spent the whole afternoon searching through the books on subjects I couldn't even spell correctly. When I returned, I was just in time for the wine tasting evening, where I sat at the corner of the room for half an hour until I felt it was polite enough to go to bed.

It's not that I had a problem with people drinking. They're free to live their lives the way they want, I suppose. It's just that I'd never felt comfortable drinking myself. Maybe I was put off by the endless scare campaigns I saw when I was in school, shocked into nonconformity by a horror-show of diseased livers and drunk-driving accidents, and I was scared that if I started that one day, that could be me. Maybe it was because most of the kids in my class looked like idiots when they were drunk. It doesn't really matter. By the time I was eighteen and matriculated at St Andrews, I'd already adopted 'non-drinker' as a central part of my personality. I wasn't cool enough to be 'straight edge', but saying I was 'teetotal' made me think of coffee mornings for blue-rinsed grandmas, but I didn't see any point in putting a label on it. I just didn't drink. I was happy with that. It made me feel special, distinct from everyone else.

But it did make my first semester at university difficult.

It wasn't all bad. I settled into a routine once classes started and made some friends that, like me, preferred to stay in rather than go out.

But even among friends, there was no way I was going to avoid Raisin Weekend.

No matter who I asked, no one was able to fully explain to me what Raisin Weekend was about. As far as I could piece together, it was an old mentoring tradition, held in October, where the first-year students put themselves up for 'adoption' by third-years, who would take responsibility for the well-being and tutelage of their academic 'children'. In practice, like most things in the St Andrews student body, it was about drinking. But on Raisin Weekend, the levels of drunkenness reached a new level of excess as entire gangs of first years would meet with their academic 'parents' for round after round of booze. The sense of debauchery about the event was only worsened by the tradition of giving 'receipts' that the children 'found' to present to their parents in gratitude for taking the children under their wing.

By 'found', I should make it pretty clear that I mean 'stole'.

Most of the thefts were pretty low-key and innocent; a brick taken from the street pavement, or the ubiquitous traffic cones. The bolder freshers might make an attempt on the shopping trolleys stacked outside Tesco, so the more sensible shop owners made sure they were housed inside. But some of the hauls were genuinely spectacular. I heard from one incredulous fourth-year who swore up and down that he'd once seen the amnesty skip outside St Salvator's Quad contain a set of traffic lights that a pack of brave students had removed from the roadside with a hacksaw.

I was never sure why it was that the university, the town or the police put up with this, except that St Andrews had always been a town that felt like it belonged in another era, and the locals living there had adopted a fatalistic 'kids-will-be-kids' mentality, and put up with the students for the most part.

I tried to avoid Raisin Weekend as best I could by staying in my dorm room and studying, but my hall-mates wouldn't leave me alone until I relented and agreed to head out with them.

The typical St Andrews pub crawl, I'd noticed, had a particular pattern to it. starting in the Union while it was still quiet, where the drinks were cheap, then proceeding, in an anticlockwise circle south and east, until eventually you lost momentum and ended up drinking in one of the pubs. It was common knowledge that the places you chose to drink said a lot about who you were, and who you wanted to be friends with. If you frequented the Whey Pat, you were likely an old man. If you went to the West Port, your dad was probably a baronet. And if you went to The Rule, you were probably lost, or on a dare. We must have been halfway through the night by the time I noticed we were in Drouthy Neebors, a snug little pub on South Street that was trying too hard to present its Scottish credentials. The walls were plastered with quotes from Burns, filled with incomprehensible words like 'sark' and 'blethering', and the place was lined with shelves stacked with golfing memorabilia and car-boot-sale collectable kitsch. There were maybe two dozen people in the group with us, too many for the pub to hold comfortably, and a good number of them were almost strangers, whose only shared experience was a strong need to get plastered. There was the tall guy from Norway, the plummy-voiced pretty boy from Norwich, and the shouty lass from Aberdeen who no one could quite understand.

The only one there that I kind of knew was a woman named Kirstie, whose hair shone like leaves in autumn and whose voice was a murmuring burr that buzzed pleasantly whenever she made an R-sound. I'd had seen her a few times during meals and thought of coming up with an excuse to talk to her, but now that I finally had the opportunity to get to know her, I found I had nothing to say.

I hadn't planned on drinking much until Kirstie pushed a shot of something blue and sweet-smelling in front of me.

"That's okay," I said. "I don't drink."

She smiled and flung back her hair, revealing a turquoise pendant shaped like a dolphin hanging around her throat. "Ey man, one drink's not gonna kill ye."

And she flashed me a smile that would have made a devil cry. I drank the shot.

It burned down my throat like a trail of napalm, made the inside of my mouth taste like candy floss. But it felt good. Everyone around me cheered like I'd passed a tribal initiation. After that, the shots kept on coming, round after round, tiny glasses materialising on the table, spreading like bacteria as we downed each of the drinks. My head felt light enough to float away from my shoulders, and my bladder swelled so badly I thought it might burst and spray all over the table. By now it was too late to turn back. I was committed. And for some reason I kept thinking about something I'd heard a teacher tell me once. "Eat, drink and be merry. For tomorrow you'll have to pretend you're an adult."

By the time we left Drouthy's I was having difficulty seeing straight. The cold outside slapped me in the face like a concerned friend staging an intervention. I should have brought a coat, but I'd wanted to look good. Who, exactly, had I thought would be impressed by shirt and jeans? I'd dressed for Ibiza, not Scotland, and now it felt like Scotland was punishing me for my hubris.

I couldn't keep track of the rest of my fellow celebrants. They seemed to melt away the way people so often did on nights out, splintered and atomised into smaller groups to move on to other bars, or disappearing into the toilets, never to return. A few of those that remained threatened to return to the Union and brave The Bop, the dance floor in Venue One

189

where old pop music went to die. For myself, I was starting to feel a little restless. Part of me, the little voice that sat in judgement of me for getting drunk in the first place, was screaming that I should get home, that it was starting to get late, beginning to think that I should head home while I still could. I checked my phone, tried to focus hard enough to make sense of the screen. Not yet Silly O'Clock, I told myself. Still plenty of time left in the evening before I had to get some sleep.

When I looked up, everyone had moved on. I couldn't see them anywhere. But there was no telling where they might have gone. Damn.

I started to stumble way down South Street, hoping that I didn't look too incapacitated. It was an odd feeling. I'd never been this drunk before, had never really even *been* drunk, didn't know if I could handle it. It wasn't unpleasant, exactly. The whole world felt like a soft cocoon around me, a suit of cotton wool around me, making everything feel unreal. I passed a gaggle of students heading up back towards the Union. They hollered a good-natured greeting at me, which I returned by walking into a lamp post.

I kept walking, acting as best I could like everything was normal. The funny thing about the east end of town, though, was that the further I went, the darker things seemed to get, the weaker the light from the street lamps felt, as if they were spaced further apart, and as I kept walking further away from the main centres of the university, the streets began to feel empty, devoid of the gangs of merrymakers you'd expect to see on weekend nights. I was starting to feel tired, but I still wasn't prepared to head back to halls, which were a good forty-minute walk away. On this side of town, the complexion of the streets changed. St Andrews felt less like a rowdy playground for over-privileged kids, finally free of Mummy and Daddy, turned loose on an unsuspecting world. Here the streets were darker, colder, narrow winding paths, the withered arteries of the medieval town.

In the distance, I heard the moan of a church bell. I tried to count the peals, lost track at around six or seven, but they kept on coming. It was pretty late, but not yet past midnight. I couldn't pinpoint exactly where it came from. It could have been any of the half-dozen or so churches on South Street alone. After alcohol, churches were the thing that St Andrews had in abundance. The town had the highest ratio of churches per capita in Britain, or so the orientation guide said. Every denomination was represented: Anglican, Catholic, Church of Scotland, Free Church of Scotland, I Can't Believe It's Not The Church of Scotland. Even the Greek Orthodox church held a hymn service in the chaplaincy on Saturday mornings, though they had to work out a time-sharing arrangement with the university Jewish Society. I had noticed, though, that in a town of twenty thousand people, there wasn't a single mosque, which didn't seem fair.

By the time I reached the Pends, my bladder felt like it was on fire, and I knew I had to relieve myself somewhere or risk a trip to the health centre. But there was nowhere with a public toilet this far from the bars, which left me with only one unpleasant option. I took a moment to make sure the coast was clear and that no one was going to see me - though by now my head was spinning so fast I could easily have missed someone - and when I was sure that I was alone, I unzipped my jeans, and went loose on the wall of the cathedral cemetery.

As I let the discomfort drain out of my body, I looked over the railings at the ruins of the church. Less than half of St Andrews Cathedral was left standing, the rest had fallen prey to centuries of religious reform and a few opportunistic builders looking for materials. The ruins that were left stood in the glow of floodlights like the skeleton of some impossible creature that had long rotted away. The church was, by all accounts, extremely haunted. I'd heard most of the stories during Freshers' Week of ghostly encounters in the churchyard, of ghostly monks and of dead spinsters, and campfire stories of students who'd stayed there overnight only to awaken when cold hands grabbed them out of nowhere. I'd never really believed in any of that, but as I looked over at the decaying ribs of stone in the cold October night, it seemed entirely possible.

Then, just for a moment, I thought I saw something in the space between the pillars of the cloister: a brief flicker of light, a flash of colour. As I looked for it again, I became aware of sounds rising from inside the churchyard. The rumble of drums. The merry melody of fiddles. Voices singing, clapping. The sound of celebration.

Once I'd finished marking the territory and fastened my jeans, I followed the railings that closed off the churchyard from the rest of the town. The gate was locked, of course, but that just made me all the more curious. It meant that whatever shindig was going on inside the graveyard was unsanctioned, meaning they probably wouldn't mind another body showing up uninvited and unticketed. Still, a booze-up in a cemetery on Raisin Sunday was going to draw attention, even from the tiny and famously dopey police force of St Andrews, so I figured that I'd better get in on the action before PC Plod showed up to shut it down.

Scrambling over the fence was easy enough, the railings were over a century old and full of gaps that no one had bothered to repair. Inside, though, it was hard to make anything out, as the light from the spotlights emphasised the shadows in the churchyard. I tripped over something hard in the shadows, and fought to keep my balance. It wasn't easy with a head still saddled by the booze. I tried to be careful, ease my way between the old headstones as they loomed at my out of the black. Their placement was irregular, and I collided with a few, felt the coarse texture of stone choked by lichen and age against my fingers, as I headed towards the flickering light.

There, in the shadow of St Rule's Tower, I saw them, on the green formed by the remnants of the cathedral cloister. A bonfire was burning at the centre of the green, flickering golden flames casting shadows on the dead stone of the church. The light was so bright that it took a moment for my eyes to adjust and to see the figures moving around it, smaller shadows circling the fire like cold planets around the sun. In my drunken haze I couldn't have counted them even if I wanted to, but if I had to guess it must have been at last two dozen, maybe three, at a guess. I couldn't tell anything more about them, whether they were old or young, male or female, only that they were naked, in defiance of the chill October night, their flesh shining golden in the embers of the fire. They danced like moths in a hurricane around the flames, a swirling tempest of flesh and sweat and passion. There were no onlookers, no bystanders, no audience taking a step back. There were only the revellers, the dancers and the singers and the music-players, their voices and bodies offered up in service to the enjoyment of each other's company.

I hid, crouched behind one of the larger tombstones as I watched them, transfixed. Part of me, the sensible, sober part, wanted to get out of there, to run screaming in the direction of home and a safe, warm bed. But another part, loosened and emboldened by drink, was fascinated by it all. In the end, some impulse, some drunken, animal need to understand whatever was going on, made me step out from behind the stone and walk towards the celebration. As I strode closer, I dismissed the nagging worry inside me, the fear that I might be intruding on some secret gathering that I hadn't been invited to. Right then, I didn't care. I wanted to be a part of it.

Then they saw me. For a moment I wondered if they were going to tear me apart and eat me in some drunken fury, but they didn't. Instead, they smiled, stretched out their hands like they wanted to welcome me. One of the figures stepped out of the shadows towards me, and my heart near froze when I saw her, a slight, female shape, with hair that shone like leaves in autumn, flashing me a smile that would make a devil cry. Like all the others she was naked, her body glistening with sweat in the moonlight. It was as if she had thrown off a mask, sloughed out of her skin like a snake, discarded the quiet thing she used to be, and became reborn. I barely had time to stammer out one of the questions that were burning in my brain before she reached out and grabbed my hand, pulling me towards her, into the dance.

My body rolled around the fire, dragged along by the strength and momentum of the creature dragging me by the arms. Kirstie laughed and whooped as we circled the fire, her face ravenous and bestial, her features draped in the strange half-light. The only thing she was still wearing was the dolphin pendant, shining blue and gold in the campfire's light. I couldn't say how long I danced with her before she flung me free, and another dancer caught me. This time it was an older woman, silver-haired and handsome, and just as naked. We continued to spin until she threw back into Kirstie's howling embrace. And so it went on, as I was hurled from one partner to another like a sack of meat. It was dizzying, and it felt like I had to steel myself from throwing up, but I held on. My feet burned, my muscles ached, my lungs burned as they fought for sustenance in the thick, cloying air. I wanted to stop. I *needed* to stop. But when I *tried* to stop, I couldn't. It was like my muscles were obeying someone else, and I was just a puppet on someone else's strings, doomed to dance forever like a top until I broke.

Then I looked into the faces of the dancers around the fire, and my heart almost stopped.

The faces staring back at me didn't look like anything I'd seen before. They didn't even seem like they were alive or ever had been. Gaunt, skeletal grins leered out of the shadows, their skin almost melted away, leaving only bone grinning back at me, looking demonic in the blaze of the fire. Their flesh had sloughed off, leaving only the rictus remains. And their eyes had gone completely, replaced by dark pools of infinite nothingness.

I knew then that I should have died. Maybe I already had. Maybe my heart had stopped, or I'd slipped on a wet gravestone and hit my head, and this was the last sputtering workings of my brain as it stopped functioning altogether. I could barely even feel my body any more. My legs seemed like lead weights, as stiff as old bone as I jerked awkwardly around the fire. I made one last effort to try and stop them, but it was as if I was a prisoner in my own skin. I tried to scream, but my throat was petrified shut. The laughter of the mob of demons rang in my ears, terrible and mocking, and I knew there was no way out. I would dance until these monsters dragged me back to wherever it was they had come from, and I would never see the sun again.

Then, from far away, like it was happening in another world, I heard the tolling of a church bell. For a split-second it pierced the world of the madness that spun around me, filling the churchyard with holy power. I held on to every toll like a drowning man reaching for the shore, thirsting for order in a world of chaos. I counted each toll and saw the sky in the distance, over the sea. The first rays of the sun were glistening over the waves, lighting up the sky and banishing the darkness. The figures around me looked to the east with despair and tensed at every ringing of the bell. They began to slink away in horror, back into the shadows.

I knew this was my chance, and I knew it would not come again.

With their spell broken, I felt the sensation returning to my body. I tore myself away from the grip of the banshee holding my arm and ran as fast as I could towards the rising sun.

My heart pounded in my chest as I scrambled over the wall and sprinted down the long stone steps towards East Sands. I raced along the beach, kicking sand into my face with every step, not daring to look back in case I saw the things from the churchyard following after. All I could do was to keep staring ahead, hoping my feet could keep up until, at last, it was too much, and my legs buckled beneath me. I fell forward, planting my face into the sand. The taste of salt filled my mouth as the pain that I had been suppressing caught up with me and flooded my body like a wave. The spell that the creatures in the churchyard had cast was shattering, and my muscles shut down. I had to fight to make myself stand up, and got as far as forcing myself onto my knees before I threw up on the sand and passed out.

When I awoke, the sun was high in the sky and shining on my face. I staggered to my feet, feeling groggy, and with a headache far worse than anything I'd ever felt before, though I decided, on balance, it was probably a good thing. It meant that I was still alive.

I shambled back to the halls of residence and managed to

crawl into bed. One of the small mercies of Raisin Weekend was that lectures were cancelled on Mondays, so I had the whole day to catch up on sleep. When I awoke, I made myself a piece of toast and looked out of the window for a while.

I swore off drinking after that. Sometimes people would insist I have a bevvy or two, just to be social, but I never felt tempted. Even if I was, the smell of alcohol alone was enough to bring the memories flooding back of that awful night when I danced with the dead. I never told anyone what happened. I figured they wouldn't believe me. To be honest, I didn't really believe it myself. The only way to stay sane, I told myself, was to convince my brain that the whole thing hadn't happened, that I'd simply had too much to drink, and it had given me some odd dreams.

I didn't go past the cathedral churchyard much after that. Fortunately there wasn't much reason to go that way, and where possible, I tried to take a different route. It wasn't difficult. St Andrews was small enough that I could go just about anywhere without passing the cathedral if I didn't want to go there. The one time I did go back on purpose was a few days later, after several nights of not sleeping. I don't know exactly why I started heading back towards the churchyard. Maybe some part of me wanted to reassure my waking mind that I'd made the whole thing up, that it was all just some drunken bender filtered through the half-light of the cathedral spotlights. Or maybe, just maybe some part of me wanted it to be true. It didn't matter. I made myself head back into the churchyard, into the square of grass bordered by the cloister, in the shadow of St Rule's Tower. The sky was grey, and there was a light rain that added an air of melancholy to the tombstones. But for all that, I didn't find any evidence for the strange, demonic festival I had seen only a few nights earlier. The grass was green and unblemished where it should have been blackened and burned, and the headstones remained pristine, untouched, with no sign that anything untoward had ever happened.

I breathed out a sigh of relief, feeling like I had somehow exorcised the worst of my fears. There had been no fire here, at least not recently. That meant there had been no dancers, no diabolical figures cavorting in the graveyard by moonlight. My drunken brain must have imagined it, or at least had exaggerated whatever real celebration I had interrupted. It wasn't enough to banish the memories of that night entirely, but it gave credence to the notion that I had imagined the whole thing.

Feeling glad that I had made the return journey, I decided to walk back home. But as I turned to walk away, I felt something crack underneath the sole of my boot: something hard but fragile, like the snapping of a twig under the weight of my body. Instinctively I looked down at the ground, at the space where my foot had been, and as I did so, my heart froze. There in the imprint of my boot, lodged in the muck and covered in flattened grass, was a shard of something hard and pale. My hand was shaking as I reached down to pick it up for a better look, and I saw that the edges of it were blackened as if they had been warped and burned in a fire.

There was no mistaking what it was. It was turquoise pendant, shaped like a dolphin.

Patrick Welsh is an emerging fiction writer from northern England, specialising in fantasy and horror stories. He studied Creative Writing at the University of Edinburgh and his work has been featured in gothic horror anthologies and mental health websites. In 2012 he was a finalist for the Scottish New Writers Awards, with the panel praising "the boldness and ambition of his writing" and in 2019 he won the Jesmond Library Creative Writing Award for his short story "Love Interest." He is currently living in Newcastle Upon Tyne next to a Victorian cemetery.

Visit his website - www.pbewelsh.com

The Clock

Tom Halford

Lenore hated the clock. Edgar loved it.

It stood in the corner of the room, tall and wide, made of oak, the machinery ticking and tocking behind the glass. A relative of Edgar had it shipped from Scotland, explaining to Edgar that no one in the family had room for it. Most of the McAllen family lived in apartments, and only Edgar, their cousin in the colony, had enough space for a grandfather clock. He loved the connection to his father's family in old Scotland, that he had an object to remind him of them here in Nova Scotia.

"Ba Boom! Ding! Dong! Ba Boom!" sang Lenore. "That thing is loud."

It clanged every half hour. Lenore's imitation of the sound was fairly close, but for Edgar the 'ba boom' sounded more like 'go home'. It was as if the clock was trying to speak to him, reminding him of his roots.

"That's the sound of my family history," said Edgar.

She rolled her eyes. "Oh, wow, man," she said. "You're like so Scottish."

"I am so Scottish," he said.

"You were born in Canada, and you grew up in Canada," she said. "You're Canadian."

"I'm proud of my family heritage," he said. "What's wrong with that?"

"Honestly, how different is Scotland from Nova Scotia?" she asked.

"That's not really a question. You're telling me it's not different at all. And that's part of the appeal. They have England to the south, and we have America. They have a proud history of education and progressive politics, and so do we. The connections between here and there are what I love. So many Scottish settlers landed on these shores and made a life for themselves. That's a beautiful thing."

"It's a beautiful thing unless you were already here," she said, laughing at him. "Before New Scotland, it was called Acadia, and before that it was called K'jipuktuk. The Scottish and the English were colonisers here. Plain and simple. Could you imagine going to a place and calling it the new wherever-you're-from? Arrogance. Plain and simple. That's all that is. Imagine someone moving into our house - Martin from across the street - he moves in, and he proclaims that our house is now New Martin. That's the Scottish in Nova Scotia."

"Get off your high horse," he said. "The gleoc stays."

"The gleoc?"

"It's Gaelic for clock."

"Well, if the gleoc stays - " she said, and stopped herself from finishing the sentence.

Edgar was startled. He had to admit that the gleoc was certainly not quiet. It had been affecting their sleep, which was already bad.

Both he and Lenore were insomniacs. Lenore would spend hours on her phone, scrolling through various social media sites, reading about the world, and Edgar was obsessed with TV about the occult. He stayed up watching shows on alchemy and the undead, vampires and werewolves.

One part of Edgar felt tortured by the lack of sleep, but another part thrived on it. If he could stay up late enough, then he would have the opportunity to see the Spoon.

It was always after midnight when the Spoon appeared. Luminescent, it floated into the room and hung over top of him. A fierce eyeball was at the center of his mother's wooden spoon.

When she had died, he had taken the spoon from her kitchen and stuffed it in his back pocket. Now it was safely hidden in his sock drawer. The night after the funeral, the Spoon appeared before him. In the dark, late at night, when he thought he was asleep, there it was, always the eyeball at its center, glaring.

It was furious at him for letting Lenore make light of his heritage. His father had talked about Scotland so often and so fondly while Edgar grew up. He was proud of where he was from, and what was wrong with that?

Edgar watched the Spoon.

It scolded him. It told him to stick up for his father. The clock was more than just an object. It was a piece of his family history. His father would be rolling in his grave if he knew that Edgar had let that woman speak about his family in that way.

The clock clanged downstairs. "Go home! Go home!"

Edgar sat up, and the Spoon was gone.

***

Edgar and Lenore had first met at an insomniac support group, which was held bi-weekly in the basement of a Baptist church in downtown Halifax. The meetings were always at midnight. The organisers would put on massive pots of coffee, and those who were suffering would sit in a circle and talk about their struggles with sleep deprivation. Then after the meeting they'd tell each other ghost stories or go to a bar together to drink themselves into a stupor that would hopefully lead to something resembling sleep.

The second Edgar saw Lenore, he felt as though he had been struck. He couldn't stop looking at her. She was wispy and light; something about her complexion made him think of fresh whipped cream. She sat there during the meeting with a handful of vanilla wafers, crunching through them one by one. Afterwards, he asked her if she'd have coffee with him, and they went to a bar and sat in a corner sipping on their drinks and chatting. He was fascinated.

Then he didn't see her for a month. When she finally came back to the insomniac support group, and he asked her what had happened, she said she'd nearly died. She'd become sick and had been in a coma for three weeks.

"I never felt so rested," she said.

They started dating and eventually moved in together. They bought a house, and both had good jobs. Things were going well.

When the clock arrived, they thought it looked somewhat regal standing in the corner of their living room. It almost made them feel like they were both finally adults. Edgar took it as a sign that he should propose soon. They were ready for the next step.

***

There came a knock at the door. It was Martin. He was planning a trip to London to take part in a climate change rally. He was wondering if they would look in on his house while he was gone. He held up a key. Edgar and Lenore both readily agreed. They liked Martin. He was down on his luck. His wife had left him (but according to Martin, for good reason), and his son didn't seem to visit very often. All of that was to say Martin needed kindness in his life, so it felt good to help him out.

Before Martin left, the clock rang out and startled him. "Boy, that's loud," he joked. "Nearly scared the life out of me."

"That's what I've been saying," remarked Lenore.

He thanked them again and left.

"Do you have to make such a big deal out of everything?" asked Edgar as he watched Martin cross the street.

"I don't make a big deal out of everything," she said.

"Every half hour when the gleoc goes, you roll your eyes or you repeat the sound," he said.

"Oh you mean Ba Boom! Ding! Dong! Ba Boom!"

"You shouldn't make fun of my family," he said.

"I'm not making fun of your family," she said. "That gleoc was made in Baltimore. And on that note, can we stop calling the American clock by a Gaelic name?"

He didn't believe her. She walked over, crouched down and pointed at an inscription on the bottom of the clock. It was indeed made in Baltimore, and that only annoyed Edgar more.

Then she added, "Besides, like you're so easy to be around. Oh, look at my heritage. I'm so Scottish. Why in the world would you be proud to be Scottish?"

"The first Prime Minister of Canada was Scottish," said Edgar. "Sir John A. MacDonald."

"Yeah, what a legacy he left," said Lenore. "See how he treated Indigenous peoples here. You're proud of that goon? I was reading about him last night. Do want to know a direct quote from your old Scottish pal?" She opened up her phone. "Here it is. *I want to get rid of the Indian problem.*"

"You just left that open?" asked Edgar. "All night and all day at work, you've been waiting to unleash that on me?"

"I'm reading here," she said. "Old John A. said, *Our objective is to continue until there is not an Indian that has not been absorbed into the body politic.* He said that! He said it! And that's what you're proud of!"

"How in the world could you honestly think that?" asked Edgar. "No, I'm not proud of that! I'm proud of other stuff. He was the first national leader to try to give women the vote! You're just cranky!"

"Cranky? Yeah, I'm cranky because I never sleep," she said. "Because all I hear every half an hour is Ba Boom! Ding! Dong! Ba Boom!"

"Stop shouting at me!"

"You're shouting at me!"

"You're just jealous!"

She laughed, and once she started, she couldn't stop. She had to sit down, she was laughing so hard. It was starting to feel obnoxious, and she wanted to stop, but she couldn't understand why he would think that she was jealous. Jealousy was the last emotion she felt towards that clock. Annoyed, exasperated, destructive, these were all more appropriate words.

She heard Edgar slam the door shut, and he was gone.

***

The Spoon and its all-seeing eyeball was hovering over him again. He had come home after a long walk through the park. He had planned to stay out longer just to make Lenore think about the way she had spoken to him, but a raven started to follow him, and it had made him so uncomfortable that he decided to return early.

The Spoon was still upset at him. Storming out of the house was not nearly enough to stand up for his ancestors. Did Lenore have no respect for his heritage? Did she know nothing of the Battle of Culloden, where the English slaughtered some 5,000 of Edgar's people? Did she know nothing of the Highland Clearances, where so many Scottish were forced from their own homes? How dare she laugh in the face of all this suffering?

The clock clanged downstairs. "Go home! Go home!"

Edgar sat up.

The Spoon disappeared.

***

The next day she cooked him a breakfast and rubbed his shoulders while he ate. As he chewed and slurped his coffee, she said, "I'm sorry I made fun of your clock yesterday."

"Thank you," he said and continued to chew and slurp.

He didn't say anything for the rest of the meal.

That was it? They had both argued. Then she had apologised, but all he could say was thank you. Thank you? Then he went about being grumpy all day.

The clock clanged loudly and reverberated through Lenore's jaw.

She was in the kitchen washing the dishes. He was sitting at the table with his arms folded, still looking as cranky as ever.

"You know what? I'm not sorry!" she said.

"What?"

"If you're not sorry, then I'm not sorry," she said.

"You only apologised so that I would apologise, too. You know what that means? That means you're not really sorry!"

203

"Then I'm not sorry!" she shouted.

"Fine," he said and shrugged his shoulders.

She grabbed the key that Martin had left behind and stormed out of the door. He could do it, so why couldn't she?

She jogged across the street and walked up to Martin's door. He had flown out the previous night, so she didn't bother knocking. She just unlocked the door and walked in. The house seemed cozy. She looked around for a few seconds, opened his fridge, used the bathroom, and then sat on his couch. There was a blanket draped over the back. She took it and wrapped herself up.

"I proclaim this house to be New Lenore," she proclaimed.

She had such an atrocious sleep the night before with that stupid clock clinging and clanging. She would let herself nod off for a few minutes. There was no harm in that. She almost never felt this comfortable.

***

Edgar couldn't believe she was gone. With each half an hour the clock seemed to get louder and louder. He hated to fight with her. He hated it, but there were some days where he didn't know what she wanted from him. The clock rang out.

He hoped it was calling out to Lenore, calling out to her, wherever she had gone. "Go home! Go home!"

Why did it sound like that to him? Did it sound like that to Lenore as well?

The wind picked up outside. Edgar was sure that he heard something tapping on the back door. He walked to it and opened it up. There were leaves rolling against the house. They rolled right into the hallway.

Edgar slammed the door shut. He went into the kitchen and flipped up his laptop. Watching a TV show on haunted houses and thinking of Lenore, he sipped on a cup of tea. The narrator talked about ghosts and how they haunt a person or a home for years after their passing.

The curtains over the sink blustered open. They looked

like a spirit, pale and full of life. Edgar stood and slammed the window shut, and at the shutting of the window, he took the life out of it.

The clock rang out. "Go home! Go home!"

How was this a home without Lenore?

Edgar walked to the front window and looked out for her. He took his phone from his pocket and texted her.

I'm sorry. Come home.

He paced around the living room, waiting for her to text back, and when she didn't, he went to the kitchen table and turned his show on again.

Out in the yard he could see a raven staring at him, and that raven seemed to know him. It was the same one that had been following him the night before. Edgar stood up and looked back at it.

"What do you want?" asked Edgar.

It looked inside of him, and it knew exactly what had happened to Lenore.

The raven cawed out. "Go home!" And then it flew at Edgar, smashing into the kitchen window. A wicked thud echoed in the kitchen and the window cracked. Edgar fell back.

The Spoon hung over the top of him, the eyeball glaring into his soul, and it told him to listen to the raven. The raven knew everything, and he knew nothing. Then the Spoon swooped down, thwacked him in the forehead and was gone.

When he stood and looked out the window, the raven was back on its feet and waddling to where it had been perching. It cawed out again. "Go home!"

Edgar wondered if the raven had been able to hear the clock. Perhaps it was able to mimic the sound in the same way that a parrot could. He googled it, and it was true, ravens could mimic sounds. He kept reading. Ravens were smart, apparently. Ravens attacked people they didn't like. He glanced at his cracked window. He didn't care what the Spoon said. This raven clearly did not like him. He couldn't trust it to be right about anything.

It was perched in its tree, staring at him.

The clock clanged again. "Go home! Go home!"

The raven repeated the refrain. "Go home! Go home!"

He had thought that he was home. This was the house that he and Lenore had been keeping warm, looking after, keeping tidy. This was the house that they had been living in and paying for, the one that Lenore had abandoned him in. Where had she gone? When would she return?

"Lenore!" he shouted. "Lenore!"

There came a knocking at the front door. He ran to it and swung it open. There she was, looking as beautiful as ever. Lenore! Lenore, standing at the front door.

He grabbed her and kissed her, and he wanted to kiss her more, that beautiful, spritely Lenore. She fell back in his arms, and that was the end of his little war, his little war with the lovely Lenore.

***

Edgar and Lenore made a compromise about the clock. Edgar bought her a pair of noise-canceling headphones. Lenore didn't feel like it was a compromise, but she didn't want to argue with Edgar anymore.

The truth was that Edgar was getting sick of the clock. He kept hearing its echoes everywhere he went. It started with the raven. "Go home!" Then he heard it in the creaking of the steps. Each time he went upstairs, he rhythmically heard, "Go home. Go home. Go home." All the way up or all the way down.

When he got in the shower, which was becoming less and less frequent, each little drop of water seemed to slap against him whispering, "Go home. Go home. Go home."

Every sound built upon the last. And then the loud bursting of the clock rang out, cutting through and ascending above the rest, silencing them for a peaceful few seconds afterwards.

Then the sounds would begin again, slowly getting louder and louder.

He couldn't bring himself to tell Lenore. She knew

something was off. He was more tense than usual. He caught himself shouting at her over nothing. One day he said, "Have you checked on Martin's house today?"

"Not yet," she said.

"Not yet!" he shouted. "It's almost midnight! When were you planning to go over?"

"You could go over too you know," she said.

"Like I don't do enough around here," he said.

"That's not what I'm saying," she said. "I'm not putting up with this. You've been shouting at me non-stop. I deserve better."

She got out of bed and left the room.

He sighed and called out a few minutes later. "I'm sorry."

She came back to the door, and when she opened her mouth to speak, the clock rang out. "Go home! Go home!"

"That friggin' clock," he said. "I'm sorry, Lenore. Each day, I'm sorry more and more. Come to bed, my lovely Lenore."

***

The next day, when Edgar returned home from work, the clock was gone. Lenore pulled into the driveway a few minutes after him. She was smiling and said, "Before you say anything, hear me out."

He stared at her: "You sold the gleoc?"

"I got a thousand frickin' dollars!" she said. "Let's go to Cuba, baby! Pina Coladas on the beach!"

"You sold the gleoc!"

"Stop calling it that! It's a frickin' clock! From Baltimore!"

"Without asking! You sold my family history!" He was shouting again, and he wanted to stop, but once he began shouting, it was impossible to calm himself down. "You have no respect for me or my belongings! You think you're so smug and superior!"

She held up both hands. "I'm not doing this anymore," she said. "Let me know when you've cooled off."

She walked out the front door and crossed the street to Martin's house. It had been a longer trip than Martin had told them he'd be gone for, and they hadn't heard from him or his family. That was odd. Maybe she would text him. She took the envelopes crammed into his mailbox and walked into the house. She sighed. She knew that Edgar would forgive her eventually. She was certain that he secretly hated the clock. She wasn't disrespecting him. She was liberating him. If only he could see that.

She turned on Martin's TV and sunk into his marshmallowy soft couch. She relaxed and watched the TV. How long would it take for Edgar to calm down? She wasn't worried about that. She was too comfortable. She knew that if she kept sitting like that, she would fall asleep. That was a good feeling for an insomniac, to know that you were going to fall asleep if you just stayed still. She couldn't pass that up for anything. She felt her eyes close, and she let herself fall into a deep, peaceful sleep.

***

The clock was gone. Edgar would have been relieved if he wasn't so angry. How could she just take something of his and remove it? How did she physically move it out of the house? She was so thin! What kind of power did she have in those sinewy arms?

He texted her.

How did you move the clock? Did you have that dork from your work help you? Did you have him in the house behind my back?

She didn't reply. He looked around the house for some sign of the dork from her work. Nothing. No dude smell.

He looked out the window and saw a dolly in the yard. That's how she'd done it. He thought about it for a moment. What was wrong with him? Why did he get so angry, make so many mean assumptions about her? She wanted to live with him. She put up with so much of his nonsense.

"Go home! Go home!" the raven cawed out in the

backyard.

He'd had enough of that noisy animal. He hauled open the kitchen window and shouted, "No! You go home! You stupid bird!"

That crow never liked him anyway. He ran up to his bedroom and dug the wooden spoon out of his sock drawer. He could tell by the way the raven looked at him that it didn't respect him. He would teach it a lesson about respect. He ran out to the backyard, and shaking the Spoon at the raven, he screamed at it to shut its mouth.

The raven cawed back at him. "Go home! Go home!"

"I am home!" he shouted at the thing and tried to strike it with the Spoon.

It hopped up and flew away. He chased it down the street, but it flew too quickly. There was a cab driving in the opposite direction, he hailed it and said, "Follow the raven."

The cabbie was an elderly man who was tired from a long day of driving people around, and he didn't take kindly to this young man's strange request. So he drove Edgar to the airport and said, "That'll be fifty bucks."

Edgar passed the man his debit card. He paid, stuck the Spoon inside his pants, and he got out.

Finally it all made sense. Go home. Perhaps the raven was looking out for him after all. Everything had been a sign up to that point. He needed to go back to his ancestral home. He needed to get to Scotland. He went into the airport and looked at the massive electronic board with its list of flights. There was one to London that was leaving that night. He found a woman standing behind a desk and booked himself a flight to London. From there, he could get on a train and head north.

"Do you have your passport, sir?" asked the woman.

She sounded French.

He said he didn't.

"Well, you better get it before your flight leaves," she said.

He ran out of the airport and got the elderly cabbie to drive him back to his house, found the passport and got the cabbie to drive him back.

"That'll be one hundred bucks," said the cabbie.

Edgar passed him his debit card again.

He paid, and he got out. As he walked through the airport, he wished he had left a note for Lenore. A mean part of him thought that maybe this would teach her a lesson, but he decided that he was done with that sort of behaviour. He loved her too much to play any more games. He would text her.

"*Going home. Love you!*" he wrote once he was seated on the flight.

He was in a row by himself. He stretched out and felt himself falling asleep. He'd text her again once he landed.

***

Lenore woke in the dark. Martin's TV was still on. What time was it? She shot up and looked at her phone. It was three in the morning. She saw Edgar's text. *Going home.* Where had he been? Had he been out drinking? Was he with that nerdy girl from work that was always sending him emails?

She tried to focus on the positive. Things had been so tense between them since the clock had come into the house. It was cursed. She was sure of it.

She got up from the couch and walked out of Martin's house. It was freezing outside, so she darted across the street and into her own house. She would crawl into bed with him, nuzzle in and cuddle up. Everything would be fine. He loved her, and she loved him.

When she got into the room, she was surprised to see that the bed was still made. Where was he sleeping? She looked in the spare room, and he wasn't there either. Not wanting to wake him, but feeling like she had no choice, she called out, "Edgar?"

Outside she heard the cawing of a raven. Normally, she would ignore it, but there was something in the sound that the raven made that was incredibly similar to the word 'home'.

She told herself that her mind was playing tricks on her.

There was no way that the raven was repeating a word from Edgar's text.

She walked down to the kitchen and looked out the window. There was the raven, perched in the tree, staring at her and cawing, "Home! Home! Home!"

The wind burst the curtain out, and the raven flew head first at Lenore through the window, its claws grasping at either side of her face. She felt the thing's beak cracking down on the top of her head. She screamed and fell back, swatting the raven off of her and running back up to the bedroom.

What on earth was happening? She heard the raven shuffling around the house. It was still on the main floor. It was as if the world was turning on her. First the animals would attack, and then what next?

Where was Edgar? He said he was going home. Was he dead? Was he a ghost? Was he the raven trying to win one last argument with her?

She opened the bedroom door, and she walked cautiously down the steps. She could hear the raven's movement in the kitchen. She peeked around the corner and got a good look at the thing. In her exhausted mind, she could feel some presence, something in the black, beady eyes that made her certain that it was her Edgar.

"Edgar!" she shouted. "I'm going to open the back door, and you need to leave for evermore!"

The raven cawed at her. She took that to mean a yes. She sprinted to the kitchen, swung open the door, and then ran to the safety of the stairs. She listened to the thing eventually find its way outside. Then she ran and shut the back door.

She felt the cold wind blowing through the window. There was no way she was going to sleep again after that.

_____

211

Tom Halford *lives in beautiful Corner Brook, Newfoundland, Canada. He and his wife, Melissa, work at Grenfell Campus Memorial University of Newfoundland. They have two amazing, hilarious kids who enjoy Pokemon and superheroes.*

Tom holds a doctorate in English Language and Literature, and he studies representations of surveillance. His first novel is titled Deli Meat, and he hopes to finish another novel before too long.

Follow Tom on Twitter @tomahalfordnovel

Fortress of Shadows

Caoimhín de Paor

It is in that first grey breaking of the day, before Lugh's light is upon the land, that he is most beautiful.

He does not wait for the morning to come, for he is more radiant. He wakes in the still room, when the birds have yet to begin their song, his body draped gently by the sheet like a great master's sculpture, showing the relationship of form and fabric entwined. He stretches and dresses quietly, his muscles sketched by moonlight as he pulls his tunic over his head, and takes up his weapons. He pauses at the doorway to look back at me. I feign sleep in the bed where he lay. Then he vanishes into the thick mists that cloak Dún Scáith. I linger a moment in the void he leaves behind, small and tired, so ordinarily human in every regard, struggling to muster the strength to rise at this hour. It is not long before his absence weighs heavier upon me than the need to rest, the need to see his almond skin and smell the honey sap in its pores, and I am drawn to him like the chariot behind a horse. I follow in his footsteps along the gravel path from the castle to the shore. I follow him in all things. I will follow him until the end of time.

He is upon the storm-washed rocks, his fair hair aglow, and the favour of the gods upon his shoulders. All of the flowers are turned to him; the mist rolling in from the sea swirls around him. This morning he has been swimming. His clothes abandoned, he sits cross-legged on the tallest of the boulders, salt water streaming from the curls of his hair, off his shoulders. His skin dries in the wind. The first light of the morning breaks in the east on Alba, and it sets him alight. And though we have lived on this island for a year now, I am still breathless by the sight of him, enchanted by the lie of the land, and how he sits framed by the snow-capped mountains, their tallest peak. They will surely be named for him in the years to come, the legacy he will leave upon this landscape.

It is criminal to interrupt this divine scene with my mortal touch. But it must be done. No less is expected of each other, and the Shadow could be watching us from afar. Lir's breath blows in off the sea, and I stalk across the boulders downwind of him. I wait until the waves crash down before making longer leaps, the spray raining down upon us as I plant my feet, and look up to see if he has heard me. His eyes are closed in a deep meditation still. Some rocks are loose, but I know the ones to mind; some are slick with seaweed, but I use them to glide swiftly around the pools. I crouch down thirty paces away. A comfortable striking distance. Fingers closing on the grip of my hurl, I leap towards him, swinging.

His eyes open; two distilled droplets of a blue sky. He rises in a spin, shaking off the last of the salt and sea from his hair, and catches the ball soaring towards him firmly in an outstretched fist. There is a loud slap as it digs into his skin, but he is not in pain. He smiles.

"That is the closest you have gotten, Ferdia." His words are carried to me as delicately as the ocean washes through the rocks around us, sea foam bubbling between them. I am weakened at the knee by their melody for a moment, and this he surely notices, launching himself to his possessions before I can react. Hurl in hand, I bear down upon him, but he rises with his own and blocks my strike. The ash handles clap together like thunder, ringing out between the mountains.

He springs into the sky, soaring with arms outstretched like a bird, and comes down balanced on the next boulder, one foot planted, one extended. His hurl is clasped between his toes, and there resting on its end is the ball. Pure showmanship. A display of dexterity and timing few if any on this earth could match. But I must try. And so, with a deep breath, I chase after him as the next wave comes crashing down, and from rock to rock we leap, the two of us like playful stoats, up and down, in and out of the terrain. He does his best to shake me but I read him well, and I swing for his ankles, swing for the ball, but I am always a pace or two behind his immaculate speed. I would only find an opening if he were to willingly leave it for me. It is futile to try and find his faults, as holding the ocean in cupped hands. He crosses the beach quickly, stopping on the last of the rocks before the tall grass, and here I catch him, knocking his hurley away and taking the ball in hand. It is uncharacteristic of him to concede so easily; he could have contested the blow, parrying me off him, or dodging at the last moment, as he so often does. I had been expecting him to, and I am unbalanced now, tumbling forward over the edge and crashing into a shallow rock pool. The water is cold and heavy with seaweed, robbing me of my breath and the grip to rise, and I am thrashing like salmon as he lands upon me, pinning my arms to the rock. Truth be told, I commit little to fighting him back. His blue eyes are upon mine, and in them I see another world and its swirling clouds, another world wholly separate from this earth, where we will never need to use the terrible skills we have learned here, where there is no need for war masters like us, and we are free to be young again, artisans and lovers.

His lips are slick with salt, but I can still discern his sweetness and warmth in their taste.

Winter's chill is upon the mountains, its long arms reaching down towards us, but there is some warmth still in the glow of Lugh's light, and we sit in it, drying off. The tide is returning to Lir; the rock pools drain through each other with the pleasant pouring of a fountain. It is his favourite sound. I learned this in our first week here, when I could so rarely find him, until I searched the beach, and here he would always be, still as a statue upon the rock. I glance at him sideways, looking to read his features. He is staring out across the water, unblinking.

"We have been here for a year this day," he says. It is clear then where his thoughts lie. They are, of course, of home. Though there is a dark ocean and many isles between us, Éire is out there; too far to be seen, even for one smiled upon by the gods as he is. But it is there, rising out of Lir's realm, as sure as the mountains of Alba do. Today its green hills feel closer than normal, and this is comforting, even to me. I do not want to return. Here I am needed by him. Here I am his sparring partner, his confidant, his closest friend, the most intimate love he has known. I have tried not to imagine the voyage that awaits us, for it may well be the last day I spend at his side. He will be welcomed back to Emain Macha, to walk in the gardens of Lugh. He will once more enter the hall of Forgall Monach, to eat bread and olives and drink sour wine, and ask again for the hand of his daughter, Emer. This time, he is a fully realised man. He is *more* than a man. He cannot be refused again.

It is difficult to imagine them wed. I want to take his face and kiss him again, and convince him there may be more yet for us to learn here, no end to our training, another year and a day at the very least. But we are not alone. He rises and turns, as one of the Shadow's daughters crosses the grass toward us. She calls from the edge of the path, her voice lilting across the wind with a beautiful high register, her hands folded on her chest, pressing the notes.

"The Warrior Maid summons you for an audience, my lord Ferdia."

He turns to me then, his face suddenly hard and braced like a shield, and without another word he gathers his weapons and sets off across the rocky shore away from me. He leaves small and shallow footprints in the sand. I wonder what I have done to displease him so. I want to call after him, to shout his name from my core, to declare my love for him in the light of the gods and the presence of others as I would when we were alone, *Cú Chulainn*. But I do not. I walk with the daughter back towards the castle, in silence. And as we pass beneath the dark battlements, I can feel a cold touch at the base of my neck. A sensation I have not yet grown used to. I look up to the sky, shielding my eyes from Lugh's light. There, between a slit in the stone parapets, I can see the Shadow. She watches me from inside the folds of her cloak.

Dún Scáith has grown quiet in our last days. Many of its halls are empty now, the Shadow's servants and daughters sent away. I walk the narrow corridors and touch the weeping stone walls, remembering the nervous first few times he took me by the hand when we were around a corner, the places he kissed me when we were out of her sight.

She is waiting for me in the doorway of the armoury, flame raised above her head. Her black garments do not absorb the light, and she looks to be a continuation of the darkness from the room, save for her ghostly pale hand and its black nails, gripping the shaft of the torch. It is cold always in this castle; it is colder always where she stands. She moves aside, indicating for me to pass. I hesitate.

"Are we not to wait for Cú Chulainn?"

"This is not a lesson," she says. I walk slowly past her into the room and she follows, cloak sweeping across the stone, then shuts the door behind. She begins to light the rest of the torches, bringing a flickering glow to the room. The hanging blades and axe heads glitter in the light. Upon the table at the centre of the room there is a long iron casing with ornate etchings and an exquisitely-crafted latch lock. As she walks between the torches, the Shadow speaks.

"There is a legend of two sea creatures, older even than the gods, monstrous in their size and ferocity. The Curruid, scorpion-like, had talons that could penetrate any hide, and with them it sculpted the earth that rose above the water. The Coinchenn, swirled like a snail, had armoured plates that locked like chain-mail, making it impervious to all strikes. With them it split the currents that shaped the sea. They sparred endlessly in the deepest depths of the ocean, where the seabed drops away and the light of Lugh himself cannot reach. They were two unstoppable forces of nature."

She comes to the table and reaches over to open the case. I lean in to see. It contains a long, milky-white spear, thin but beautifully crafted. Though difficult to tell in this light, it does not appear to be made of any metal. It is dull and unreflective by the flame. I am certain, whatever it is, it is not fragile. It is well-designed and sculpted with a naturally smooth finish. I had never seen such a unique or carefully-crafted weapon.

The Shadow continues. "After centuries of conflict, the Currid finally delivered a fatal strike. It enwrapped the Coinchenn and passed its barbs through the chinks of the armour, slaying its eternal foe. But to do so left their bodies in an unbreakable link. The Currid sank into the black depths, and the Coinchenn was dragged with it. And in death, they were entwined together for evermore."

She waves her hand over the spear. "This is the Gáe Bolg. It is all that remains of either of those legends."

I study it closer. It is indeed made of bone; a long rib piece perhaps, although with many sinewy strings wrapped around its head. The strings are laced with sharp nodules like teeth that pierce both into the bone and out, like the jagged rocks on the shore.

"Centuries passed before a storm washed their tangled forms upon the strand, and they were uncovered by a champion, Bolg Mac Buain. He was a famed fighter and a skilled blacksmith of equal measure. He found that their bones and barbs could not be separated; instead, he crafted with a mind to keep them together, and the Gáe Bolg was formed."

I understand now that this was not one of their bones, but both. The barbs of the Coinchenn, attached to the bone of the Currid. A razor-sharp spear, barbed like a thorn.

"This is one of a kind," I say. She nods. "And you would offer this to me?"

"Yes."

"Not Cú Chulainn?"

Her face remains still. The torch crackles in her hand. "If you do not wish to take it, I will offer it to him."

I skim my fingers across the shaft of the blade, wary of its thorn-like barbs, unable to determine where its grip lies.

"How do I hold it?"

"You do not. Given the nature of the bone, it is buoyant. It will rest on the surface of a still lake, and float in the current of a stream. It is designed to be grasped and thrust with the

218

foot, by its base where it is thinnest."

As incredible as it sounded, now that it had been explained to me, I could see it being used in this manner. The spear did taper towards a thin end like a pick-axe, narrow enough to be gripped between toes. Many weapons could be enchanted such that they could only be used by a unique master - in the same vein, could they not be enchanted to be used in a unique way? It would take me years to master, of that I am certain. But Cú Chulainn might be better able. I remember the way he stood on the rock this morning, his hurley in toe.

"To use it, you must be willing to destroy absolutely those that you would wield it against."

I look up to the Shadow's veiled face. "What do you mean?" I ask.

She indicates toward the head of the spear. "Upon contact, the wire extends from the head of the spear, in search of your enemy's body. The barbs will embed themselves in their every limb. To be separated from the spear, their flesh must be cut loose."

I shake my head. "I do not understand. When will such a weapon prove useful?"

She is silent for a moment. In the torch light I can see her eyes flickering amber and feline in the flame. The faintest hint of tears glistens beneath their surface, giving them a sparkle like gemstone.

When she speaks again her voice surprises me. So often biting and authoritative, now it is no more than a whisper.

"Tomorrow, you and Cú Chulainn leave Dún Scáith. There is nothing more for me to teach you but this."

I nod. It is an eternity before her next words, as though she weighed them for some time in her mind.

"Once you return to Eíre in the morning, you and Cú Chulainn will not see each other again for many years. But your paths are fated to cross one more time."

She speaks on, but I hear little else, her words muted as though I were submerged in the rock pool once more. I feel the earth sinking in upon itself beneath me, the stone slabs falling out of the floor one at a time, all of them hurtling into a dark void until there are just two left beneath my feet, and when they drop I go with them too into a darkness with no end, no impact at its base. I shut my eyes, fighting to control my breath as it comes in short portions. Her words hurt more than any wound I have known. While I refuse to accept them, I know them to be true. Mortal though I am, I know the tone of prophecy when it is spoken. My heart rings out endlessly in my ears.

"Ferdia?" she says, taking my wrist, grounding me. I shake free.

"Listen to me, please. There will be a battle in the years to come. The armies of Ulster and Connacht will face each other, divided by the ford that marks their border. Cú Chulainn will stand shin-deep in its waters and single-handedly hold the forces of Queen Méabh at bay, dispatching champion upon champion in single combat." She pauses. "Until she sends you."

I open my eyes, astounded.

"I would never fight him."

She considers this, breaking my gaze for a moment. "Maybe so. Prophecy always occurs, though so rarely in the manner it is predicted."

I shake my head. It is inconceivable that I would ever do him harm. And less likely still that I would out-skill him to do so. "Even if we were to battle. He would defeat me easily. He has the measure of me with a spear."

"And you have the measure of him with a broadsword, with your taller stature. Make no mistake, Ferdia; were a god not born to us in the snowfall upon Emain Macha, you would be the greatest fighter in all of Ulster. That you have stood shoulder to shoulder with him in many aspects of your training is most commendable. And with the passing of time, I predict the disparity between your skills will even out. I do not see a victor in a contest between you."

I look at the spear.

"And you consider this weapon will give an edge in such a contest?"

"I do not stand in the way of prophecy. The Gáe Bolg has

passed through the hands of many masters, but always leaves blood and death in the soil where it is cast. Fate has seen fit that it came to me, and now it is before you both today."

Eyes shut, I imagine the scene; the light of Lugh, high in the sky over the fjord that splits two empires. Water flowing across my shins, pebbles in the riverbed rocking beneath my feet. And as I step forward, Cú Chulainn gives no ground, beautiful in his soft features, dazzling in his gold armour, and then we both twirl and parry, employing skills as we have been shown on this island. My weapons lock with his, and time and time again we are at an impasse. I would only find an opening if he were to willingly leave it for me. The armies of Ulster, the armies of Connacht, watch on wordlessly as dawn becomes dusk, until I change stances and balance to launch the hidden spear underfoot, low under his shield, striking him squarely in his chest. And his beautiful face melts away; first with a look of shock, a gasp of disbelief at such an unfair tactic, such a betrayal, and then the shock melts away unto pain, like a wick burning through a candle, the wires of the spear's barbs extend and embed themselves through each of his limbs, and he collapses, vanishing beneath the surface of the flowing water. My eyes begin to burn. When I open them again, my vision is doubled and glossy with tears. The Shadow is unmoving. I back away slowly and point to the spear.

"I would not use this on my worst enemy. Let alone someone I love."

"It is honorable," she says. "So be it." She shuts the lid of the case, returning the pieces of the beasts to darkness, and the finality of my decision rings out in the room.

"You understand I am to make him the same offer."

The taunts now became too much to bear. I wanted to spit this foul taste from my mouth, to smash through the table and charge her, dashing her small frame against the cold wall. The Shadow had extended to me the length of her knowledge, and now I knew more than she, of that I was certain. I am confident I would prevail in a contest between us. I no longer considered myself her guest here. This was her final lesson, and I had heard it.

"He will say the same," I say, venom pouring from my lips. "He is proficient in every weapon. He can become a beast strong and horned like an Ox. He does not need this. He will deny you."

She fixes her eyes upon mine, and in them I can see the most insulting of all her slights this day. She feels sorry for me.

"He might," she whispers.

And with that I turn from her, certain I will never see her again, and if I would, it would be her end.

***

What right do the gods have to speak of the days yet to come, in the same manner that the common folk joyously reminisce of the past? What right do they have to laugh and measure out the lives of the honest, the hard-working, like lengths of cloth to be cut and traded amongst each other?

I had always thought that I had come here of my own accord, that I crossed the roughest stretch of Lir's domain to train with the Shadow and become a champion in my own right. I would return to Éire and forge my own destiny, my hands upon the young and malleable earth. I was so green, so foolish to think that it could ever be so. I wonder of my father, who gave me the inspiration for this quest. I wonder of Forgall Monach, who challenged Cú Chulainn to this similar fate. Are they really without agency in the wars to come, or strung up like rag-dolls by the divine? How entangled am I?

I spend the rest of the day carting crates of my things to and fro, castle to boat, wearing the path anew with my sandals. I want no force to delay me come the morning. I want to be away and never return, for the boat to veer off course and take us both far to the east, to the land where Lugh's light rises, and that we may never know another day of darkness again. And if it cannot be so, I would wish the boat capsize and drown us in the depths of Lir's domain, our bodies entwined together forever more like the Currid and the Coinchenn.

He returns late and undresses in the moonlight, and though I might wonder what he decided when pressed upon by the Shadow, I cannot bear and bring myself to ask. Instead, I lie awake, watching him, as each of his garments fall to the tiles, sober with the thought that this is to be our last night together. I imagine the judgement of each of the gods in turn. Their wrath and endless wickedness inflicted upon me. And I decide there is no force on this earth that could compel me to stand against him, none that could make me strike him in anger, maim him, even break his delicate skin.

As he climbs into the sheets beside me and wraps his body with mine, I wonder if he could say the same.

Caoimhín de Poor *is a writer from Cork, Ireland based in Edinburgh. A geology graduate, the natural world usually trickles into his work in some way. His favorite mediums are flash fiction and short stories.*

Visit Caoimhín's website - www.kevinjuly.com/

Strikers of '84

James Gault

Lenin was sitting in the pub, head down, checking the roster for the picketing of the Kilmuir pit. His usual half pint of heavy lay on the table in front of him, hardly touched. Most of the miners thought he was a big lassie when it came to the drink, but none of them would have dared say it to his face. He was a shop-steward who ruled with a rod of iron. It wasn't just the bosses that got rid of recalcitrant employees; several ex-miners were stacking shelves in the local supermarket because they had refused to toe the union line. Mining was effectively a 'closed shop'. Lenin had just about as much power as the Russian who had lent him his nickname – and he was just as ruthless.

The door of the pub was flung open and Grilla stumbled in. The noise caused Lenin to look up. Grilla was already well into his campaign to render himself legless before lunch. Lenin shook his head and went back to inspecting his roster.

"Four haufs; a' in the same glass, pal," Grilla's voice boomed as its owner staggered to the counter.

Wee Rab glared at him, wondering whether to serve him or throw him out. Grilla was an enormous beast, but Wee Rab was an ex-Scottish lightweight champion. "Just the yin, and then you're oot o' here, Grilla. You've had just aboot enough."

Grilla glared back at the diminutive barman. The few regulars scattered along the bar knew what was going on. The big man would be weighing up whether or not to tell Wee Rab to stuff his drink and walk out, but he wouldn't do it. For one thing, he had nowhere else to go; he was barred from every other pub in the area. Besides, he had a pathological need to spread a bit of aggro wherever he went. He'd hand over his money, down the whisky and insult a few of the customers. Then he'd nip down to the Co-Op to blow the last of his strike pay on a half-bottle of vodka.

He took a gulp of his whisky and surveyed the clientele. "McGahey and Scargill are a pair of eedjits," he announced. "Fucking wankers," he added, giving his opinion a steely edge.

The men at the bar looked over at the table in the corner, but Lenin didn't flinch. The silence didn't last long. These miners needed to keep well in with their shop-steward, and quickly jumped to the defence of the revered leaders.

"If it wisnae for them, ye'd have nae stike pay."

"You should be grateful they're fighting tae keep oor jobs."

"Who else can save us from that Yankee traitor, McGregor? He's gonnae shut doon a' the pits if we're no' careful."

"Aye, Arthur and Mike are the boys tae sort him oot; him and his boss, the Iron Maiden."

Grilla was unimpressed. "Ye're a' wimps. There's no' wan o' ye able to staun' up to Lenin ower there, and a' his Commie pals. And this," he held up an enormous fist and shook it, "stauns behind whit I'm sayin'. Aye, I'm callin' ye oot, you shower o' cowards. Ony o' ye gonnae take me oan, or whit?"

Wee Rab came back to the bar beside the troublemaker and leaned over towards him. "Swally the rest o' yer whisky and get the hell oot o' here afore I chuck ye oot masel'." His voice was calm: not so much threatening as matter of fact.

Grilla gulped the remnants of his whisky and thudded his empty glass on the counter. "I'm finished up here, onyway," he mumbled and tottered out through the pub door.

Lenin looked up from his papers and addressed the room. "That boy's gonnae get himsel' intae big trouble one day soon. If any of you are his pal, you could do him a favour by having a wee quiet word in his ear."

***

Like all UK policemen stationed in mining areas in 1984, Police Sergeant Alan Baird of the Dalneuk Constabulary was

225

wallowing in unexpected wealth. Overtime was there whenever he wanted it, and even when he didn't. He wasn't spending much time with his family, but his account in the local Savings Bank branch was swelling, and the Branch Manager greeted him with more and more deference every day. On the other hand, his relationship with his wife was deteriorating in spite of the money.

"It's a' right for you, Alan," she told him one morning when he had some rare time off, "you're oot a' day, awa' breakin' up some picket line or beatin' up some workers just oot trying to protect their livelihoods. I'm the one who has to meet the neighbours, take the weans tae school and get the messages. They a' hate us, Alan, and it's me that has tae put up wi' the sneers and the snide remarks behind my back. You're never here."

"The law's the law, May. It's my job to carry it out."

"Aye, and rake in the cash at the same time. Don't imagine the folk roon here don't ken whit's goin' on. They can add two and two and get four. And the greedy way we're keepin' the money a' tae ourselves isnae helping either. Haulf the folks roon here are starvin'. Nane o' oor ain family are talkin' tae us, even."

"What do you want me to do, May? Both our parents are retired, they've no worries. An' your sister's married onto a teacher up in Glesca. She's doin' a' right an' a'."

"Whit about your brother? I see his weans at school every day. They're nae mair than skin and bones. I slip them each a wee corned beef piece every mornin', but they're still no gettin' enough. And his poor wife, she's that skinny ye can see through her. You could bung him a couple o' quid from time to time."

Alan Baird sneered. "My brother! Gordon the Gorilla. His wife and weans don't go hungry just because o' the strike. He's a waster. Even before the miners came oot, he spent a' his wages on drink and left Wilma to get by as best she could. And if he worked two days, it was a good week. I'm amazed he kept his job up at the pit. Any money he got from me would go straight to the publican or the off-licence. Me stuffin' the odd tenner in his pocket isn't gonnae help his wife and weans."

May gave her head an ominous shake. "A' the same, if anything happens to them, what wi' the strike an a', you're the one who'll get the blame. The whole thing's a bloody mess, and before it's over it's gonnae turn to shit for all of us."

***

Lenin folded up his roster and shoved it into the breast pocket of his jacket. Twelve thirty, time to make his way to the pit for his shift on the picket line. He looked over at the bar to see which of his crew had turned up early and nipped in for a pint. Only two of them. He supposed the other two had run out of readies and would be waiting for him at the car. "Cadger! Shankly! Time tae go!" he shouted. They followed him out of the pub.

"Thanks for the pint, Shankly," Cadger screeched as they walked to Lenin's car.

The big man who ran the village football team just grunted. His real name was Scott, but he had been bestowed with the name of the local hero in the hope his local miners would emulate the successes of Liverpool F.C.

There was no one waiting for them at the car. Lenin looked at his watch and frowned. "Where are they? This'll no dae. It's no' fair on the early shift if we turn up late."

Cadger coughed quietly and looked at the ground. "They're no' comin'," he whispered.

Lenin scowled at him. "Whit dae ye mean, they're no' comin?"

Cadger cringed. "Fat Willie says tae tell ye he's got a touch o' the 'flu, and The Moose sent yin o' his weans roon wi' a message that his wife needs him this afternoon."

"Whit?" Lenin's face turned an angry red. "Oh, for God's sake. We're a skeleton squad as it is, withoot havin' two 'no shows'. The blacklegs are hangin' aboot, just looking for a chance tae slip back intae the place. We need every man we can get tae keep them oot."

"Aye, well, we've been oot for a long time, Lenin,"

Shankly suggested.

It wasn't the kind of excuse that went down well with the shop steward. "That's nothin' tae dae wi' it, Shankly. Solidarity. Solidarity and courage. We cannae give up noo. This backsliding'll no dae. I'll need tae get Tiny Tim n' his boys to go roon and have a word wi' them two. And don't either of you two even think of body-swerving yer shifts."

The other two men said nothing. If they had had any ideas of having an odd afternoon off picket duty, it had taken flight. They both knew what Tiny Tim and his boys were capable of.

***

Cadger was dying for a fag. The craving was enough to drag him out of his warm house and into his freezing, misty, November garden in search of a benefactor. The Strike Committee was too socialist for his liking; the strike-pay fund was destined for the family, and the single man only got a pittance. If only that bitch of a wife hadn't taken the weans and slunk off to Glenmore to bide up wi' thon smarmy shopkeeper. Bloody wee gold-digger.

He shivered and exhaled clouds of white breath as he considered his options. Shankly next door was normally an easy touch, but Cadger had been getting the signs he had used up all his credit there. That pint in the pub yesterday had been given grudgingly, and on condition it was the last until he paid back some of the money he owed. The Moose was the only choice left to him. The hen-pecked wee bastard didnae smoke, so he would have to wheedle the price of a ten-pack oot o' him. Cadger wasnae too sure he would have that much cash on him; the whole village knew his wife took a' his money and spent it on their fancy house, fancy furniture and the fancy car that sat on the pavement outside his gate. Their 'new' motor widnae even be ten years old, for God's sake. So he was probably wasting his time trying to tap The Moose, but 'nothing ventured, nothing gained', as his wise old granny used to say.

He negotiated the unkempt undergrowth that had invaded his front lawn, peeked around his gate, and all his hopes evaporated. The Moose's motor, the pride and joy of his life, had been desecrated. There was no chance of Cadger's neighbour being in a mood to dispense handouts now. If Cadger wanted a smoke today, he would have to call on his emergency supplies: an old packet of *Rizla+* and the tin of mixed-blend tobacco liberated by his never-ending scavenging in the local pubs' ashtrays.

Cadger surveyed the damage to the street's most luxurious limousine. The back and a couple of the side windows had been put in. The pristine waxed blue paintwork that The Moose shampooed and dried once every Saturday, and twice on Sundays, was daubed in bright yellow slogans: '*UP THE MINERS*', '*SAVE THE PITS*', '*THATCHER GO HOME*' and '*BLACKLEGS BEWARE*'. Cadger recognised the hand of Tiny Tim and his boys all over the vehicle. That Lenin could be a right bastard when he put his mind to it.

***

On the basis of a phone call he had received the night before, Lenin had spent the morning visiting his members in the village. He passed on the same message to all the militants. "The polis are coming mob-handed tae the pit this afternoon. They want tae break the picket-line and have the lorries wheel oot loads of coal for the power stations. We just cannae let that happen. Three-line whip for the pit gates afore two o'clock."

To Lenin's chagrin, not all union cardholders were committed supporters of the industrial action. He had a different message for those non-militants. "You're on my list, ye scab. If I was you, I'd start lookin' for a new job right noo'; I couldnae vouch for yer safety if ye come back tae the pits after the strike. An' I'm just taking this chance tae remind ye that life'll no be worth livin' for anyone daft enough tae become a blackleg."

His canvassing had had the desired effect. By two o'clock the gates of the Kilmuir pit were protected by an army of the faithful. All his regular pickets had turned up, and even some of the waverers, who had experienced his earlier threats and decided not to chance falling out of favour. The numbers of locals were inflated by volunteers from the neighbouring pits. The miners had their own secret service, and it worked ten times better than MI5.

The cops had begun to line up about a hundred and fifty yards down the road from the entrance to the mining complex. The hated locals were there, truncheons at the ready, Grilla's brother at their head. Their ranks had also been reinforced from outside. About a dozen mounties on each flank, some of whom may even had made the journey all the way from Glasgow. Then there were the Special Forces, two rows of them in black riot gear with helmets and shields. They even had artillery: two water cannons lined up behind the infantry.

The Battle of Kilmuir Colliery was brewing up nicely.

The two armies faced each other, each waiting for the other to initiate hostilities. Lenin, appointing himself General for the day, had found an old crate which he placed near the gatehouse. He stood up on it to direct manoeuvres. Someone had unearthed the NUM banner of the local branch and was brandishing it just behind the front line. A plethora of posters gleamed like spears in the warm autumn sun. Choruses of *The Red Flag* broke out from time to time.

The ranks opposite stood immobile, in stony silence, waiting for the arrival of the lorries. When the first one trundled up the road, they parted to let it pass. It drove up to the barrier of miners blocking its passage. A lone picket strode to the side of the cab and shouted something which the onlooking policemen couldn't quite hear. The miner stepped away, the lorry executed a three-point-turn and made its way back to the waiting constabulary.

Sergeant Alan Baird stepped out in front of it, held up his hand and engaged the driver in conversation.

"What happened up there, then?"

"Official picket. They'll no' let me through."

"Wait here. We'll clear a path for you."

The policeman ignored the driver's shaking head, took out his truncheon and raised it aloft. "Forward!" he shouted. The whole constabulary army drew their weapons, swept past the stationary lorry and advanced up the hill.

The driver of the lorry took advantage of now being at the rear of the front. He put his vehicle into gear and fled the scene, signalling to all the upcoming trucks to make a U-turn and follow him. None of them wanted to cross a picket line. In terms of preserving the integrity of the picket, the miners had already won the battle.

Ignoring the fact that their objective had been lost, the hordes of navy-blue-uniformed infantry swept on and engaged the enemy. Heads were broken, faces bloodied, noses bitten and ears torn off. There were casualties on both sides; the police were bigger and better-armed, but the miners were tough men with the strength that comes from years of hard graft.

General Lenin stood on his perch with a pair of borrowed binoculars, shouting encouragement to the combatants while at the same time keeping an eye on the road. When he saw the last of the trucks disappearing back in the direction of its base, he shouted, "Get oot o' here, lads. The lorries have scarpered." The miners scattered in all directions, taking their wounded with them. A few policemen made half-hearted attempts to follow them, but gave up after a few yards.

Sergeant Baird and Lenin were left facing each other, hatred oozing from each pair of eyes.

"I'm arresting you, Lenin. Disorderly conduct and causing a riot," Baird roared.

"Awa' and gie us peace, ye stupid bastard. There are hunners of witnesses that can testify I never lifted a haun' tae anybody, and it wis you and your heavies that started a' this. Why don't ye dae yersel' a favour and fuck off hame tae lick yer wounds. You've made a richt arse of yersel' the day, and the best thing you can dae is get oot o' here afore ye make it worse."

The policeman knew the wee shop steward was right, but he was determined to have the last word. "Don't think this is all over, Lenin. Bet yer life on it, I'll get you for this"

"No' if I get you first," Lenin retorted.

***

Cadger was feeling pleased with himself. Not a bad day yesterday. Lorries seen off, picket line intact, and a few coppers wi' sore heads and suppurating bruises, or worse. And he'd played his part fully – him and Shankly. They'd singled out that polis who seemed to delight in lying in wait for them every time they went in for a wee bit of poaching up at the estate. Cadger had tripped the cop up and Shankly had broken his arm with his own truncheon. A good day's work.

He was pretty certain the invalided copper would never turn them in. If he did, he wouldn't be able to go out anywhere on his own. Tensions between the miners and the agents of authority were running high. So he was a bit surprised when his front door knocker was rattled loudly and Police Sergeant Baird's voice boomed through his letterbox. "Open up, Cadger. I want a wee word wi' you."

"Bugger off an' annoy someone else, Baird. You're no' welcome here."

"This is official business. Open the door or I'll break it down."

"Talk to my lawyer." The nearest thing Cadger had to a lawyer was Lenin, who had the trust of the whole mine when it came to dealing with authority. Cadger knew the police sergeant hated the shop steward, and was a wee bit scared of him as well.

Baird tried softening his tone. "No need for that. I'm just looking for some information on a crime reported to us by your next door neighbour's wife. It won't take a minute."

Cadger put the chain on his door, opened it a few inches and poked his nose out. "Whit?"

"We're looking into a report of criminal damage to your neighbour's car and wondered if you heard or saw anything."

"I noticed he had been making some modifications to the vehicle," Cadger replied, pompously.

"There were slogans daubed all over it."

"He's a loyal support of the cause, The Moose is."

"And how do you explain the broken windows?"

"Maybe he was a bit too energetic wi' the paint brush. The witch is always oan at him tae dae up the place, but he's really no' that great at the DIY."

Policemen do not like to be mocked, and police sergeants from Dalneuk particularly so.

"You're hiding something from us, Cadger, but we'll drag it out of you eventually. Where the hell do you get your cheek?"

This was a red rag to the striking miner. "Where do you get yours, Baird? Turnin' up in this part o' the toon where you're no' wanted, stickin' yer nose intae things that don't concern you. You're public enemy *numero uno* roon here, pal. We a' ken whit you're up to, lining yer pockets while the real workers are starving. No' even lookin' after yer ain. It's aboot time ye pit your haun' in your pocket and gave a leg-up tae your poor brother and his family, afore they a' drap deid frae malnutrition."

Cadger slammed his door shut, and the pride of Dalneuk's constabulary found his nose up against the faded flaking paintwork that typified local authority housing stock.

***

Grilla had locked himself in his garden hut, preparing for his planned adventure. He'd salvaged an empty ginger bottle before Wilma chucked it in the bin and poured in the full half bottle of whisky he'd managed to nick from the Co-Op when the wee serving lassie's back was turned. It wouldn't be enough to see him through the day, so he added the remnants of a bottle of methylated spirits. He gave the mixture a good shake and gulped a mouthful to try it. It wasn't bad at all, so he had another. Then another and another, stopping only when he felt truly fired up. There wasn't much of the concoction left by then, so he poured it into an old hip flask that used to belong to his father.

He headed for the house to finalise his preparations, taking the hip flask with him. Wilma glared at him as he passed through the kitchen on the way to the bathroom, but she could see his eyes had gone so she kept her mouth shut. Up in the bathroom, he stripped to his underpants, pulled his wife's make-up bag from the shelf and got to work on his warpaint. He started on his face, using lipsticks and eyeliners to trace red, black and blue lines across his cheeks and brow. After a quick glance in the mirror to check his handiwork, he repeated the pattern across his bare chest. Next he lifted two hand towels and folded them over into his underpants, one hanging down at the front and the other at the back. A headband with a feather would have been good, but he didn't have anything that would have done the trick.

On the way downstairs again, he stopped off in the bedroom to pick up his shotgun and his sheath knife, stuffing the hip flask into the gun case. Wilma's mouth fell open when she saw him. He was well known for his drunken eccentricities, but she'd never seen anything like this before.

"Whit the hell are you up tae noo', Gordon?" she shouted.

Grilla stood stock still in front of her and raised a hand aloft. "Silence, squaw! No shout at Big Chief."

"You're no' goin' oot dressed like that? It's freezin' oot there."

"Me brave Brave! Strong! Fearless! Cold no problem."

"Gordon, for God's sake, stop this. Where do you think you're goin'?"

"Big Chief go hunting! Bring food! Feed family!"

Wilma's voice was becoming desperate. "No, Gordon, don't. Don't go poaching. Don't go anywhere near the estate. The polis are always there, keeping a look out."

"White man no frighten Big Chief. Big Chief fearless. Make way, Squaw!" As he said this, with a wide sweep of his arm he knocked his wife out of his way, and she stumbled against the kitchen sink. Grilla didn't even notice. He stomped, stomped, stomped out of the house and on into the wilderness. He was still wearing his miner's boots.

***

The two constables sat on a tree stump at the edge of the forest on the Kilmuir estate. They were cold, miserable, and not at all convinced they should be there. Was hanging about on the off-chance of a poacher a good use of police time in this period of unrest? The problem was that the laird up in the big house had a lot of influence, and the Sergeant wouldn't have dared refuse his request. They both looked at their watches at the same time. Another half an hour and they could go home. It couldn't come quickly enough.

It was the singing that grabbed their attention. Floating across the fields. *'I wandered today to the hills, Maggie'*, in a tuneless off-key voice that made Sydney Devine sound like a diva. A figure was coming towards them, and it was carrying a shotgun.

"Plan A, Tam!" Constable Wullie said, and the two defenders of the law moved into position. Wullie concealed himself behind a tree at the edge of the wooded area, while Tam hid further into the forest.

The poacher passed Wullie and stopped in the clearing just in front of Tam. As he surveyed his surroundings, sniffing to detect the smell of any possible game, *'When you –oo- oo and I-I-I were young'* echoed through the trees.

Tam stepped out and shouted, "You're under arrest."

At this point the criminal should have turned tail and fled towards the other cop, waiting with handcuffs at the ready. Instead, he reached into his gun bag, raised his shotgun aloft and shouted, "Death to the White Man. These are hunting grounds of the Sioux, stolen by Whiteys. Geronimo!"

As 'Geronimo' pointed his gun at his colleague, Wullie realised he had to do something real quick. He threw the handcuffs to the ground, took out his truncheon, ran up behind the gunman and struck him as hard as he could on the back of the head.

'Geronimo' fell to the ground, face down, blood pouring from his skull.

Tam, who had just missed being shot, breathed deeply. "Thanks."

Wullie didn't answer. He turned the wounded man over onto his back to look at his face. The stench of meths and alcohol made him gag. The red, blue and black stripes stood out starkly on the whitened skin. He sat there looking at that face until his colleague spoke.

"Looks like he was on something. Know who he is?"

Wullie was too busy feeling the poacher's pulse to answer. Eventually, he nodded. "Aye, I ken him fine. He's the sergeant's brother. And I think I've killed him."

***

The locals gathered in Wee Rab's pub after Grilla's funeral. They were up in arms about the killing. Grilla had been a wastrel and a troublemaker, but he was one of them. A Brother of the Lodge, even. The official story did nothing to placate the striking miners.

Criminal killed while resisting arrest by an unnamed officer. Police enquiry concludes no foul play.

'*No foul play*' just wasn't believed, and '*unnamed officer*' drove them into paroxysms of fury. The powers that be were even trying to protect whoever had wielded the bludgeon.

Not that it made much difference. The village had already decided who was to blame. In general, the NCB, the Thatcher government, and the police; and, in particular, the 'heid yin' in the Dalneuk Police Office: Sergeant Alan Baird, Grilla's very own brother.

"He wisnae even at the funeral, the rat. Does that no' tell ye something?" Cadger asked.

"Guilty conscience," was the universal reply.

"An' look at the way he stood by while Wilma and the weans were starving tae death. Money comin' oot o' his ears and he did nothin' for his ain family," Cadger added.

"Aye. At least noo Grilla's gone, the strike committee's ta'en his family under their wing. They'll see they're a' right, nae worries," Shankly said.

Even The Moose put in his tuppence worth. Mrs Moose had given him a rare pass-out so he could attend the funeral of a colleague and neighbour. He offered his contribution to the discussion. "He's nae friend of the miners, that Sergeant Baird."

There was a murmur of general agreement. "Are we gonnae let him get awa' wi' this scot-free?" Shankly asked the assembled company.

Cadger followed up his pal's comment and continued to push for retribution. Their leader had been sitting on the fringes, saying nothing. It was time for him to take responsibility. "Well, Lenin, whit are we gonnae dae aboot it?"

Everyone turned to look at the shop steward. They were expecting him to take action. If he didn't, he would lose them and the strike would fail. Not that it was a hard decision, anyway. There was no love lost between him and Police Sergeant Alan Baird.

"It'll be taken care of," Lenin announced. "I'll have a wee word wi' Tiny Tim and his boys."

***

A week later, at two in the morning, under a stormy moonless sky, a dark grey Transit van pulled into a field beside the river, a few miles outside of Glenmore. Two hefty lads got out, opened the rear doors, manhandled a heavy plastic bin bag to the river bank and heaved it into the water. It wasn't well hidden, but that didn't matter. They intended it to be found anyway. The two heavies then jumped back into the van, drove it back to the Doonmouth car park from where they had stolen it, and left it in exactly the same place. Unless the owner was one of those nerds who assiduously checked his milometer every five minutes, he wouldn't even know it had moved.

Lenin already knew about this incident: both that it was supposed to happen and that it had happened. So it was no surprise when his phone rang and his contact from the Strike Committee's intelligence arm whispered down the line.

"I don't know what's been going on in your area, but our informers tell us the authorities up there are buzzing over something. Don't go to the pit today; stay by the phone. We're keeping an eye on the nest, and we'll keep you posted on what the wasps are up to."

Lenin had been waiting for this news. He wasn't worried. When a local policeman gets knocked off, his compatriots move heaven and earth to find the culprit. But in the current circumstances, heaven and earth wouldn't be enough to do the job. Lenin fully expected the local police to be all over the village in the next few days, asking questions, but he was equally certain they would be met everywhere with stony silence. There may be some residual sympathy for May Baird, but her husband was universally detested and whoever had done him in was a hero to the local populace. And if they were hoping that forensic evidence might help them, they were in for a disappointment. Tiny Tim was a professional who had been getting away with murder, both literally and metaphorically, for years.

The next call from the union's spies came through a couple of hours later. It didn't surprise Lenin either. "We understand your local police have discovered their sergeant's burnt-out car somewhere on the Glenmore Moors."

That had been part of the plan too. Tiny Tim would have torched it to remove all the evidence and abandoned it just off the road in the middle of nowhere. There would have been a suggestion of a road accident, but not a very convincing one.

Lenin knew the body had been disposed of elsewhere. It was found later that afternoon. His union contact called again. "A contact in the Doonmouth police has just told us they have found a body wrapped up in a plastic bin-bag in the river an hour ago."

"Thanks for the information," Lenin told them, as if he hadn't known.

"There's more. The local cops were told to hand the body over to a Special Branch Inspector and forget the whole thing."

Lenin hung up. So the political police were involved. A national inquiry, no stone to be left unturned. The whole area would be swarming with secret and not-so-secret police in a couple of hours.

But no policemen appeared in the village. Instead, the local TV news carried a report towards the end of the next evening's bulletin.

Local policeman in tragic road accident. Earlier today, the body of Police Sergeant Alan Baird was discovered in his burnt-out car in a remote part of the Glenmore moors. It is understood that Sergeant Baird, who had been prominent in policing the miners' strike in this area, was on his way to a case. He is survived by his wife May and his two children. The police are not looking for anyone else in connection with this incident.

The deaths of both Alan and Gordon Baird had both been swept under the carpet at Dalneuk Police Station.

The strike carried on for many more months, social division deepened, tragedies were enacted everywhere. In the colliery villages throughout the country, hatred and distrust lingered on long after the miners' jobs had disappeared.

James Gault *is an award-winning short story writer, poet and novelist, born in Ayrshire in Scotland, now living in SW France. His fiction career began in 2007, when he won the writing prize from the British Czech and Slovak Society for his short story 'Old Honza's Day Out'. He has since written eight novels, some political satires and several psychological and philosophical thrillers. He has also published several short stories and from time to time he dabbles in poetry.*

In addition he is the author of books on English Language Teaching and other non-fiction. Many of his articles and papers on language teaching, travel and philosophy have been published in magazines and journals.

His main interests are philosophy and politics, but he loves anything that makes him smile. He writes to amuse, so:

If want to laugh till your face turns blue
Wee Jimmy's daft stories are made for you.

The Cottage

Samuel Best

The forest was light and sparse, with spongy moss underfoot. Tom, Michael, and I walked slowly, chatting and laughing, our warm breath clouding like ghosts before our faces. Although our rucksacks contained little more than cheap beer bought by an older brother (and, in Tom's case, a bottle of whisky stolen from his parents' drinks cabinet), the tent and sleeping bags we wore with straps slung over our shoulders made us feel like wilderness explorers. So far we had hiked a couple of miles through dry, flat farm fields, and the sun had guided us ever further towards the horizon. Over there somewhere, Michael told us, there was a forest, and if we walked through it, and followed a certain trail his brother had mentioned, we would find the old mill cottage.

Michael's brother had been to the cottage loads of times, he said, and rumour was that it was abandoned after the last owner had shot himself. Being teenage boys, we wanted to explore in case we could find any gun shells, treasure, or pieces of bone. Michael's brother had found the old man's wedding ring, he told us, and sold it back in town for a song. Michael's brother had done a lot of things. There was a small part of us that knew, even then, that we were only friends with Michael for the vicarious *coolness* that came from the connection to his brother. But it was worth it to hear those stories.

As we pushed further into the forest I shared out three of the beers from my bag. We had been walking without a break for so long that our legs and throats burned and the lukewarm lager was a welcome relief. The bottles were stubby and made of cheap green glass. Tom used an attachment on his penknife to pop the lids off one by one. They fell like breadcrumbs behind us and although we walked on, a small part of me remained there, crying guiltily about leaving a trace. We had told our parents that the camping trip was something to do with Scouts, and while this was a lie, it felt wrong to break such a cardinal Scouting law. Drinking and smoking were fine to dabble with, but as each bottle-cap landed on the dirt I felt I could hear our Scoutmaster tutting sharply.

The trees began to grow even more sparsely as we drew closer to the edge of the forest. It felt like we were so far from home that we could stake the land as our own, as though we were the first people ever to set foot there. The moss was dented occasionally by hoof-prints from deer or sheep, and I wondered aloud whether anyone owned the beasts, the land too, or not. Michael replied "Of course not," and reminded me that in Scotland the law was different. Something about public land versus private land. His brother had told him there was no such thing as trespassing because technically all land belonged to the people, or something like that. So if any angry famers caught us camping we could explain that Scottish law was on our side, thank you very much.

But that didn't mean that we weren't being careful. None of us wanted to have to explain ourselves to a shotgun-toting farmer, a nosey passer-by, or (worst of all) the police. The weight of the alcohol in our bags and the knives in our pockets seemed to grow whenever the thought of police passed us by. Would they take us to jail or back home to our parents? None of us could agree on which would be worse.

We began to walk more slowly, casting our eyes around for cars winding along the road in the distance, or farmhands ploughing nearby. The coast was clear though, as it had been all morning, and we left our beer bottles like bowling pins next to a fly-tipped refrigerator. Rusted and dirt-dappled, it must have been there years, sinking deep into the verge that ran alongside a dirt path, a jolting reminder of civilisation over the nearby hills. I felt my heart sink a little at the thought. A part of me, probably the same part stinging about breaking Scout laws, loved the childish adventure of the day so far. We were *Stand By Me*, *Lord of the Flies*, *The Fellowship of the Ring*, even. Boys left to their own wild devices. We could have been anywhere in the world, never mind the Riccarton hills.

The dirt path next to the fridge took us from the forest down to a little glen where the cottage sat brooding by the bank of a small stream. We trekked on, thirsting already for more alcohol and a rest, but a dizzying excitement now filling us, the cottage so close. The path was uneven and our shoes slipped and stumbled over the stones. Bottles clinked in our bags, and when Tom slipped, it was his sleeping bag that cushioned him (and them) from the hard stone earth.

Then, as we wound further down the glen, the cottage came into view. A small, rough, stone house, it had a patchy slate roof and every window was boarded up. The front door, we realised as we drew closer, was nailed shut with three long planks across the frame. We set our bags down next to a battered barbed-wire fence and took it all in.

"It's bigger than I thought," Tom said. "More secure-looking, mind you."

Michael was nodding like an architect appreciating every stone.

"Did your brother say how to get inside?" I asked.

"Round the back," Michael replied, hoisting his bags to his shoulder. "Which is where we should be anyway. We're wide open out here on the path."

We weren't, what with the hills either side and the tall shrubs to the south. But as soon as Michael said that, I felt it, like someone was watching. Again, I imagined coming home in the back of a police car, charged with breaking and entering now, as well as underage drinking and possession of a Swiss Army knife. The looks on Mum and Dad's faces. I flinched and lifted my rucksack, the tent and sleeping bag knocking against my legs as they swung behind me.

Around the back, the stream widened like a python,

circling close to the cottage wall, and there were three stepping-stones leading across to more shrubbery on the other side. There was enough room for the tent and no more, and I remembered Michael explaining that his brother had said we should camp there. The stream would give us some protection from anyone who might come across us, buying us time to make a break for it, he'd said, and under no circumstances should we try to stay the night *in* the cottage. Even he hadn't gone this far, and that's saying something: Michael's brother had jumped from the highest cliff in the old quarry last summer without even hesitating.

Michael walked up to one of the windows and wedged the fingers of one hand under a split in the wooden board. Tom and I saw the muscles in his arm strain as he moved it enough to put his other hand under. From where we were stood it looked like the cottage was slowly swallowing him.

"Give me a hand, will you?" Michael called, and Tom and I ran over.

We took hold of the board and pulled. There was a loud groan from the window frame as the tacks were wrenched from old holes. Rust-stained and free, the board fell to our feet and we grinned, high-fiving with splintered and dirty hands. Turning back to the window, we fell quiet and looked into the gaping blackness. Although the sun was beaming, reaching its peak above us, the cottage seemed to drink up the light and we couldn't see much further than the empty hole in the wall. Beyond the window frame there could have been anything. We bristled with nerves, the house stretching on and on like a gullet.

"Who's first?" Tom asked, and I looked to Michael.

"Well it was your brother who told us about this place," I said. "So it seems right that it's you."

"Don't tell me we've come all this way and you two are wimping out on me," Michael replied. There was a challenge in there, a threat, and I regretted speaking.

I took a breath and looked back to the cottage. I tried to get my eyes to focus on the shadowy room but still there was nothing. Something about the shadows seemed to shift, like the house was taking a deep breath, but the darkness was too thick for me to make anything out. I steeled myself, the weak beer in my bloodstream doing little to halt my nerves.

"Fine," I said, kicking my bags to the side and walking up to the house. I gripped the window frame and tested its strength. It was solid but uncomfortably high. I would need to haul myself up as I jumped in order to gain enough momentum to make it. I began to rock, priming my muscles. I could feel Tom and Michael watching me, testing me. I jumped.

I heaved myself into the room, catching my hip on the window and tipping clumsily onto the floor. Dust-covered, I pulled myself upright and wiped myself down as my eyes began to adjust. To my left, against a wall, there was the frame of an old couch, the cushions long-gone. Ahead of me was a stone fireplace filled with old beer bottles and crushed cider cans. Above it, where a mirror or picture frame used to hang, was the scrawl and doodle of graffiti. To my right was a door, cracked open, the daylight fading to a deeper darkness beyond. I coughed, batting a cloud of dust away with my hand, and turned back to Tom and Michael outside.

"Who's next then?" I asked.

***

Hours later and the tent was erected in the garden and the cottage explored fully. We hadn't split up – an unspoken rule – but searched each room of the house as a team, eyes peeled for any grisly remnants from the last owner's suicide. We were unlucky, though, and as the day drifted on and we sat in an empty bedroom upstairs, drinking beer and writing lyrics from our favourite songs on the peeling wallpaper. We agreed that Michael's brother's find was a one-off. A part of me was relieved, I suppose. There had been a dead fox on the road on the way here and my stomach had lurched at the sight of it. Maybe human bones would have been too much to handle.

As I stared up at the ceiling, picturing the fox again, Michael finished drawing something in the centre of the room and began fishing around in his rucksack. He pulled out a cigarette lighter and a bag of tealights. I hadn't noticed until then, but the little daylight which did manage to penetrate through the hole in the roof above us had begun to wane. It cast the edges of the room, and the hallway beyond, back into shadow.

"Just don't burn the place down," Tom laughed, peeling the label from his beer bottle and tearing it into confetti.

"No no no," Michael said. "We're going to be careful. These aren't just any old candles, you know. I got them from a magic shop."

"What, like the kind of place that sells wands and top hats with rabbits inside?" Tom said, draining the last of his beer before flinging the empty bottle past Michael and into the hallway. It landed somewhere in the darkness, unbroken, and there was a cyclical sound as it spun in shadowy circles.

"No, like the kind of magic that is actually real. The kind not for kids," Michael said. "I've been reading a lot about it."

He lit a number of candles and placed them carefully on top of his drawing, eying the arrangement carefully. Next, he pulled out Tom's bottle of whisky and held it up like a taster examining the hue. He unscrewed the lid then, and took a long, pointed gulp.

"That's the stuff," he said, fighting the urge to flinch.

Tom and I both scrambled over to him for the next drink but Tom beat me to it, pushing me to one side and toppling himself over, bottle now in hand, at the same time. He took a series of short swigs before holding the bottle out to me. I didn't take it though. I was too fixated by Michael's drawing on the floor.

A circle of runes surrounded a five-pointed star. Michael had drawn it with a thick marker pen, and I could see the bits where the dusty floor had clogged the pen. He had gone over the same spot a number of times. It was messy, and the runes were unintelligible, but the pentagram was instantly recognisable.

"Isn't that a devil sign or something?" I asked, but at the same time Tom gently swung the butt of the whisky bottle and it dunted against my temple.

"Never mind that and have some of this," he said, grinning.

My eyes lingered on the star for a second, but then I took the bottle and drank deeply. There was only around half of it left, but judging by how much it burned, I figured it would be plenty. We still had another bag of beers too. As the booze hit my stomach, I found my nerves about Michael's drawing dissipate.

Michael, meanwhile, had pulled a small book out from his bag and was flicking through it. He was clearly looking for something, and had to leaf through the pages more than once before he found it. When he did, he checked his drawing again before handing more beers around.

"So I was reading this in the shop," Michael said, "and I found this section which talks about dark magic. Scary magic."

Tom snorted and popped the lid of his beer with Michael's penknife.

"I'm serious," Michael said. "It's really interesting. It talks about all these people throughout history who have done this one spell and then become really powerful."

"Like David Copperfield, you mean?" I said, and Tom dribbled his beer from laughing.

I took the knife from him and opened my own, drinking half in one go. My head was growing hazy and the beer washed the whisky down nicely.

"Like Napoleon, Winston Churchill, Julius Caesar," Michael replied. He leaned over and took his knife back. "So the first part is you draw this symbol and light these special candles. They have something in them which is supposed to draw power towards you."

Tom and I were still laughing and drinking, but as Michael's voice grew quieter, we settled into a sceptical hush. Above us, the sun was setting. The hole in the roof was blood-red. We were listening carefully when there was a wooden creak from somewhere in the cottage. Michael fell silent and we stared at the bedroom door, at the blackness beyond it.

My heart was suddenly galloping in my chest, despite the breath frozen there. I could hear the pulse throbbing in my ears, but apart from that, the house was still. Somewhere in the cottage, I imagined, an angry man mirrored our movements, listening for any sign of intruders. I could picture him downstairs, his shotgun loaded, his finger on the trigger, ears eager for us.

"Can you hear anything?" I whispered, and Michael and Tom shook their heads.

"Go check," Tom said to me. Another challenge. A challenge I was drunk enough to accept.

Slowly I exhaled, and next to me a row of candles flickered, sending shadows darting across the room. Michael went back to his book, reading it aloud under his breath, and Tom shuffled closer to get a better look. I stood, taking ginger steps towards the hallway door. Inside the tent – downstairs, outside, and across the stream – was my torch, and I cursed myself for forgetting to bring it with me. As I got to the doorway, a floorboard creaked beneath my trainers and I baulked. My mouth filled with burning, beery vomit.

I turned back to Michael and Tom but they were engrossed now. Tom had taken hold of the book while Michael flicked his penknife open and shut, open and shut. The candles around them continued to flicker, and just for a moment I thought that Michael looked like somebody else, *something* else. I blinked hard, realising truly how much I had had to drink. A deep breath, a long exhale. I willed myself sober and took another step so that I was out in the hallway. The floorboards here didn't creak and I felt a wave of relief break over me.

Slowly, like an evolution, I adjusted to being swallowed by the shadows. My eyes changed, and the hallway grew before me like an illusion. I stayed quiet, listening to Michael and Tom's whispering behind me, far-off as though they were miles away. I could hear the sound of something moving around outside. A distant rustling of plants, just audible over the gurgle of the stream. An animal maybe. The shake of a bush again, more violent now. I glanced back to the bedroom before walking along the hallway to the stairs.

Downstairs, in the living room, I crouched by the window and peered out. The sun had fallen below the horizon and the sky was merely embers. There was just enough light out to catch the stream though, which glistened and babbled softly. Something about it reassured me. It was idyllic and peaceful, almost enough to make me forget why I was down there. I set my half-drunk beer down by the couch frame and waited long enough to be sure that whatever had been moving around had gone. Then I hoisted myself back over the window frame and dropped outside.

My shoes landed in the dirt and I staggered. I held onto the wall for support and walked over to the stream. I crouched by the water's edge and dipped my hands in up to my forearms. The cold was sharp, like broken glass, and I cupped my freezing hands so I could drink from them. I slurped the stream water and splashed my face, wiping at my eyes, still wishing myself sober. My stomach was beginning to bubble and churn with vomit again, and I felt sweat blistering across my hairline. If this was getting drunk, I decided, I wasn't going to do it again. I dipped my hands once more, cupping another mouthful of water, but when I raised them up to my face the water looked different. I stopped dead, horrified at the wriggling, twitching insects that were swimming in my hands. They flitted and flicked, splashing my face with tiny drops from their claws and tails and antennae. I unclasped my fingers, pouring the filthy water over my knees, and flicked my hands at the stream, moaning from a disgusted, primal part of myself.

Scrambling backwards, I spat and spat, convinced my mouth, throat, and stomach were filled with parasitic worms, writhing and frothing and gnawing away at me. I pictured them burrowing through my insides and pouring out from my nose, my mouth, from under my fingernails. I pictured their eggs hatching and bursting through my skin.

When at last my stomach had emptied itself and I was vomiting nothing but bile, I looked to the tent. In my bag there was a change of trousers, water, and my torch, and I desperately wanted all three. More than anything, though, I wanted to go home. The thought of spending the rest of the night in that tent made me want to die. I had come up to my knees before what I was actually seeing stopped me.

Our small nylon tent, grey and red, a shared purchase of our pooled pocket-money, was ripped apart. The tent door was still zipped shut, but the fabric had been cleaved open by three smooth gashes. Although there was no breeze, the tent rippled, as though the violent momentum was still echoing through the poles. I spun back to the house, terrified of some rabid clawing beast that might be lurking in the shadows around me.

I looked up to the second floor window. For a moment, my eyes tricked me. Instead of plywood and rusting nails I saw an image of glass. And looking straight back at me, behind the glass, was a monstrous figure. Silhouetted by candlelight, I could only make out the shape of two twisting horns, and a shaggy, wolf-like pelt. It breathed a hot, rabid puff that clouded the glass. I felt my breath catch in my chest and, as I blinked, the form was gone. Instead, a blank, wooden panel was fixed in its place, exactly as I had expected.

My heart shuddering, my blood burning like acid, I tore back to the house, desperate, more than anything, to be in company. Regardless of any great fear, something deep within me knew I would be safer with Michael and Tom than I would be alone. I hurdled the window frame and kicked over my beer bottle as I ran through the cottage. I took the stairs two at a time, my thumping footsteps like hammer blows in the silent building. Then, as I reached the bedroom, I heard laughter.

I slowed to a walk and, panting, pushed the door wider. Michael and Tom were sitting, passing the dregs of the whisky between them, taking hearty slugs and chatting about old rock 'n' roll bands. The candles were still shining, but two had been knocked over and now burned horizontally. Wax poured over the floor, smothering the runes and pentagram with thick gloops. Michael's book sat, cast aside, under the boarded window, the pages spilled open, words catching in the flickering candlelight.

"Are you okay?" Tom asked, as I pushed the door firmly shut behind me.

I glanced around the room again, eyes scouring the shadows for the wolf-beast, before answering.

"I'm fine. Fine."

"Are you sure?" he asked, offering up the remains of the whisky. "You look like you could use a drink."

I took the bottle and drank deeply, forgetting my earlier vow of sobriety. The alcohol bubbled in my stomach like a witch's potion, and my throat burned more so after being sick.

"We gave up summoning the Devil," Michael continued, nodding to the book. "Nothing was happening. He must be busy tonight."

He laughed as I swirled the last of the whisky around the bottle and I was about to speak, about to describe what I saw at the window, what had happened to the tent, when I heard the sound. More real than our imaginary farmer from earlier, this was a tangible, definite sound. Below us, something was heaving itself across the wooden floorboards in the living room. The slow creak and drag of something heavy. It was unmistakable. I looked to the other boys and they were sitting still, blurry eyes now stuck sharply on the door, listening intently. We waited for the sound again, and there it was. A slow, steady pulse, like a heartbeat.

Drag, creak. Drag, creak.

Across the hall. Up the stairs.

I glanced at the book and caught sight of the diagram Michael had drawn. At the bottom of the page, scribbled in messy, teenage pencil, was the monster I thought I had seen at the window earlier. Turning, I looked towards the door. Michael and Tom exchanged a glance. Breathless and silent, we waited, as the door was pushed open and the candles blew out.

———————————

Samuel Best's short fiction has been published in magazines in Britain, North America, and Scandinavia. His début novel, *Shop Front*, has been described as "A howl and a sigh from Generation Austerity" and he founded the literary magazines *Octavius* and *Aloe*. You can find him on social media @storiesbysamuel.

Visit Samuel's website - www.samuelbest.weebly.com

Thank you

Thank you for purchasing Dark Scotland. We hope you enjoy it.

All royalties received will be split and donated to two Scottish charities: **ME Research UK**, and **The Halliday Foundation**.

The publisher is grateful to those who have contributed to the publication of the Anthology. Their work has been done without payment.

Fantastic Books
Great Authors

darkstroke is
an imprint of
Crooked Cat Books

- Gripping Thrillers
- Cosy Mysteries
- Romantic Chick-Lit
- Fascinating Historicals
- Exciting Fantasy
- Young Adult Adventures
- Non-Fiction

Discover us online
www.darkstroke.com

Find us on instagram:
www.instagram.com/darkstrokebooks

Printed in Great Britain
by Amazon

58137242R00149